a dance upon the level shore

By V P FERGUSON

> Who will go drive with Fergus now,
> And pierce the deep wood's woven shade,
> And dance upon the level shore?
> Young man, lift up your russet brow,
> And lift your tender eyelids, maid,
> And brood on hopes and fear no more.
>
> *W B Yeats*

contents

Almeria, Spain. May 1937

the widening gyre

ceremony of innocence

a rocking cradle

human child

darkness drops again

pavements grey

of self and soul

a lonely impulse of delight

a sudden blow

dropping from the veils

know the dancer from the dance

a ghostly paradigm of things

rough beast

the crime of death and birth

dark cloths

a battle fought over again

before a looking glass

a sufficient end

uncertainty of setting forth

through summer and winter alone

and flowed from shape to shape

to trouble the living stream

the sailing seven

glory of changeless metal

crooked thing

human dignity

take the roses

catch-cries of the clown

shy in the gloom

the leaves grow on the tree

dreading and hoping

wither into the truth

one by one we drop away

nobody wise enough

hand in hand

the merchant and the clerk

the pale unsatisfied

truths that are your daily bread

Appendix

  References

Almeria, Spain. May 1937

"El lisiada," asked the man, 'quien es el? Su rosto es familiar"

The cripple? Who is he? I know that face.

His companion turned his head to look down the long corridor, deeper into the tunnel.

"English. Se llama Donaghue, " he replied in his accent, heavy with the intonations of Catalonia. "Came on the road from Malaga."

"He's not here to fight then?"

"What good is he in our fight if he can't run."

The man's lips smiled; his eyes didn't. He turned and then tugged at the rough breakfast bread he held in his soiled fingers. Flakes of crust settled in the stubble of a new beard.

Instinctively the man's hand reached down to his own leg. His fingers pressing the moleskin of his miners trousers into the pale scar tissue that ran from his hip to his knee. His souvenir of the fighting outside Madrid. His own reason to be stuck here; working not fighting; digging tunnels deep underground again.

In the stillness he looked back to where the broad-shouldered Englishman worked. If the cripple had come along the road from Malaga he would have had to run. He would have had to run and hide, to dodge and cower, his pride buried by fear, his eyes wild-blind by terror, his hearing deadened by the German's shell's shock-quake and the cries of the dying and maimed. He knew the cripple, however damaged, however slow, would have had to run and run fast.

Perhaps he would have run bravely; steadfast in the beginning; but as the fascists and the dark Moroccans of Spain's African army chased the crowds of refugees he would have faltered and fast limped away; his boldness abandoned and replaced with shame. Having known the same shame, the Catalonian fell softly into remembrance of his own journey.

Starting long ago in the green hills and valleys of Ourense, Galicia he had followed his father to the tin mines at age 12. He had followed his father each day. Waking early and walking the three miles to the head of the mine. Working late into the afternoon, deep underground, then following those tired footsteps homewards.

He had followed his father when a strike was organised. He had followed his father's cheap coffin, weeks later, and helped dig his grave in the thin soil of the hill above their home. His father shot dead on their doorstep by a member of the Guardia Civil, a uniformed assassin working for the mine owner to break the strike.

From there he left home and travelled to his countries capital and joined the Government's army. In the trenches dug across the streets of Madrid he was joined by the weekend warriors who bussed out from the Centro after Mass on Sunday. With sandwiches and beer they came to fight the fascists sharing a rifle and gossip with the comrades from their barrio.

He laughed at them as they arrived. A coloured rag wrapped around their left arm as their regimental badge. They left for their homes as the sun went down. He shook his head at the departing trams and busses in the evening gloaming that took them back to a life's normality. Then on a bright Tuesday morning as he walked to the HQ dreaming about his breakfast he had wandered idly into the range of a snipers rifle. A bullet had ripped across his leg cutting into his thigh and maiming him from the fight.

Now, he was digging tunnels into the volcanic rocks of Almeria. Air raid shelters for the town's people. Discharged from the army he still wore with his regiments blue army tunic and cap.

"Manex. Manex?"

He heard his name being said softly. He felt a heavy hand on his shoulder. He shook himself free from his thoughts. A grin-grimace settled on his face in vain attempt to hide the humiliation he felt from his friend.

"Your back with us, primo" His companion's hand wrapped around Manex's neck and squeezed him forward into his shoulder. Manex pulled back. He didn't like to be touched.

He looked at the man. Sensed the offence in his eyes and apologised lowly, ' Lo siento.'

"De nada."

"No, Andres, I am sorry. Solo un sueno."

"More than a dream. You're eyes went dark. Maybe a nightmare dressed as a dream."

Manex shrugged. He reached for the bottle of water and swigged deeply scouring the dust from his throat. His thoughts, his fears, his memories were his own. To be kept buried deep.

The second shell from the Admiral Scheer hit the city a quarter of a mile from the Ramblas just after 7am. The first, a split second before, crumped into the warehouses surrounding the port.

The Scheer, a German pocket battleship, sitting off the coast, blockading the ports and isolating the Republican army within shelled the city daily. The population hiding from the barrage in the tunnels of Almeria mined into the rock.

Manex knew in that moment. Fate and fear, understood.

He dropped his water bottle and moved to go deeper, safer . The shockwaves from the blast ran through the bedrock of the city. The roof of the newly shored up mine above Manex's head crumbled and fell. He had reached the crippled Englishman and his companion when the sand and dirt enveloped him. He fell as a rock struck him above the temple. He was dead before the sand, soil and debris covered his face. It filled his mouth and hollowed on his eyes.

Another shell fell. Further away. Followed by another thud. The barrage, like the darkness of a thunder storm moved over the town. The tunnel shuddered; a beam shifted but held. A shaft of light lit the darkness, layering the dust filled air

The crippled man moved away from the depression in the tunnel wall that provided him with shelter from the collapsing roof. At his feet was the contours of Manex's body. He knelt down and wiped the face clear of dirt; he pushed his strong fingers into the mouth, pulling sand moist with saliva from teeth and tongue. He listened at the still chest. Nothing. Dead.

The crippled man leant back and looked at the man's death mask.

It was his. The dead man's face was his own. And in that moment the dreams of his childhood softened and became air.

They rose, spectre like, in the alternate bands of darkness and sunlight that cross-hatched the mine and, with the motes of dust, lifted into the nothingness.

the widening gyre

At the south end of the hall, above the eight fluted columns of the grand entrance where Britannia, in decorative frieze, her arms open offering olive branches to the peoples of the world, a herring gull stood arrogantly cruel over a vulnerable squab dove. The gull had pulled the small bird from its nest by the wing, breaking its fragile fritillary feathers. Then with its hooked jaundice-yellow beak it stabbed at the nestling, leaving a scarlet smear on the pale grey of its breast. Now the gull cocked its flat dead-fish eye, presenting the red blood smear of its bill to the sunlight to consider its victim with the frown of a hanging judge. Then with the cruel predictability of nature, it advanced again with open wings, darting forward to deliver rapid clipped slashes. Bloodied and shocked the dove lay still, bowing to fate, waiting for death, calm in acceptance of the inevitability of life's order.

The soft down feathers of the dove, plucked by brutality, were caught in the light wind, to rise and pirouette in dance before settling to drift downwards in the space above the unknowing heads of the crowd below.

That August morning of 1911 had been bright and blue, and the people from all quarters of the city had settled on the flat plateau in front of St George's Hall. They had been welded into a mass by the heat, bonded together in the quadrangular confines of the stately neo-classical facades of the city's prideful buildings.

The high sky, hard and impenetrable, had a thin range of pale white peaks that washed down its western rim. With little wind, the cloud remained pinned in place to the hem of the horizon. Now, as the afternoon settled into the day, the heat coated the crowd's faces, although shaded under dark caps and brimmed hats, with a glaze of perspiration as they stood listening to the orators from the platform between the stately columns of the hall's entrance.

In side streets hidden from view, infantrymen stood in steadied ranks, legs astride at ease, their rifles already bayoneted, arms at rest, blank faced, with busy minds racing in anticipation. A corporal walked stiffly between the columns, talking low and calmly, encouraging his men in the need for absolute discipline and obedience in the meting out of casual violence and force. "Don't," he said, his eyes dark threats under the brim of his helmet, "ever forget whose side you are on."

At the north corner of the square, alongside the shop fronts that ran up and away along the London Road, a line of uniformly sized grey gelded stallions stood in disciplined rank. On their backs were men in olive green cavalry tunics and breeches. They too were uniform in size and colour, each wearing an essential moustache as a badge of class distinction. In front, half a length proud of the ranks, the officer's horse stamped its right hoof repeatedly, idly impatient to play. The officer, flat capped and braided gold, bore a scar that cut through his left cheek and upper lip, lifting his mouth in permanent contempt. He leant forward on the neck of his mount and patted dust from its hide with white gloved fingers. From beneath the brim of his cap he cocked his own flat dead-fish eye at the crowd gathered before him.

The line of cavalry bore that particular air of diffidence that set them apart from the rest of the troops. They exuded confidence and public-school brashness, though many were barely literate men originating from farms or small holdings. They were educated and trained in one thing: to follow orders to a man and never to question the authority of that command.

The horses, dull eyed with boredom, the men bright eyed with expectancy, were watched by a crowd of men and women on the far side of the road. A man dressed in his Sunday suit and worker's boots caught the eye of one of the cavalrymen and holding that contact, leant forward and spat into the dusty gutter.

On the cobbled street, between the horses and the people, irregular sorties of mounted officers of the police force clopped past; full of self-importance and spite, their helmet badges bright shields flashing in the sunlight. They nodded or tipped their spiked helmets to the waiting cavalrymen who stared arrogantly ahead, blindly aware of their fawning servility.

Thousands of soldiers had been drafted into the city over that summer. It was commonplace to see them drill, rifles sloped on khaki brown shoulders, around the city streets and greenspace. When at ease, they strode the pavements with a swagger of disrespect, contemptuous of the populace, over familiar with their past role as brutal warders for the British Empire. Parklands to the north and south of the centre were under army control, bivouacked with rows of white canvas pup tents; the better hotels of the city had been commandeered for the officer classes. The basement of St George's Hall had been stalled and straw-lined to be used as stables for the cavalry elite. Out beyond Liverpool Bar at the mouth of the Mersey, two naval gunships impatient for involvement rode the flat grey waves of the Irish Sea.

In the summer heat, the minutes passed, dry and dust filled. The clock ticked slowly towards three. As the throng stood in the piazza to the south, peacefully listening to the speeches, the mounted forces of the government sat straddled with false aplomb, sweat drops dripping into their uniforms, waiting. Their begloved hands expectant and twitching on sword hilt or baton grip. The officer's horse pawed its iron shod foot on the flag and raised its head. It smelled the leaking adrenaline from the soldiers, wall eyed, a tremor twitched its flanks and it side stepped, clattering on the cobbles until the officer reined it back with soft hands.

ceremony of innocence

Inside the watery womb, the boy turned to listen. Through the fluid and flesh, heavy with blood vessels, he could hear the murmur of the crowd and the steady flutter of his mother's heartbeat. He could feel her hands cradling her swollen form, supporting him now, as she would he hoped, for evermore in this life and the next. The rhythmic noise of footsteps ebbing and flowing, the low conversations of men and the quiet laughter of women permeated his amniotic waters and soothed the nearly formed child.

In the last few hours, he had sensed a change in the stream of nutrients in the blood as it passed from his mother. He knew he would be soon starting on his journey through her body's raw red tunnel to that night's destination of the rough crib that lay in the corner of her bedroom; freshly laundered rags of soft swaddling waiting ready to envelop his small form.

His mother rested her body against the abandoned vegetable cart that had sat empty for weeks outside the hotel that fronted Lime Street Station. No fresh vegetables had been allowed past the pickets in the months since the workers on the docks, the sailors and the railwaymen had been involved in wildcat strikes. Only milk and bread had been allowed into the city under the governance of the workers' councils. Parties of striking men and women had been sent to the farms and estates lying on the Lancashire Plains and they had returned with stolen vegetables, fruit, and livestock. These were distributed equally amongst the poorest families at the different workers' centres that had been founded in the halls of local churches.

The vegetable cart she leaned upon was being used as a table for her husband Joe, and his pamphleteers who were washing the city with papers, hurriedly printed, still wet with ink, to plead for the continued support of the people for the strike in the face of overwhelming propaganda from the newspapers. The cart stood on the pavement in front of the Northern Hotel, the façade heavy with boarding to save the ground floor windows and the etched ornate glass of the heavy oak doors. Upstairs, on the second floor, a self-congratulation of union officials watched the gathering from a broad window and drank freely from the porter and ale provided from their members' dues.

Below on the street, the pregnant woman Bridie, and her daughter Shelagh, watched as her husband, fresh off the boat from Dublin in early June, handed out piles of leaflets to small boys. Shoeless and dirty 'street Arabs' in the low broil of an August day, sweated as they weaved amongst the crowd. They ran the messages for the heads of the strike committee, those men watching from the rooms of the hotel above, to the organisers at street level. They distributed the pamphlets calling for true democracy, universal suffrage, union recognition and bread for all. They were the eyes and ears of the controlling cadres, brave and fearless of the authority of the government agents, police and army patrols that were clotting the arteries of the city.

Bridie looked out over the plateau of pavement and the road ahead of her. She had been distracted by the shifting life inside her body, beginning to feel a change, feeling warm patches of milk moisten her breasts and sensing the need to return homewards.

Now in front of her, the crowd had swollen further. Heads topped by flat caps, straw boaters and stiff felt hats turned to face towards the speaker. He was standing on a high platform between the Corinthian columns of St George's Hall. His voice, carried by the rising air of the heat, strayed away from their ears. Men and women around her leaned themselves forward into his words, as they drifted loose through the August air, corralling the defiant words together into lucid meaning. As the words formed in their minds' eye, heads nodded approval and voices were raised in support. Then applause, and now bolder voices joined in, rising to a clamour, and calling out loudly the objects of their hatred, the oppressive capitalism of political parties, and the detached ruling classes.

Inside the womb, the noise made the child become excited. He kicked and pushed against the drum-skin of his mother's side. He wanted to escape, to add his unformed vocal chords to the cries of discontent. He wanted to flex his soft muscles and harden them, linking arms with the fellow workers, united, forming a chain to march together. He wanted to open his eyes to join a world seeking understanding from those blind to change. He wanted to swagger and sing aloud the protests and songs of unity he remembered but whose words were lost to him, confined within his watery dormant state he could only move thin pale lips and contract his limbs in spasmed time to once remembered music.

A stronger discordant rhythm began to snare, drum beat through the parchment skin to his all listening senses; a striking of metal on cobblestone, a cymbal ring of horseshoe on tram line, vibrating through the bones of his mother's legs, to the bowl of her hips and onwards, wrinkling waves through the waters of her womb to his ever receptive ears.

The noise grew without; the voices outside of his warmth became silenced and fretful. The inner waves of expectancy and possibility were replaced by swells of anxiety and nervous energy. The unborn boy strained his ears, his body quivered bow-string tight in expectation. The sunlight, that moments before had radiated pink through his liquescent space was now shadowed by uncertain storms of doubt.

The dissonance disturbed his balance. He sensed the change in atmosphere outside his sanctuary. The crowd murmured their fear, some shouted alarm, women cried in panic and above it all, one voice spoke loudly, a tone of a different cadence, a strict sturdier tone, the guttural bass, a measured beat of urging command and instructions.

From the junction of London Road, the shouted orders came from the officers of men. A captain of a squadron of dragoons on horseback spurred his men and their horses onwards. The lines of infantrymen followed, their corporals and sergeants marching them forward with a vinegar and sugar meld of obscenity and blessings. Before their bayonets, the crowd, child, woman, and man alike, panicked and broke into confused chaos.

Swords, purposely blunted, hacked at the backs of the massed crowd. Horses barrel chested the slow of foot to the floor and iron shod shoes cut into skin and broke brittle bone. Those quicker of mind and body, those familiar with the ways of justice, escaped into doorways or side streets. Hiding, cowering, pale skinned with dread. Behind the mounted soldiers, the troops marched, steady rhythm of metal toed boots tramping the flagstones, a bass line beat of bullying intimidation.

Inside the woman's womb the noise grew nearer. His mother's body tensed, and the near-formed boy felt the race of blood through his body and the anaesthetic ebb of adrenalin that calmed his foetal panic. There were screams all around him. The lights in the womb flashed red to blue, then to cold pale yellow. Then darkness. He was scared and vulnerable. His finger tendrils moved inside his mouth seeking comfort, he drew on their tips, sucking hard.

The rush of cavalry swept through the mob; the soldiers, barbaric, on foot cleaned the pavement of the people. In the space following, another line of mounted cavalry. These calmer, high stepping their horses in procession, their swords shouldered to take military control of the street and set a line across the square. To their right, from the cavernous rooms inside St George's Hall, more policemen spilled on to the highest steps and, with wooden baton and stave, slashed at the protestors around them.

The crowd, panicked into the surrounding streets, now began to regroup. The men, dockers and carters, with labourers and navvies thrown in for good strength, began ripping cobbles from the streets to send a lethal barrage of stone and blood onto the troops. Braver souls stood up to the baton waving police and bloody fights broke out about the streets. In places, those on horseback slowed and separated by the mass of the crowd became the hunted. Surrounded by anger, they were dragged from their horses and beaten in bitter bile-filled reprisal.

The child wept unseen tears as the noise of inhumanity filtered into the womb.

At his moment of despair, he felt his water-filled hollow swill and wash. His mother was being pulled. Her daughter had taken her hand and was, with the strength of fear, dragging her down to the level of the street and the sanctuary that lay beneath the standing cart. Bridie swept her dark shawl around herself and allowed Shelagh to hide her and her unborn between the wooden-spoked wheels. Through the planks of the cart's bed she watched, as the horses of the cavalry wheeled and spun, hooves sparking, iron on flagstone, while flat blades ground retreating strikers to the floor with bruised blood seeping from wounds. She enveloped her arms around her baby to protect him, to send to him a steadying heartbeat pulse of maternal love.

Inside the boy felt a hollow beneath him. It was a new sensation, a magnetic pull downwards to hidden worlds, through the paper strewn street, beyond the compacted dirt and gravel, beneath the stone slab, he sensed an echo of escape. As his mother's belly pressed the floor, he recognised space below and, in that space, security. He pushed his arms and hands against the flesh of his mother's stomach that held him trapped. He formed a soft fist and pattered a soft urgent plea against the walls of his gaol. He felt his mother gasp with the Morse rhythmed pain as her hand instinctively reached for his.

Bridie felt as if she had been stabbed. Her hand went to find the wound and found only foetal fingertips pressured against her skin. As she held her baby's rounded place, she felt him push hard against her and the knuckles of her hand brushed something hard on the rough gravel beneath them. With fingers scratching through the dirt she found the heavy ring, inset in concrete, that gave way to the entrance where the draymen used to barrel ale into the cellar of the hotel.

Again, her unborn pushed her down. She pulled on the door and it opened far enough for them to slip into the safety and dark of the tunnels of the cellar. She sat on the dirt floor and held her daughter close. In the dark it seemed that the noise receded, the peace calmed, and in her ears and heart and mind all she felt was the rhythmic pulse of her unborn's heart as it beat out the word 'sanctuary'.

As her breathing levelled and she began to look hard, blind eyed, into the surrounding darkness, dim forms began to shift into recognisable shape. She saw stacked crates of bottles and barrels of ale and demi-johns of raffia basketed wines. The dark cellar walls were lichen green with damp and water stains.

Her daughter stayed close, burrowing into her side, seeking quiet, succour and comfort.

Then without warning, a pale shadow of shock slid across Bridie and she felt her waters break. The flood from her unborn's underground river spilled, unchecked between her legs, and pooled at her feet. Her baby was ready. He had found escape to the cellar and now was ready to leave his mother, replacing one sanctuary for another. He was ready and under his own will made his way through the fleshy canals, swimming with each of her natural spasms, searching for the first breath of air. He rushed her. Her breathing became laboured and short, in sudden seizures he pushed outwards and arrived eel slippery, under her long skirts, the wet wool soft and yielding. His mother, shocked and wan pale, lay back against the wall as her daughter reached into Bridie's damp clothes and brought to her mother's tear tracked face, her child.

a rocking cradle

Above this mother and child reunion, drifting if you could upward, through the cross section of plaster and brick, dirt and paving stone, to the lobby of the hotel in Victorian splendour of tessellated tiled floors and flying aspidistra and then, higher through the ornate plaster cornices and scrolls, through thick floorboards and carpets to the room where, under clouds of tobacco smoke, important men watched in grim horror as the scenes played out below in the streets.

The military lines of police held the crowd at bay. Penned in the well of the cobblestones in the plaza, a pressed mass of humanity swayed back, trying to avoid the stepping horses. Behind them the police and plain clothes agents swiped at the heads and legs of the people with batons, forcing them downwards into the throng. Laying alone, unconscious now to the unleashed brutality, limp figures of men and women, paper cut-outs decorated the steps, pools of crimson enwreathing their shape.

In the streets that fed the flagged square to the front of the North Western Hotel, men were organising themselves into gangs to protect the women and children from the raiding police attacks. The women were busying themselves by helping the wounded and injured with scant regard to the dangers and threats around them.

Silence lay heavy in the room of important men. From the hallway, a noise of commotion turned the heads of the men, and for a moment, they were frozen. Seconds later the door opened, and half a dozen plain clothed policemen swarmed in and fell, with lead saps, onto the men. Bleeding and unconscious, they were dragged to the hall and down the sweeping grandeur of the stairway to the kitchens below. Then out to the yard. With rough vicious violence they were forced into wagons, handcuffed and chained, to be transported to the local Bridewell.

Joseph Donoghue was searching the crowd ahead of him. As he stood on the overturned cart with his hand protecting his eyes from the white sunlight, he scanned the crowds and the clutches of people the police were leading away.

"Bridie," he called. He called again, shouting louder into the crowd. A mounted policeman rode his horse towards him, causing him to duck under the swinging baton. The men on the pavement, anger rising like heat from sun baked stones, launched themselves at the horse. Its rider realising his isolation reined his horse and wheeled away to the safety of his own.

"The bastards have taken my wife and daughter," Donoghue shouted at the men staring up at him. "They've taken my Bridie and Shelagh, a child of eight years and with my wife ready to give birth and all. The feckin' bastards."

He stepped down. His heart hung nadir low. A man he recognised from the Union Hall, came to his side. "The agents have taken White, Ventre and Tillet. They came in the room and have taken them away to the lockup."

"What about the papers?" replied Donoghue.

The man shook his head and taking Donoghue's shoulder led him through the pavements' litter to the side entrance of the hotel. The pair took a set of servant stairs to wend their way, unseen, to the room. Past the splintered wood frame, where the brass lock had shattered the tight grain of the mahogany door, the room was a riot of upturned furniture and strewn mess. A hat sat on the floor, its crown dented and flattened.

"Mother of God." Donoghue said, toeing a line of bloody dots on the thick pile of the carpet.

"What are we looking for?" asked the man.

"It's a red leather bound hard backed book. It's yea big." Donoghue indicated with his hands the length and width of the book. "It has the list of all the strike's supporters. The combined lists of all the union men, the highs and mightys, the convenors and shop stewards, right down to every working man. It has, against each name, a tallied amount raised for the strike fund. We can't let it get into the hands of the gendarmes. They'll have each and every one in Walton Gaol before we can spit and throw a curse down on the devils that they are."

What he didn't tell his companion was that at the back of the book, in loose cipher, was another list. This list contained the encoded names of others. These others were from foreign or domestic contacts, fellow travelling organisations or individuals with vested interest in this small war of revolution. Against their titles, the pound sum of the monies they had contributed to the cause. The size of these sums of money dwarfed the pittances collected by the union men.

In silence, lifting coats, cushions and chairs, the men searched the room, growing more frantic by the moment. If the government agents had found the book, then the arrest of the contributors was imminent. If the money dried up, then the strike couldn't be funded. The meagre monies distributed to those most needy would be unavailable. They would soon be forced back to work through starvation. The strike could crumble and be broken. No amount of pickets and calling out the scabs would stop a man returning to work when deprived of the basics needed to provide for his family.

"I have it," shouted Donoghue's companion, holding the book above his head. "It was hidden at the back of the bookcase. Somebody was quick witted enough to keep it from the agents."

"Make sure that all the pages are there." Donoghue walked towards the man who held the book open for inspection. Donoghue took it and laid it on a table. Taking the sheaf of pages, he used his thumb to rasp through the sheets from the back of the book to the front. On the reverse side of each page, in the bottom corner was one letter from a poem by William Blake taken from his epic book on Milton. It spelt out in rapid succession the words of the lines '*And did these feet in ancient times…*'. When all the letters had been exhausted a series of individual stars flickered into view shaping into the constellation of the Starry Plough over and over again until he reached the first page.

Donoghue riffled through the pages again, this time more slowly, his lips forming the words of the poem and double checking the formation of the constellation as he neared the front.

"Aye, it's all there, right enough. Now let's put some miles between us and the police before they return."

As they descended the stairs, a hotel porter came to them.

"Joseph, your wife. She's in the cellar. She's had the baby."

He had forgotten them. "Sweet fecking Jesus." Without waiting for a response, he took the book and helter-skeltered down the stairs and into the depths of the cellars. He called out to Bridie repeatedly as he wandered the rooms, before he heard the voice of Shelagh, his stepdaughter, calling him.

"Da? Da? Is that you?"

He came into the room and could smell the dry damp that sat on the sandstone bricks and the stale ale that had leached from the kegs. He saw in the half-light the large figure of the porter's wife, her skirts black and ballooned around her, leaning over his wife who lay on the dirt floor. The porter's wife turned and showed him the small pink head of a child, the only part visible from the towel the new born had been wrapped in. She scowled at Donoghue.

"And where were you when your wife was having your child? More important things to do in the world of men, eh? Useless articles, that you are." She said, her face sour as lime juice.

"Don't be giving out about me, ye old cow" said Donoghue. As he moved towards her a smile cracked wide open on his bearded face. She smiled back, showing her gums black with pyorrhoea and her loose teeth, life's milestones, set at all the angles in a turn.

"You, Joe Donoghue, don't deserve such a beautiful baby. It's a fine boy, you have."

He took the child and looked into his knowing eyes. The baby watched back, and Donoghue felt his soul expand and shook his head with small wonderment.

"It's God's own truth," he answered, his eyes in communion with the child's, unable to wrest away from their worldly gaze. He felt as if what he held in his arms was the wisdom that mankind had lost; as if he could spend eternity asking the imponderable and without hearing, understand all the child's answers. The knowing and the unknown, the possibilities of forever and the heartache of the unknown future. It was a bond formed in the empathy of the intimate moment of a man realising, at last, he had become a man.

The child stared and he knew his father in that moment. A moment that would fade with time but was there immutable and undeniable; a pair of eyes, the iris, hen-speckled brown and with the glint fractioned light of opportunity, that showed his soul to his father and was reflected back. The slow blink of shared understanding from the baby's eyes broke the spell. Donoghue looked to the floor where his wife lay still.

"Bridie? What of Bridie?" he asked, "is she well?" and with that he knelt at her side and placed the all-seeing new born to her breast. The woman stirred, the scent of her child awakening her instinct to nurture. With a slow smile, waking her lips and eyes, she reached for the baby. Her fingers touched her husband's and the smile quickened.

"He's a grand little man, darling Bridie." He whispered. He had turned soft and gentle, a spun cocoon thread, wisp quiet. A thousand miles and more he would have walked for the love he felt for his wife and child at that instance. Her eyes drank from his unspoken promises and she became giddy on the feeling.

Her eyes fixed on his, she fumbled at her blouse and the boy fed on her milk and finally closed his eyes, the spell breaking the bond his gaze had engendered between the three.

A moment of quiet contentment passed.

"What of the streets, Joe?" said Bridie. "I saw the Dragoons. There was a terrible carnage, but the people fought back. Did they prevail, Joe? What's happening now?"

"They've taken the committee to the Bridewell. Anthony Ventre, Davy White and Ben. All arrested. We have the ledger, but at this time, I'm not concerned of the outside world.

"All I have is here."

"Aye," said Bridie, "we know how long that will last, Joseph Donoghue. All you have is here, sure enough, but we'll still be here after. Go now, Mrs Jackman will see to us.

"Leave the book with me, it can rest with me and Shelagh and the little man. No one will look under the dresses of a woman with a little scarecrow at her breast. Away and find out the world. Be back in an hour or two, mind. Me and Shelagh and this little fella will be wanting away home soon enough."

Donoghue nodded, pushed the book to the porter's wife and with a kiss to the white fingers of his wife, the pink head of the babe and the rose flushed cheeks of his stepdaughter, he ran to the stairs.

human child

As the faint light that entered the cellar rooms from overhead gratings dimmed, and the afternoon sun dropped from the sky, Donoghue had returned. His wife and their child, secure in the tunnelled folds of her shawl, had slept deeply unaware of the unrest in the streets above.

The crowds had been dispersed by mounted cavalry, with the forming mobs chased away up the slopes that dropped to the city centre. On Mount Pleasant, skirmishes between strikers and the horsemen, supported by yeoman infantry, had led to barricades of burning mattresses and furniture from nearby houses and shops being thrown across streets. Bayonets had been drawn on Brownlow Hill and a line of soldiers marched, under a cloud of stones, to clear the road. In the small side streets that ran off main thoroughfares, groups of men fought stand up battles with policemen. Around the North Western Hotel groups of armed soldiers stood apart from the people, hostile and belligerent, warily smoking thin cigarettes with faces of mistrust.

Donoghue approached three of them and wringing his cap between his hands asked, with eyes to the floor, if he could right the upturned cart that they were now slouched against.

"You're a 'Mick' aren't you?" said a corporal, thin lipped and jaundice yellow from poor diet. He had the touch of intolerance upon him and was brave before his men.

"Aye. I am. But I'm not part of this rabble." Donoghue had lied. "I'm only after my cart so I can take it home. I have a wife who's just given birth and I'll have need of it to push her and the boy homewards."

"Aye, well, Mick, you and your potato headed wife can bloody well fuck off," said the corporal, pulling his shoulders back so his chin stood proud.

Joseph Donoghue stood still. Inside the fuse was primed and the touch paper smouldered. There was the tiniest wisp of smoke, but he refused to let it spark into the rage he hid. From under his brow he glanced at the soldier, then looked away. He wouldn't rise. He waited. The corporal stood, his neck scratching against the hard wool of his tunic caused him to tick his head sideways repeatedly. Behind him, his men sucked hard on their cigarettes, their cheeks sallow and hollowed, and watched. Donoghue stood still.

Other men, watching the small band of soldiers, who had been disinterested before, now moved forward, wanting to be involved. They stood together, a little way behind Donoghue's figure of supplication, passing knowing looks and balling their fists in readiness.

The corporal's eyes flickered around him and he dropped the butt of his cigarette and used the toe of his boot to stamp its fading glow. He turned his back on Donoghue in false bravura and ordered his men to shoulder rifles, and sloped them away from the broiling tension.

"Aye, fuck to ye as well, you fecking gobshite of a man," Donoghue said to their backs.

Then, turning to the men, he asked them to right the cart back onto its wheels. As it had been set aright on the cobbled setts, he thanked them and entered the hotel with his cap pushed back, jaunty angled on his head.

"Come on now, Bridie, Shelagh, let's up the wooden hill. I've got you a carriage to take you both, and the brand new baby home."

They gathered themselves up, and with the help of Mrs Jackman, the porter's wife, who Donoghue thanked with a kiss and a sixpence, they took themselves upwards to the surface.

Bridie sensed the atmosphere in the streets had changed. Over the hours, the oppression of the armed forces had deflated the crowd's aspirations. Where once hundreds of thousands of people had stood in carnival mood, there was instead an empty space. Sentries on horseback, in police blue or the khaki green punctuated each street junction. On the high table before St George's Hall that had been audience to the orators of the strike, higher rank army officers, flat capped, braided and in wing legged jodhpurs swagger-stick strode the flags. In front of them a line of Wolseley saloons, their soft tops down and their drivers standing to attention by their side.

"Up you get, Mammy," said Donoghue, as he lifted Bridie and her bundle of humanity onto the bed of the cart. Shelagh was holding the two handles at the front to balance the precious load. He took the weight of them off her as she joined her mother. He turned the cart, so his wife, child and baby were facing the front, and strained to start them up the hill to their home on the Kensington Field roads.

Joseph Donoghue, though landed only for a few weeks from Dublin, had spoken at a number of the rallies and gatherings held in support of the strike. He had travelled from the Irish city at the behest of the Irish Transport and General Workers Union and its leader, James Connolly. He had shared a stage with Tom Mann and had thought he'd been as eloquent as the leader of the strike. Different styles, he'd give you, but his speech was more passionate, Mann's address more measured; both equal in conviction, gravitas and inspiration. As he lay into the weight of the task, he was recognised and, with a nod and no-names mentioned, men standing behind the front lines, began in their twos and threes, to push the happy load onwards. As they reached the brow and the land levelled, the men with a touch of their forehead, left the cargo to Joe his self, and he saw them tired but happy, to the small-terraced house they lived in.

darkness drops again

The room in which the child awoke the next day was filled with muted grass light, filtering through the swards of green cloth that served as curtains to the large window. He lay wrapped tight, as was the custom, in light cotton in the wooden crib his father had made from the thin wood slats of fruit boxes. He had slept, growing imperceptibly in each second of his slender grasp on time, with dreams of a far gone life. He half remembered people, gone from his life in the shadowed memory of death, that had clung to his dreamlike consciousness unwilling to fall away. As the night wore on and the dreams broke and faded, he was left with eclipsed memories of fathers and mothers and his own children speaking to him from afar, their voices silent, drifting away into the hush of the void.

His eyes opened and he knew, but didn't know, that he could tell of things long forgotten. In this nascent promise, he could only talk with his eyes. As each second formed and disappeared, he grew and his memory of the past faltered.

He knew, but he didn't know, that before he could begin to speak of all that he had lived through, it would fade like smoke in the air. The slightest residual trace would remain, always a fingertip away from his understanding, until the experiences of this life grew dense and untidy, covering them and hiding them away.

His mother and father lay in the double bed above his crib. His sister, half-sister, lay clothed on a thin mattress by the far wall, covered in a red blanket, save for her stockinged feet crimped toe-tight together, that extended onto the bare floorboards.

He could hear a woman coughing from the other room. He knew

it was the consumptive wrack of the dying. He listened, his eyes searching the air above him for death. He saw nothing. It wasn't yet her time.

Bridie Donoghue awoke sore and stiff, her legs and hips swollen, empty belly flaccid and soft. She reached for her child unconsciously. She pulled him to her, and his lips sought her milk and he fed greedily and grew. With each moment he began to forget. She cradled him to her chest until he fed no more and fell again into a forgetful sleep.

Later, after she had washed and dressed, she woke her daughter and shooed her downstairs to prepare the range to cook their breakfast. Her husband lay asleep, his head hidden under the bolster.

She went next door to the bedroom where the old lady, Mrs Murdoch, whose house they shared, was propped up on the pillows. Her eyes were closed. A web of white phlegm had spun itself between the fine white hairs of her chin, into a lace mesh of spittle. Her breath came grudgingly and went away complaining, her chest rising and falling in slow time.

Bridie watched the eiderdown's small swell rise with each of the old woman's inward gasps as she searched for life. Then a wait, eternity passing, before the breath fell back with a despairing sigh, that dismissed the possibility of her enduring life. It was mesmeric.

Bridie remembered days on the beach at Seapoint, just south of Dublin, where fascinated she had watched the pulse of the waves. She had sat with her father, Jack Hayes, on dull sandy shingles. He had told her that if the waves failed, then the world would end. She had watched them roll in over the pebbles, and then fall back into the sea. Incessant.

She had said to her father, as he rolled his cigarette paper between nicotine-stained thumb and finger, "A tiny part of me wants to see the wave stop. The sea to fall still."

"Fuist, child, hush now. Do you want the world to end?"

She couldn't answer. The smallest part of her child like wonder did. To see the stars fall and the moon fade, the dead rise and Heaven take them from hunger and want to the white bliss promised by the priests. And it was so for Bridie again now, with the old woman's breathing. It hypnotised her. Waiting, watching the rolling breaths of life to cease. Waiting in bewildered anticipation of what death looks like when it visits.

The spell was broken by the call from her husband and the sound of him creaking out of bed to cast his shadow over the child's cot and exclaim to the world. "My storeen bawn, my little man. Have you ever heard the great poet's words?"

He recited from his heart the words of Yeats, his favourite.

"Come away, O human child! To the waters and the wild.

"With a faery, hand in hand,

For the world's more full of weeping than you can understand."

When Bridie came back into the bedroom, he had lifted the boy and was looking into his eyes.

"For the life of me, I'd swear that this child had already seen all of the world's weeping."

She brushed his words away. "Don't be more of a fool than you already are, Joseph."

"I swear on my own grave his eyes are holding something," he replied, continuing his gaze, "there's a depth to it. Like those bottomless pools in the mountains of Connemara, there's something in there, like spiritual. Do you get me?"

"Quiet now," she said. "You'll be naming the boy a faery himself. It's not the time of the world to be having faery boys, however deep and magical they are, floating in the air of this city.

"You're just drunk with the thought of your first born. I hope he fulfils his own dreams, let alone yours, but you're right. This world is full of sorrow and he's got to get through that with a dry eye. Now give the wee thing to me. It's either him that needs a change of his nappy or it's you, Joseph, that stinks to high Heaven."

After a breakfast of tea and bread and dripping, they had begun to dismantle the cart that had spent the night outside the front step. Donoghue had removed the split pins holding the wheel and had laid them to rest against the side of the gas lamp post. With a large spanner he had undone the nuts and bolts that held the yoke in place, and the bed of the cart had been separated and lay square on the cobbled street.

"It'll come in," he had told Bridie, with a smile of bedevilment. "We will keep it in the yard by the privy. Possession is ten points of the law. We can say to all and sundry that I've reclaimed it in the name of the revolution."

Aye, thought Bridie, the revolution. And if the cart is found, do you not think, you'll be jailed and me and the children left to fend for ourselves. The revolution won't feed me and the baby.

Through the front door and down the long passage to the scullery, and then out the back door to the small yard, Joe and his mates had hefted the parts of the cart. They had been placed in the small yard and covered with a tarpaulin, making the night time trip to the dank hole of the toilet even more perilous.

That afternoon, after the family had attended morning Mass, two men arrived in the street outside. The day had turned overcast and the once strong shadows muted as the sun paled. They passed the house and turned at the corner and then, satisfied they were themselves alone, backtracked, to knock on the door of the Donoghue's home.

Shelagh opened the door, recognised one of them, not the other, and in mute silence beckoned them in. Joseph had been in the yard. On hearing the front door, he came in with a knife in his hand and flecks of paint on his arms and in his hair, from scraping the name of the fruit merchant from the side of the cart. Bridie sat in a chair with the child. She looked up and smiled at the visitors.

The taller of the two came forward, took off his wide brimmed trilby and, pushing away the blanket that wrapped the baby's head, he chucked the mite's chin.

"He's got your looks, Bridie. Luckily, he hasn't the face of yer man there. We can thank the good Lord for that blessing."

It was predictable but Bridie feigned a pale smile. She patted the seat of the chair next to her and dutifully, her husband came to her side. As he sat, she entwined her fingers in his.

"Shelagh, find Jim and his friend a seat, would ye," said Joseph, and they shook hands with the steady firmness of working men. The men courteously half bowed their heads to Bridie in acknowledgement.

They all waited until the girl came back and the men were seated. They were both dressed in a similar fashion, high collared stiff shirts and a black tie under a tweed suit. Sunday best. Jim Larkin wore a dark raincoat with the collar upturned to hide an unwaxed and unkempt moustache. The other man was clean shaven. He had blue grey bruising beneath his fidgeting eyes and held a slim leather briefcase tight to his chest.

"So, Jim, this is a bit of a surprise to me," said Joe, "I didn't even know you were coming to Liverpool for the Strike."

"Ah well, it was thought wise to travel, like, incognito. Not quite disguised, like, but use a bit of nouse and keep a dead low profile." He unconsciously stroked his moustache. "I came over on the boat to Holyhead and then collected and driven home by car. I was there yesterday on the piazza, and I'll be going back to Dublin in the next day or so."

"No more need be said. Just be careful when you leave, there are some sleven nosey biddies in this street. And if they think they might earn a shilling from the Guards, they'd put the finger on you no problem."

Larkin laughed. But there was no humour in the sound. "Aye, Joe, I'll be careful but as yet I'm not a traitor to the Crown. Not unless you know different?"

Donoghue shook his head. "I'm just advising caution, that's all. Are we to be introduced?" Donoghue indicated with a nod the man accompanying Jim Larkin.

"We are thinking that it might be best to keep some names a secret. I'll add it's not a matter of trust, for those in this room are all friends, but as you say caution is a good thing, and there are secret agents everywhere. Even by my old home in Toxteth, the Bethel Presbyterians are taking a poor view of our work. I've been warned to take all possible care."

Donoghue slowly nodded. "Well, tell us now Jim, what was the conclusion of yesterday's action? As you'll have heard we had to leave early but we left with the prize. Two prizes to be fair." His eyes touched his wife's with tenderness.

He then indicated to Shelagh to fetch the large red leather tome that had been hidden behind the Welsh dresser. He pushed the book towards Jim who raised his hands in refusal.

"It would be better if we sent someone for this. We came on one of the few trams running. We'd be easy target for the police if we were seen to be carrying this. You're right, it is a prize. It should be kept safe, remain hidden, until we can deliver it to the people who need it."

Donoghue nodded and looked to his wife for agreement. She rocked her child slowly as he awoke and murmured his introductions to the group.

"The tram?" she said to the men, "is it running with the knowledge of the Strike Committee and the Syndicats?"

"It is, with their permission. The tram is running to take people back and forward to the infirmary. There were hundreds damaged yesterday when the Warwick Regiment, or whichever of Churchill's generals was involved, ordered their men into the crowd. Prior to that it was peaceful. It took just a few rowdy ones to give the excuse the magistrates needed to call riot and send in the police.

"It didn't take long to become quite the war scene," said Jim. "We were fortunate indeed, that there were no deaths. Some of the beatings handed out by the police, and the plain clothes amongst them especially, were beyond brutal. I saw women felled by horses, lying on the flags only to be beaten by the bobbies, scum that they are, as they tried to raise themselves up. Anyone who helped them got beaten as well."

The baby was awake. Half dreams, fleet to memory, pervaded his thoughts. *Red flags, gun shots and drums he heard on a salt wind coming off a storm driven sea. His fists folded and unfolded, creasing tiny palms into the mapped roads on his skin that later in life would be divined and studied, touched by one searching for his mystery. The child heard the prayers of the dying, spoken in a foreign tongue, rise into the steady gusts of air bearing the smell of dried seaweed, then sink into silence, replaced by a keening cry as the wind syphoned through marram grass on the dunes that lined the estuary. He tasted the dust of dry red earth and the metal of blood in his mouth. He saw shadows of corpses in a sun bleached arroyo, shoeless and half clothed, fed on by feral pigs while a pack of dogs slept in the shade, replete from their meal.* Again, he tried to reclaim his memories, but they faded, small typeface overwritten by emboldened fonts as his new story was authored and took their place.

From these voices of the past, in this new life, he listened to the words. His unconscious recording them deep within.

The demonstration in the city was the centre of a countrywide strike that had been organised in the early part of the year.

Workers in different sectors of industry had realised that the elected bodies, the Labour Party itself or their representatives on the Trades Union Councils had not followed their members' appeal for action. The Labour Party voted for by those enfranchised workers in 1906 had aligned itself with piecemeal reform of the ruling Liberals. The move to the left, needed for the growing numbers of unemployed, the marginalised working classes, the poor and impoverished, and expected to be dynamic following the election became a turgid limp towards moderated values.

It had been left to agitators, those who believed in the French method of Syndicalism to motivate the workers. It hadn't been difficult. Years of rises in prices had eroded the living standards that many had reached through the benefits of industrialisation. The expansion of the railways and coal mines to feed the avarice of the economy had initially benefitted the worker. The workers organised as they grew and formed the union and labour movements. Slowly, as the years passed and the heads of these radical organisations became staid through the machinations of politics, the ordinary workers found themselves again on the outside.

Not surprisingly those at the front line of the workforce, faced with the objection of their own political allies and the intransigence of the owning classes, felt differently. The wildcat strike, sudden and disruptive, became the tool of the organised workers. Although many belonged to the unions, they ignored the official line and withdrew their labour, sometimes with bloody consequence. With little control, heady individuals would strike and lead workers off the factory floor, the dockside, or the rail track. If the owners tried to use scab labour to keep the production lines running, the docks clear of cargo and the rail passengers moving, the strikers took violent reprisals. Across the country, from Glasgow to London, from Hull to Merthyr Tydfil, strikes had almost halted the economy. The government's response had been to try and break the strikes by supporting the scabs and the owners by using the police and the military as wings of their own executive. The boundaries had been writ large and double underlined and each faction knew where they stood.

The child innately understood more than just the words spoken. He drank in the sentiment, the bitterness contained in one, the sweet taste of another, his mind filled with the senses of the words and of man's possibilities, and man's injustice. It was a heady cocktail of emotions that coursed through his small veins and settled effervescent in the soul of his heart.

There was a silence in the room. From upstairs, came a rattling chain of coughs from the old woman.

The American man leaned forward. He spoke in a long lazy drawl that mystified those in the room, hearing its fluttering cadence for the first time.

"The violence was pretty much limited to the crowd in front of the station during the afternoon. It turned even worse later. There were squads of those bobbies, some in plain clothes, scouring the streets afterwards. If they came upon a group of men, they'd whale on them. Beat them senseless and throw them into the wagon. For a long time last night, all through the city you could hear the police whistles as they caught up with groups of protesters, and they weren't all strikers. I saw a family, quite the well-dressed group, be fallen upon, men and women alike, all because they tried to stop a fellow from getting a beating."

"You were best out of it, Joe," spoke Bridie, "I know you've a temper and a half, and won't be seeing an injustice gone unheeded. It was best you were home with me and the child last night."

Joseph Donoghue looked down at his feet as he cradled the

knuckles of his right hand in the palm of the other. He blew his breath out.

The American continued. "They didn't have it all their own way though. It's one thing being the bully when you come as a mob, but we caught them a few times outnumbered, and we didn't hold back. The darker the night became, the better it got for us. These fellows knew the streets and alleyways of this city better than the rats that run in them. I fell in with a band who had taken a police whistle and had used it to position traps for the police. They'd sound it and wait. You'd hear the footsteps first and then, so long as the numbers were in our favour, we'd spring out and take our revenge."

His smiling face was met with sullen disapproval from Bridie, who straightened her posture as the man spoke.

"We become as bad as them if we have to stoop to violence to get our voice heard," she said quietly.

The American shifted in his seat. Larkin continued.

"Violence is necessary, Bridie, we have the unions and the Labour Party for what they are worth, but they lie on the side of the government. They don't like the way we go about our business. They'd prefer if we acted like gentlemen, that we gave them notice of our walk outs, so the bosses can organise scab labour. If we try and stand against the scab, to protect our jobs, they send in the police and army. Do you know there's five thousand troops here in Liverpool, as well as an extra two and a half thousand police drafted in?

"Our unity as workers is only as powerful as the bonds that hold us together. They broke up a meeting yesterday, attended peacefully by nearly a hundred thousand people, and used sword and stick to beat ordinary workers, their wives and children. So yes, we have the right to fight for what we believe in. Maybe only revolution will come with the gun. It's not as if we have the universal suffrage yet, we still need to vote a party of the people into power. You know what Marx said of the Paris rioters? 'It was their own good nature that caused them to be defeated.'"

Bridie was well enough versed in the philosopher's words to know that the quote had been altered to fit Jim Larkin's purpose.

"Ah, so is it a revolt or a revolution you're after?" she said, and looked away into her child's dark listening eyes.

The American, his lips wet and shining, spoke "Maybe from the seed of revolt, a revolution will come. When there is no hope then people take to the streets. If they are put down by the agents of the State, deference is lost for authority. Then the rough men, ready to do violence on the people's behalf, appear and are seen as their champions. You know what happened at Tony Pandy last year, shots were fired by the police and that one miner was clubbed to death by a police baton. There's over three hundred injured yesterday. Some won't ever recover or walk, never mind work again, so we have no choice but to fight back. There's fresh news that Churchill has sent two gunships to anchor on the Mersey and they have orders to fire into the city if there are more troubles. Every spark threatens to light a fire. What will it take for this city and others to burn in insurrection?"

There was a dread silence in the room. The baby began to cry silently, and Bridie soft murmured him back towards sleep.

"I'm sorry to have had to talk about this. Our visit was purely to see you and the baby, to pass on our congratulations. Do you have a date to get him christened? And have you a name for him?"

Joe spoke for the first time. "Well, after our leader, of course, we are going to call him Patrick James Connolly Donoghue."

Two days later the police were transporting some of those arrested during the protest in Liverpool, notably Tom Mann, the protest's leader and main speaker, to Walton Gaol. Under a shower of stones, the police shot rifle volleys into the ranks of striking workers who blocked their way.

Two dockers, John Sutcliffe and Michael Prendergast, were killed. The christening of the baby, Patrick James Connolly Donoghue, was postponed for their funerals.

pavements grey

O'Brien took the special edition of the Echo and snapped the newspaper open from its creased confines.

He was sitting in the parlour of his home in Orwell Street, Kirkdale, comfortable in his armchair, his collar unstudded from his unbuttoned shirt, showing the soft cream undergarment. Beside him on the settee, with her sleeping daughter's head on her lap, was his wife Mary. She sewed demurely under the gaslight. The room was wallpapered in the dark patterns of damask, carpeted with rugs on the hardwood floor and furnished in the heavy oak of the time. The parlour was lit by gas, pools of light bleeding into dark space and flowing into the dim of the room's corners.

"Peter, what do the papers say of the meeting today at St George's Plaza?" she said in a hushed tone, needless for the deep sleeping child.

Her husband read from the paper.

"The mob and the rabble-rousers at their fore were cleared out by the Liverpool Police and a regiment of the Nottinghamshire's. A number of policemen and soldiers were injured."

He continued, paraphrasing the article. "It says nothing of any casualties within the crowd. Thomas Mann and Tillet were arrested and taken to the Bridewell on Dale Street it says, and other seditionists were taken into custody for questioning. Seditionists? That's a harsh word to use for this mob. They've been bound over and will be taken to Walton, to be tried later in the week. The police are imposing a curfew on the city centre. It's a terrible indictment of this crowd led by Mann. He has ignored the Trades Union Congress and the Labour Party itself. To call wildcat strikes repeatedly is damaging for business, and if business is harmed then the work for the ordinary man is affected. I am not against the withdrawal of labour, but it must not be disruptive to commerce."

His accent strengthened as he read and though the words were high, the tone lowered as his anger rose.

His wife looked at him, a question in her eye, but discretion prevailing in her mind.

She leant forward into the cream light of the gas lamp standing on the side table, covered in a heavy moss green corded cloth. She placed the sewing on a side table and picked up the small companion dictionary she kept by her side. She found the word 'sedition' and pondered on its meaning for a moment.

"I wonder if Joseph, Bridie's husband, has been caught up with that same crowd?"

Mary O'Brien, nee Hayes, knew that her elder sister and her husband had arrived in Liverpool a few months ago, but had not spoken to her in the past week. Her sister was carrying her second child, her husband's first. Bridie had an older child from a previous marriage. She had been widowed at the age of nineteen and had married less than six months later, providing her infant daughter with a new father, Joseph Donoghue. Their own new baby was due in the next week or so.

Joe Donoghue was known to be a Dublin radical, a friend of Tom Johnson and in league with the leaders, Larkin and Connolly, of the ever-strident Irish Transport and General Workers Union. He had been denounced by his parish priest as a communist and branded a socialist by the confederation of industry in Dublin. He became a pariah who could only work on casual jobs under a false name or to eke an existence from union business. It was on union business that he had arrived in Liverpool. Both the O'Briens knew Donoghue's heart beat hardest for the fight for a united Ireland.

Mary had visited the address of a rented house in Kensington for her pregnant sister and was comforted by the knowledge that a steady wage, albeit small, was coming into their household. In these times of hardship, any money from any source was a God given gift. Even her own household had been affected by the strikes. It was the women who bore the burden. She knew her sister was a strong woman. Wilfully pragmatic, with an eye for the survival of herself and her family. That had been proven, Mary thought, by Bridie's marriage to Joe Donoghue. There had been talk, within the family, that with her first husband not long in the cold earth, the marriage was hardly decent; but a father for her daughter, Shelagh, was paramount in Bridie's thoughts. Mary wondered if she would do the same if anything happened to Peter. She watched him as he read the newspaper, her needle and thread suspended above the darned sock. He'd be a hard man to replace, she thought. She sighed, shrugged her shoulders and snapped off the thread with a quick pull of her wrist.

Peter O'Brien had been a tallyman on the Sandon Dock. A tallyman or dock gateman was a position envied and despised in equal measure by the dock workers, who woke early from the cold bed and waited in line for his grace and favour nod to impartiality. It was the tallyman, the agent of the ship owner, who gave work to the men who waited to be hired.

Standing on a cart at the stand, as it was called, in front of the dock gates, O'Brien would look down on the men turned out for the everyday of the hiring fair. A hundred men or more could line up to be picked for a dozen available jobs that day. Those registered with the Mersey Docks and Harbour Board would hold a tally, a button like object that allowed them entrance to the dock system and their name recorded in the ledger. Each had already paid a pound and four pence to be registered as dock workers, many in the particular specialisms of being a stevedore or porter.

Others were casual labourers, often non-unionised, required on the docks to do the heavy lifting. If chosen they were guaranteed a day's low pay for a day's hard work, loading or unloading ships, sometimes in the dark reaches of a ship far away from daylight, the air filled with the lung choking dust of grain or coal, the footings unsure, the cargo unstable. The ever present threat of injury overhead from swinging jibs and chains, the consequence of moving shipments within the hold, underfoot unstable and liquid, a broken leg, a broken back, a broken life and a family hungrily reliant on their endeavour. The morning shift finished in the afternoon at four and the dock owner's agent, the gateman would pick another set of men to work shift after shift until the hold was empty. When the hold had been emptied, the men were paid off for their shift with no guarantee of any work tomorrow. They would receive their pay, with a touch of the cap to the gateman and take it to the nearest pub to wash away their misery and seek brief oblivion.

For the casual labourer, to catch the eye of the tallyman usually meant some corruption, minor or more, or bribery had taken place. Some accepted the temptation of cash, stolen goods or the favours of the wives of the most desperate. Some hired on religious grounds, taking members of their parish or chapel or faith. Secret signals, ribbons or signs making them known as a friend of the tallyman. O'Brien was one of the few who hadn't abused his position.

Those who weren't chosen were turned away to spend the day waiting for the afternoon shift or the distant tomorrow, taking their frustration and anger home to their families who would go to bed hungry that night.

The current strike had been called to try and stop this practice and to increase workers' pay. The strikes were called by men within the workforce, often with no union recognition, and were acted out with short notice. It was the fundamental tenet of Syndicalists that the individual should take direct action and not be beholden to the union hierarchy to negotiate for them. The wildcat strike was supported by pickets, with easy violent retribution against those scabs who sought to work when others' labour had been withdrawn. The strikes in Liverpool and the Welsh valleys had spread nationwide discontent and the heady air of revolution was oppressively heavy in the air.

"Well, for one, I'm glad that I won't be going back to the Sandon. My job at Simon and Hester at the Cotton Exchange will start in a week. There are a dozen ships, either at the Liverpool Bar waiting entry to the docks or en route as we speak. There'll be interesting times when the ships are allowed to unload their cargoes. The market will be volatile and a volatile market for a trader is usually profitable, and profit for the firm is what it's all about."

He folded the newspaper and looked at the fire, dying embers of coal holding his gaze.

"I've been told that Mr Churchill," his speech was punctuated as he spat, the distaste of the name on his lips, into the fire, "has promised his party that the dock gates will be re-opened, even if it takes gunships to patrol the Mersey and soldiers themselves to unpack the load. Though God help the soldier working in the bowels of a collier ship in the August heat. He'd wish he were back in India, South Africa or any part of the empire whipping the darkies into the black hole of Calcutta."

Mary allowed silence to dissipate the heat of her husband's soap box speech to his imagined audience and after a calm had again settled, spoke.

"Anyway, I'm very pleased myself," said Mary, "to have my husband working in Old Hall Street in the city centre. It's a fine new building. You'll need starched collars and a new suit and shoes. I imagine it'll be a different way of dressing in the Exchange. We'll have to make a donation to St John's parish. It was a grand gesture of Father Sean to intercede for you with Mr Haskin, the man you're to work for. Lucky indeed that his parents are our parishioners." She smiled at him.

O'Brien had been born in the squalid streets around Wood Quay in Dublin. His father worked as a carter and his mother seemed continually with child. In spite of her swollen stomach, or maybe because of it, he remembered his childhood as one of hunger, always a meal or two away from the miracle of enough. He had been favoured within his family by being the eldest child. He had the privilege of being given an education only available for their first born. That had been essential to his parents in order that he was able to provide for them and his family as soon as he finished school. He had left the classroom with a mind crammed of learning, a heartfelt obligation to family and a bright eye, wide open for the main chance.

Of the fourteen children his mother gave birth to, seven survived. They were all still at home when his parents, worn and damaged, were chosen to move to the newly built Iveagh Trust Buildings on Bull Alley, a purpose built tenement for the poor. Within a year of having their own front door and not having to share their home with other families, his parents had both died. Untimely death wasn't uncommon in the hard fought stations of life. It was said, at their wake, with the devil's own smile, that they had succumbed to the luxury of an indoor water closet and the rare pleasure of cleanliness, and the warm comfort of a proper bed.

Then aged seventeen, O'Brien had left Dublin, taking the ferry to Liverpool with his two younger brothers. The rest, the other children went to live with relatives, his eldest sister into the drudgery of domestic service. In Liverpool, the boys spent their first night in a loose brick hovel on Great Howard Street where the rats and lice had the better of their room. The furniture was one chair, a table and thin straw mattresses, still damp from the watermarks running through the bodies of previous occupants.

One brother had quickly embarked for New York with a heavy pocketful of shillings won in a gambling den on Islington. The other found work in the tobacco workshops in the north end of the city and waited for the call to America from his older sibling. While he waited for the call westward he and Peter took lodgings in Kirkdale, in the parish of St John the Evangelist.

Peter O'Brien had found opportunity waiting for him and being singularly educated, moved quietly from a shipman labourer to be promoted to stevedore , and upwards to warehouseman, a job normally reserved for the diligence of the Welsh Methodists. He had been taken under the wary eye of the chapel going Presbyterian master to become his preferred tallyman. The gateman who collected the dockers' tally, the button issued that gave them the right to be hired.

It was on a regretful return visit to Dublin to pay for his youngest sister's funeral, who had succumbed to tuberculosis, at age thirteen, not yet full grown, that he had met the dark eyed Mary Hayes. Smitten as he was, he proposed that evening and they were married the next day in the Church of the Immaculate Conception on Merchants Quay. The day after the wedding celebrations he brought his new wife to his home at 91 Orwell Road, Kirkdale, Liverpool.

Now, he reflected in the warm comfort of his sitting room, that when this strike had been broken, normalcy would settle and the natural order of things would resume. He would thank the priest, the good Lord, and chance, in that order, for the prospect of moving a rung upwards on the social ladder, skipping over the snakes that whispered misfortune and into the world of finance and commerce, and the possibilities therein. They would need the money. Mary yearned for more children and it was his duty, he knew and supposed, to give his wife what she wanted.

O'Brien was unsure if he shared his wife's longing. Annie, their daughter, asleep, pale at peace, her head on her mother's lap, now three years of age, had been born blind. The guilt of his disappointment at her birth still lay dark on his soul.

He had confessed his sin, hiding veiled from the priest behind a screen but in plain sight of the Church. The anonymity of the confessional meant little when the priest knew the lives of his parishioners. The priest had cautioned love. For his daughter and his wife but most of all for Peter himself. Embarrassed at the unmanliness of the thought, he had left wondering at the unlikely ability to love oneself. He had pondered the meaning and it wasn't until the following Thursday that he returned to the church to seek an explanation from Father Sean McGuire.

of self and soul

He entered the church at the main entrance on the corner of Sessions Road. The door closed behind and the noise from the street faded into inconsequentiality. O'Brien genuflected and crossed himself. There were already pews full of people, heads bent in prayer; those on the right considering which of their sins they should tell the priest, those on the left saying prayers in penance, having been routinely absolved by an undiscerning god.

Every five minutes a parishioner unburdened by the weight of sin would rise, turn to face the altar, kneel briefly in taught respect to the omnipresent, and then turn and leave the church forgiven of their trespasses. On the other side of the nave, as the doors of the confessional box opened and a relieved sinner escaped, another weighed down by the enormity of his or her trivial failings in the eyes of man and God would, with head bowed, venture into the holy abyss for absolution.

The church in the late evening sunlight prismed the light of the high stained-glass windows of the apse. The colours fell silently on the hushed church. Queues of candles, their flames shaped in the silhouette of praying hands, entreated the plaster figures of the Holy Family to answer the petitions of the faithful. Around the walls the plaster reliefs of the twelve Stations of the Cross. Each showed the devoted poor that the only way to their heaven would be to follow the Son of God's journey of pain and suffering at the hands of others.

O'Brien walked down the aisle and joined the ashamed rows of the contrite.

"Forgive me, Father, for I have sinned. It has been one week since my last confession" he said, as he knelt at the prie-dieu and made the sign of the cross. He put his closed fingers to his lips in devotion to the Holy Sacrament. From behind the screen came the low voice of the priest sitting in the shadows. Peter leant into the murmured blessing.

"Father, I have been neglecting my wife. I know she wants another baby, but I'm scared that it'll be blind, like our Annie, or in some way blighted with disease or illness."

"Now, Peter, did you not come with the same sin last week? And did we not absolve you then as we'll absolve you now; and didn't we say that you had to learn to love yourself in order to love others? Well? Why are ye here again? Have you not done as I said?"

"Well. I'm not sure what you meant, Father."

"Well, your child was born blind, was she not? But did you not love her and provide for her? Do you still love her and provide for her and her mother?"

"Yes, Father, of course."

"So why in the world of the saints would you not love the child that God will give you in the future. You are a good man, O'Brien. A child born into the world whatever shape or deformity is not going to stop that goodness. It's within your own heart and soul. You will love them, each and every one. It's for you to realise that. Come to terms with it, let you, and give yourself a tiny bit of credit now.

"Yes, you had the human frailty to see your child born blind, and of course to worry for her. It isn't that you can't cope with her blindness, it is that you worry for her, that she may not cope in the future. So, as I said last week, learn to love yourself; appreciate yourself and all you do for your family. You will begin to understand that in loving yourself you will love others more and they in turn, will reciprocate with their deepest love. And God will love you and your family. Are you with me, now? So, no more stupid guilt. It's not guilt anyway, it's being scared for the child's future. All fathers should have that concern, especially in this brave new world we are living in with cars and planes and the like.

"So, together we'll say the Act of Contrition and for your penance for wasting my time and for your own foolishness, say ten Hail Marys, ten Our Fathers and a Glory Be."

Afterwards, Peter knelt and with silent incantations of long remembered prayers served his penance. He spent a further half hour meditating on the red light that hung like a steering star above the altar. To the faithful, the light showed the Holy Spirit was present in the form of his host, in the tabernacle on the altar. In the still atmosphere of the church, O'Brien felt the forgiving comfort of its refined essence.

He rose, crossed himself, and left to go home to his wife and their bed.

In the same bedroom nine months later, as they prepared for bed and Mary lay on fresh laundered sheets smelling faintly of violets, her waters broke.

Peter called the neighbours' daughter to sit with Mary. He was sent to fetch the doctor, taking his bike through night streets filled with low mist and orange sodium light. By the time they returned, the teenage girl was sitting by Mary's side, naïve, not knowing what to do; she held her hand and patted it gently, while under the dark bedclothes and heavy woollen blankets the new born child, comfortable, wet and warm, breathed the muggy undercover fumes of his afterbirth, unaware that his journey has ended. Unaware of the journey to come.

The nurse had fussed and cut, and mopped and dried, before

handing the new born to O'Brien.

"He's a handsome wee chap," she said, all safety pins and smelling of antiseptic, "your wife is fine; a few days of rest and she'll be good as gold. I will weigh him and give you the details to register him at Brougham House in the morning and I'll be expecting an invite to the christening. What name will you give your peaceful little man, sleeping as he did under the covers?"

"Aye, nothing biblical or from the stories. He will be a plain Edward, after my own father. God willing, he will stay calm and tranquil for the rest of his life. It's a hard-enough station without adding stress to strain it."

She left him holding his future and went to feed the mother the iron-rich bottle of milk stout she always kept in her Gladstone bag.

a lonely impulse of delight

"Paddy, come here," shouted Bridie. Unconsciously her thin arms cradled her stomach.

She could see him with a group of children, playing with a ball at the end of the street. She shook her head. He's a reckless one, she thought, not the biggest, aye, and not the strongest but as bright as a new button. As she watched him, her thoughts turned to his likeness to her husband, Joe. He'd been gone for the best part of three years now. She had waited for each letter home with increasing heartache. The post boy, his bike, rattling down the cobbles of the street, had just handed her a telegram, which she held unopened, already knowing its content.

The years had tripped by, toes caught on loose flagstones, to May 1919. A stumbling step along the spiral staircase of time. She remembered each halting step and tread.

The ferment of revolution had been felt in the streets of Liverpool through the early years of the century. A mixture of the fight for better wages and conditions, the universal right to vote for all men and women, and the perplexed question of Irish sovereignty, all ingredients in the stew of discontent. Bridie's husband had been there stirring the pot.

Then mystically and magically, as attention was focused on home affairs, a distant Serbian nationalist stepped out in front of a car and shot dead a member of a vague Eastern European dynasty. One rich entitled man shot in the name of 'Unification and Death'. The Black Hand assassin's bullet had carried through the Archduke's body, ricocheting and tumbling through the countries of Europe. The bullet had settled finally, spent and smoking, amongst the piled stocks of shells and weapons accumulated by nervous governments during the years of fervent rearmament. The smouldering case needed little oxygen to enflame and set off the chain reaction to the bloodiest conflict of the century.

The men and women who had once striven against the poverty and impossibility of their lives were wondrously distracted and diverted by the flames of war and took up the call of patriotism. They put down the scarlet flag of revolution and took up the braided gold pennants of ancient regiments. With flute and drum, in time step, they had marched in Pals' regiments to the war. On the streets in front of Liverpool's Lime Street Station, they had massed. Khakied, in ordered soldier-by-soldier row they drilled on the flagstones where faded blood stains marked the places where innocent protesters had once fallen. The newly uniformed men stepped to the steady beat and boarded the same trains that had once been halted by strikes for better pay and conditions. Away then to foreign soil and a futile war that would uphold the privileges and freedoms of those that had despised and ignored them, only a moment's fetid breath before.

In the same year as those men he'd once thought of as comrades, during the rebellious Great Unrest, went off to war, Joseph Donoghue left his family and took the packet boat in the other direction. He travelled back to Dublin. He had been called back by Connolly to parade and drill another army, the ICA, the Irish Citizen Army, and to take the absent James Larkin's workload in producing the Irish Workers' newspaper.

He returned to Liverpool three times. On the first, he brought christening presents for his new child, Anthony. Unbeknown to him or Bridie, she had been left pregnant. Alone, she had looked after his children and borne the burden of expectancy and birth, while misleading suspicious neighbours with tales that her Joe was gone away to fight a war. He visited again, three months later, bringing with him his nation's characteristic fecundity and left again the seed of his next child embedded in his wife's womb. Finally, when he returned again to the house in Kensington, it was late March 1916 and the seed left had matured and now sat like a sack on Bridie's hips. The baby was late, and March stepped over into April and as Easter got closer, Donoghue became more impatient. His temper was cooled when

the baby put in an appearance on the 7th day of April. They named her after her mother, Bridgid, and they called her Young Bridie.

Then, Joe Donoghue received a message from Dublin. Two weeks after the baby's birth, he had been sitting on his front step when a man from the union offices cycled up the street. A widow from across the way cleaned her windows with vinegar and bile, shaking her head in indignant disbelief at the brass neck of her neighbour. Her sons were in France, at the front fighting, while her feckless neighbour sat safe on the threshold to his home, a traitor to the wastes of war.

In his mouth was a pipe, and in his arms was his new daughter. At his father's feet and looking up was Patrick; called Patsy by his father and Paddy by his loving mother, but always solemn, serious Patrick to himself. At age five he felt he was too old to be called by anything else.

The messenger from the union proffered Joe the note. With his arms full of the joy of his new born, he asked for the note to be passed to his son.

"Are you able to read yet, Patsy, mi laddo?" he had asked.

The boy had smiled and opened the folded paper. The words were typed.

'Forthcoming weeks will bring about great change to our country. Inform the Liverpool Volunteers that the time approaches and to embark for Dublin. However, in regard to yourself, remain at your station. In the coming time all information regarding movements of troops between Liverpool and the ports of Ireland will be imperative.

Your responsibility is to provide accurate reports from now until we stand together in a Free Ireland. Signed on behalf of the Provisional Government. J Connolly. Commandant-General, Dublin Division, Irish Citizen Army.'

The boy looked at the letters. Somewhere hiding inside the letters shaped into foreign words and his tongue tried to wrap the shapes into sound. The shapes floated and moved; his mind couldn't find the way to solidify them into hard meaning, his tongue too immature to trap the jangle of vowels and consonants. He looked up at his father's excited face and shook his head.

"Take the baby, son. Let your Da' read it."

The boy took the new child and looked into her eyes searching for something lost, something eternal to bond their souls. He had hoped the memories distant and fast faded in his mind could be found in the infant's eyes. He was seeking the hidden learning, trying to find her own unspoken memories when his Da' detonated his rage and exploded to his feet.

Paddy jumped backwards. The baby was almost dropped to the floor.

Joe Donoghue had expected to be recalled. Revolution was stirring in the Irish air. Planned uprisings were talked about plainly in the militias of Dublin and already the city's republican radicals were being armed. The news was not what he had wanted. He had expected to return to his city, ready for the coming fight for the new Ireland but instead, he was to stay in Liverpool.

'No," his father shouted, "the feckers. That fecking Connolly, that fecking Scottish gobshite bastard. He can't do it to me. I'm to brief the Volunteers here in Liverpool and tell them to sail. Feck them and feck Landy and McGarvey, the Kerrs, Pat Reid and Craven; feck them all. Fucking Connolly."

He sat down heavy on the step. Tears of frustration needled his eyes. The muscles in his jaw spasmed as he set it hard against disappointment. Behind him, Bridie came from the scullery. The woman, opposite, put her wet rags into the bucket and turned to stare.

"Joe, what is it?" She saw her son, ashen, a stray tooth holding down the side of his lip, his grimace askew. "You're scaring the boy. You'll wake the baby."

Joe Donoghue stood sharply. His rising head missing Bridie's chin by inches. "I'm not to be a part of it. I'm to stay here and report. It's that fecker, Connolly, he's jealous of me. He won't have me at his side. I'm twice the man and twice the officer he is. I've worked my way through the ranks of the Citizen Army and now I'm out of it. And through it all I'm meant to watch it go off as a fecking spectator." He crumpled the paper and stuffed it into his pocket.

Bridie knelt and put her hand to her son's shoulder as his father stamped down the street.

Paddy looked at the tiny baby, now held by his mother, and caught a light in the child's eyes and the gentlest of her small smiles. It was something he couldn't fathom. When he looked to his mother for comfort, he saw the same look. A look of shared understanding, of common background and purpose, and the undisclosed possibilities of their future life.

On that Easter Monday members of the Irish Transport and General Workers Union and the ICA, under Connolly, without Joe Donoghue but together with patriotic nationalists and fifty members of the Liverpool Irish Volunteers, took over key buildings in their city. It is said that Tom Gleeson of the Liverpool Volunteers was the man who raised the tricolour over the GPO in O'Connell Street on that revolutionary day in 1916. Dublin's unfolding drama was reported in the English newspapers and Paddy watched as his father, with tight lips, read of the different acts of the drama as they played out. Joe Donoghue didn't leave the house for those six days as the tragedy unfolded. He knew of the brave futility of the theatre being played out on the streets of Dublin. The main players were known to him and he cried for their fate. He knew that the rehearsal for the government's retribution had already been staged in towns like Liverpool and Llanelli, recently during strike and upset, and the stage directors in the British establishment were well versed in how to deliver the final act. Once defeated by the forces of the empire, the rebel men would be imprisoned. Then, onto the leaders of the men and women who took over Dublin landmarks and fought the unwinnable battle for freedom and unity; they would drop the heaviest curtain to end their valiant performances. The leaders of the uprising were duly executed by firing squad in Kilmainham Gaol. The child's namesake, James Connolly, so gravely wounded that he was carried on a stretcher to his place of execution, was tied upright to a chair in order that he receive the ultimate punishment dictated by the empire. He was shot dead, a martyr, spat upon by the Dublin crowd as he was taken to his prison, beatified, and sanctified by the very same people following his murder.

In his kitchen under hissing gaslight, Joseph Donoghue had read aloud to his family the excerpt from the local newspaper on the night of the leaders' execution. Paddy sat transfixed by the news that the Last Rites had been administered to Connolly before his death. He looked to the crucifix that hung on the wall of the room. Some pale remembered trace of his own people's ancient suffering made his eyes shy away from the stricken body of Christ on the cross, and the withered palms surrounding it, and vow never to worship at the altar of a God that didn't protect the good and holy.

In that May, the British Government had extended the conscription laws to married men. Paddy and his mother watched as his father, consumed with sour anger, availing that discretion being the better part of valour, walked away from them and on to the Great War.

Inside, Joe Donoghue, denied his part in the act of defiance by comrades in Dublin, had become acidicly bitter. Now wilful, ignoring Larkin's entreaty that no child of Ireland should fight the British war, he took up arms for the empire he once hated and took the king's tainted shilling. His eldest boy child had waved to his father's back as he walked away. His wife had cried, new born baby on her hip.

In the present that has passed, Bridie called again to her son.

"Paddy. Will you home, now." She didn't know what she would say to the boy. He came running to her. He stopped short. His eyes searched hers. He read the news in her face. Hearing it from her silent quiet despair, listening to the pain suffocating her heart; listening to the resonating keening, an echo of cello string sorrow, spoken from within.

A dripped tear landed on his bare foot. It didn't wash the dirt away. It muddied on his flesh and served as distraction from desperation. For a silent moment both mother and child stood, their thoughts pooled in a single translucent bead.

Then he fainted. He fell at his mother's feet. His eyes rolled inwards. In the glow of weak sunlight, pink through tremulous eyelids, he saw with a clarity all that had escaped him from his birth. The images flooded his mind, washed his senses in waves of remembrance, and then with the cymbal clash of a withdrawing tidal surge, against his unwilling and unopened self, were gone, subsided. His closing mind watched the collections of memories from his past drain away to disappear through the rapids of fear, denial and distaste.

a sudden blow

Paddy awoke in the Royal Children's Hospital in Myrtle Street. His bed was a jail. On four sides high bars surrounded his mattress. A thin light strayed in, grey on the beam, from a small gap in the curtains of a large window. His covers were tight around his chest; his body boiled in fever below, his arms positioned to sit on top of the white sheets, his hands folded as if he was praying or already composed in death. In his fingers were the blue rosary beads that his mother used when she went to Mass. He let them slip from his fingers and slither down the sheets until they caught in the rails. Unknowingly, he wiped his fingers on the starched sheets.

His last thoughts were his first. On opening his eyes, he tried to go back to the moments when they had last closed. He looked for the images of the forgotten life he had seen flickering like a news reel in his own intimate cinema of his mind. Then he remembered he'd shut them out, he had instinctively barred his mind to them. In dread or fright or something else? He didn't know. He couldn't remember. He fell asleep.

When he awoke, Bridie was at his side, sitting in a Bentwood chair, stained the darkest of browns with no cushion or comfort. He could see behind her, standing in her shadow, Shelagh holding the youngest Donoghue, asleep and innocent in her arms.

Bridie was looking across the ward at another child. He touched the rosary beads that had been replaced in his hands. He felt too shamed to let them go. He watched his mother. Her eyes were lined with grief; tears had swollen her face, and her lips moved with silent beseeching prayer. Prayers for him and prayers for his dead father. Prayers for the unborn, the new born and those yet to be born.

He tried to speak but his voice was a whisper of wind, a breath with no force. Yet Bridie heard and turned and looked at him. She tried to smile but instead a tear leaked from her eye. She stood and reached over the rails to take his hand. A nurse, mop capped and white pinafored, clapped her hands and shook her head mouthing the word 'infectious' with enunciated silent vowels. Bridie recoiled; the tear ran off her cheek and settled on her son's lips. His small tongue found the diamond glister of his mother's sorrow and sipped it in. The taste was ash and quiet desperation.

"Ach Paddy, my child, how do you feel?"

His voice didn't come. It was dry and scratched at his tongue. He moved his head on the pillow in stifled assent. His eyes spoke. His Da', his father?

As slow as a departing soul she spoke. "Your Daddy is dead, Paddy." She knew he knew, but the words needed speaking to lay ghosts asleep. "He died on the way home. The Spanish flu has taken him. He died on Warrington Station, thirty miles from home. He'd travelled so far to be so near. He never reached home."

Patrick Donoghue, his head sweat drenched in fever, a chilled pain in his right leg, let the rosary beads' false hope loose from his fingers. They ran over the sheets and tympanized against the side rail of the bed, a series of tiny heart beats, his faith diminishing, as they fell to the floor.

Mother and child, fingers interlinked, eyes still joined in loss, stock-still breathed together. For those moments, the echoing sounds and noise of the ward, padded-enveloped by their shared grief, remained silent in that moment of regret. Then, as if he had risen from the depths of a pool, his deaf ears undid, popped unstopped, and he was aware of everything surrounding him.

The children in beds, herring boned for the length of the ward, fidgeted in crisp linen sheets. He heard every particle of starch-whisper-movement, each soft sigh of pain and outbreath of crushing boredom. The nurses' purposeful stride, clipped on the polished linoleum, the rustle of their aprons and the deafening possibilities of life that beat in their hearts. The sharp scent of disinfectant and carbolic mixed with the weak lavender of floor polish. The light from the high windows reflecting from stainless steel and chrome instruments, and the dull gleam from each white railing-ed bedstead. The warmth in the touch of his mother's fingers.

Smiling, he let the fatigue overtake him and he fell into the depth of blanketing sleep.

Bridie watched her sleeping child, the damp cloth pressed across his pale forehead. In the peace of the ward she finally had time to think. Her husband was dead, her children fatherless and her eldest son struck down with an illness that was seldom cured. She had little money and was relying on hand outs from friends and relatives to keep the roof over their heads and prowling wolves from their door.

Inside her body she felt nature stirring. To add to her sorrows, the joy of life was being given to her. Lonely encounters with a man, kindly and attentive, who lodged with a neighbour, had created the child that grew, multiplying cell by cell, within her womb.

Three months ago, she had succumbed to her feelings of isolated desolation and the simple warmth of another's company had seduced her into his bed. She had hoped and prayed to St Jude that their precautions would undo the sin, but the prayers fell unheard. In the last few expecting days and despondent nights, even before the telegram arrived, she knew she was with child.

"Mrs Donoghue?" The voice crept into her mindfulness, derailing her train of thought. Standing at the end of the bed the ward matron stood stolid; a nurse, attentive and nervous, at her side.

"Please come with me. The doctor would like to speak with you." The matron wore a full length dark blue dress and a white high collar, stiff with starch. The collar forced her chin high and she looked down at Bridie as she stood up and made to follow the woman out of the ward. They entered a small office. Above the desk was an outsized crucifix, the eyes of the slaughtered Son of God followed Bridie as she sat. The silence of guilt allowed the smell of camphor to suffuse the room. The matron rifled through papers on her desk. A blue sheet of carbon paper floated to the floor. The nurse bent to retrieve the paper and return it to the desk. She received no thanks from the matron.

"Mrs Donoghue, your son is suffering from polio. We think we may be seeing the start of an epidemic as they have in America. The ships at the port are bringing in all sorts of new disease and problems.

"The doctor has told me to inform you that it may be some weeks before he recovers. At the moment his right leg is paralysed. We are waiting to see how far the disease will travel. Although we do have some hydrotherapy treatments, we do not find them effective for children. I'm afraid we will have to wait and see how he mends."

She continued to ask Bridie about any symptoms that may have been present in her son in the weeks before: temperatures, fevers and chills, nausea, vomiting and cramps, before carefully noting them down in neat copperplate script. Bridie sat and answered the questions until her mind wandered away. Suddenly the matron had finished and was asking repeatedly, with a rising degree of impatience "Was there anything else?"

Bridie knew what it might mean for her son if he didn't recover. She'd seen children, rich and poor, struggling to walk, their legs supported, encased in metal and leather irons. Others affected more severely, were bed bound, some not able to control their muscles to breathe and live a normal life. She knew some would succumb to the creeping stillness of the virus and die in hospital.

"No" she said, "there was nothing else."

The nurse led her by the arm back to the front door and directly Bridie found herself on the wide pavement in front of the red bricked building. She stood for a moment, herself shocked paralysed by rising fear and anxiety. An imprisoned thought escaped for a moment. It might be better if Paddy died. It rattled free disturbing, disrupting her thoughts of nurture, and disappeared with fading dread, leaving the ghost of a trace of unease. She shook her head in denial, but the trace, as faint and selfish as it was, remained.

dropping from the veils

His head laid on the wet pillow in troubled sleep...

From there he could look down inside the tunnel of tented sheets and see, above and below his trapped legs, that all was heavy grey snow. He couldn't move. He was trapped in the heat of the tunnel. He tried to move but couldn't. He closed his eyes and the heat intensified. His father's face appeared above him. A piece of paper in his right hand and the unopened telegram in his left. It swirled into a kaleidoscope of colour, red for the heat and pale blue for the ice chill felt. A band of black spiralled inside the colours, breaking and reforming as it spun.

A dismembered voice spoke as unarticulated hands pulled at his arms, telling him to quiet, to calm, be tranquil. Tranquilo, mi camerada de la brigada.

Then, air as he was lifted, a blue cold up draught, and then pain's scarlet fire as he was trolleyed through the halls and finally the cool greens of water as he was gently placed in the spa bath. Water on his face and red heat in his soul and ice in his legs. A rough towel sandpapered his body dry and wrapped him tightly in a shroud of sheet as he was lifted and wheeled and replaced in his cold sheet bed. The temperature rose. In his mind, he sat by the fire in the house. It had never blazed so fiercely. The flame licked his body, the embers touched and burnt his fingertips. He sank into the wet heat. Water pooled into the small hollows of his body. Streams of burning sweat ran from his eyes, hot liquid from his nose and searing tears from his mouth. He tried to move, to kick against the stiff linen tunnel, to swim from the sheets that drowned his body. He had no strength to surface from the depths, his breath was failing, his lungs heavy, filled with drowning fluid. His voice was still, his mind ear splittingly loud in complaint at his restraint. He could look into the tunnel.

He could see the dull grey air that surrounded his legs, suffocating movement, suffocating the escape from the snow that walled the passage. The cloth white snow, that would not be melted nor washed away, confined and held him to his future. The heat grew and grew, a stretched elastic band, pulling at his senses, his mind overreached, and voices external, extended high pitched into ranges unheard and then with a snap, silence.

He fell into the silence; tumbled into its depths, collapsed into its loud safety. All was still, all was still. Sleep took him, spinning him deeper, down to bottomless weariness where he landed soft, secure. He blink-opened his eyes once before they closed and he knew he had arrived unexpected, alive.

The fever had broken. While Patrick Donoghue now swam in sleep, through dampened pleasant dreams, the nurses changed his wet pyjamas and sheets, and replaced the soaked puddle of a pillow with fresh dry softness. When his eyes were opened, he saw the new light of the rest of his life. He drank at its source. It burnt into his cornea, hope and regret in equal luminous expectation.

Above the ordered beds of the ward, he watched the large windows flame with the sun flare of early summer.

He unfettered his arms from the tightly bound sheets and reached up to his face. Dry and soft. He ran his fingers across his nose and mouth, touched his eyes and hair in the wonderment of survival from the dreams and nightmares that had chased him, featureless faced, mercilessly grasping for himself through the past days. He tried to speak. No more than the dry rasp of the sound of 'Mammy' came off his lips, but enough to alert his mother Bridie, who sat bedside, knitting. The ball of wool dropped, paused, and pushed, moved by hope unseen, across the ward's moss green linoleum.

Bridie stood and cried, her hands to her mouth. She reached for her son and bent down to cradle his thin small body.

"I dreamt, Mam, I dreamt."

"Oh, Paddy, what did you dream?"

"Beneath my bed. Mammy. There are tunnels. Long fearful tunnels of tiled white.

"Along each of the tunnels there are rooms. Dark rooms, and night-like, half-light. Winter coverings, frost and gruel thin snow. Cold. Along the walls there are beds. There is a child on every bed.

"They were each covered with a sheet of iced mist. Quiet now, all of them, weighed down by the cold. And Mammy, they lie still, and you know Mammy, they don't know it yet, but they were all dead."

know the dancer from the dance

"I'll park here" said Isaac Singer to O'Brien.

"Do you know what this is about?"

"I was asked to bring you here by my father. He is involved in the Labour Party and I believe we are meeting two of their luminaries."

Singer was Peter O'Brien's colleague. They worked in the same Jewish firm of brokers in the Cotton Exchange. Singer was ex-army, a second lieutenant. He'd been called up in the latter years of the war. He hadn't seen active service and though it was never spoken about, it was clear he had some function in the quartermaster's stores. His father was a senior partner in the company and a brown stain of unspoken gossip preceded Singer in his career in the Exchange.

Singer told O'Brien to wait while he went to knock at the door. O'Brien extracted him from the small rear door of the car.

The new car had driven up the incline of Everton Valley and through the slum saddened streets of the lower reaches of Netherfield Road before pulling up in front of a row of grand high Victorian town houses on Shaw Street.

He stood at the corner with Carver Street. From there he had an unrestricted view over the terraced brick shanty streets of Vauxhall in the foreground, out over the River Mersey and beyond to the Wirral and the low Welsh mountains. Below him the city slouched beneath a ribbon shredded blanket of thin smoke, the late afternoon sun touched on the blades of the Leicester windmill on Scotland Road to his left and ruddyed the red stone of the scaffold clad square tower of the Anglican Cathedral on his right.

On the water, busy with ferries and lighters, larger steam ships still waited to dock whilst others were emptied and filled in the miles of docks that stretched along the river. On the Princes Dock landing stages, three ships of the White Star Line were queued, embarking their human cargoes, and stowing them each to the levels of luxury befitting their wealth, in readiness for their journey to the world without.

The arterial roads that fed the thoroughfares to the ships were choked with the cholesterol exhausts of rickety lorries or clogged with horse drawn carts and drays. A steady tide of people from the overhead railway that ran the length of the waterfront, dockers and workers returning home or turning out for the evening shifts, supplied the pulse of the lifeblood of the city's trade. Waves of office workers, clerks, secretaries, and draughtsmen invaded the streets as the clocks struck home time, heading for trams or buses

On the Pier Head plaza, the trio of buildings known to many as the Three Graces, the Liver, Cunard and the Docks and Harbour Buildings, still stood out in landmark white, their new Portland stone slow in absorbing the dirt and grime of pollution from the city that would eventually paint them burnt toast brown.

Letting his eyes follow the stream of traffic down The Strand, to his left the round cap and Palladian columns of the huge Custom House, standing authoritarian square on the original site of 'the pool of life'. Its structure had blackened; in contrast to the confidence of the Three Graces that invited the world to commerce and trade, the building that taxed looked depressingly dour.

Opposite O'Brien, the fresh town house on Shaw Street, the Woolton sandstone built St Augustine Church and its supporting Collegiate Grammar School stood stolid on the brow of the rise. The school, with its turrets and leaded windows, had been built to resemble a castle and its solidity paraded its original belief in the specific education of the Protestant classes. Despite its closeness to the large Irish Catholic areas of Vauxhall and Kirkdale, it stood defiant on the brow above the sectarian dividing line of Great Homer Street, at the end of the proudly Orange Netherfield Road. It was exclusively for the children of well-to-do Protestant families.

He was staring at the building but thinking of the people in the city; how the ebb and flow of the people working on the Mersey gave Liverpool a distinct feeling of transition. How the vagaries of trade and war and the following seas could change and in turn, as trade was its life blood, affect the lives of the thousands dependent upon it. There was no other real industry to sustain the city except trade and commerce. If a faraway hurricane or typhoon storm at sea meant a cargo was late, or a crop eating weevil devasted a harvest bound for Liverpool by way of the Cape, it eventually disturbed the rhythm of the city's life. A hurricane on distant sugar plantations could mean no food on the table for Liverpool's children. Was this why people here seemed so volatile? So unwilling to be tamed and organised?

Yet, he thought, that volatility didn't affect the wealthy. They were insulated. For all the poverty that was so distinct in the slums and cruel overcrowded courts, there was wealth. Huge amounts made from centuries of connections in trade and commerce salted away, like pork in barrels of brine, to feast on when sustenance became scarce. He needed to ensure that his family were protected from the precariousness of the river's tides and the docks' trade. He had started his journey by moving to the Cotton Exchange. He wanted to move on; to become his own boss, beholden to no one nor to the caprices of trade winds and the vagaries of markets.

Singer returned and with O'Brien, they were taken through the grand entrance of the house. Their hats were taken by a man in dark clothes with a silver striped tie. As they entered a room with a large, polished mahogany table, two men stood at the far end, silently silhouetted against the window. The farewell wave of sunlight from the west haloed the men in cigarette smoke. They both wore chalk pinstripes and white shirts. They turned in unison and came towards O'Brien. The taller of the two, moustached and eyes clouded behind thick rimless spectacles, introduced himself. He was Harford, no first name proffered but O'Brien recognised him as a local politician recently elected to office but said nothing. The other gentleman, stoop-shouldered in perpetual penitence for the sin of his faith, named himself as Fitzsimons. They sat at the head of the table.

Singer and O'Brien sat down at the faraway end, shrouded in the dust of the gloaming. Harford read from a sheet of paper.

"Peter O'Brien. Arrived from Dublin a few years ago. A docker, a warehouse man and now at the Cotton Exchange. A stellar rise from the slums." He looked up, paused as if taking in O'Brien's character in a snapshot stare, and continued. "Brought to our attention by Singer here." A downward acknowledgement of a double chin towards the man on O'Brien's left.

"Lives in Kirkdale. Three children and your wife expecting a fourth. Good letter of recommendation from your parish of St John's. Father McGuire speaks well of you and your family. So why are you interested in politics?"

From the distance of the room, both men looked up, a half-smile on their lips, inviting the right answer.

"Well. I'm as interested as the next man. I have my own views, and some are more peculiar than the common thought. I think it's every man's duty, now that we have obtained the vote, that we think wisely as to how it's used. How collectively we can, together, like, make a difference."

"Your friend, Isaac is as interested as the next man but unfortunately can't become involved. I think I'd be discreet if I said, due to certain financial indiscretions?"

This time it was Singer whose chin dropped, his hands folding in his lap.

"Let me be frank," Harford continued, "you have probably reached as far as you are going in the Exchange. Your upward ascent will be halted not by your lack of ambition but by your race and religion. Unlike Singer here, who is of one of the ten tribes of Judea, you are not.

"You could, of course, switch brokers, but they tend to be an incestuous bunch in finance. If your face doesn't fit at Simon and Hester, then it won't fit anywhere.

"I dare say with a growing family, the home in Kirkdale will become more cramped and you'll look to move. Crosby perhaps? But you'll need to earn more to have more opportunities. So, my colleague Fitzsimons and I may be able to provide you with those opportunities. Would you be interested?"

"Any man who isn't interested in his own betterment isn't the type to be interested in politics." O'Brien listened to the words as they formed, coming from nowhere in his mind, and forming a sentence he was unexpectedly impressed with.

"Well said, Mr O'Brien." It was Fitzsimons who spoke. He had flat Lancashire vowels, and spoke from deep within his chest. "This is in the strictest confidence." He paused self-importantly, to emphasise the gravity of his words.

"If anything comes out from this meeting that paints Mr Harford, or for that matter myself, in a bad light it will be denied in the organs of the press that are favourable to us, and you and your family's life made hard. Harder than you've ever known. Do you understand?" Fitzsimons smiled, the sly grin of a pantomime villain, his intent hidden behind insincere charm.

A silence. O'Brien's face remained blank, under the table his fists balled in indignation at the threat. He didn't know Fitzsimons; he knew of Harford. He knew he was heavily involved with the Irish Nationalist Party in Liverpool. The INP was formed in the aftermath of 'the Irish Famine' of the 1840s when the first large influx of the Irish starved from their lands arrived in Liverpool. Tens of thousands sailed; Liverpool the first stop on a transatlantic journey. Many sought deliverance in the New World, some moved to industrial hubs within Britain, but a sizeable proportion settled in the hinterland of Liverpool's northern docks. The irony of the masses, hounded from their farms and villages during the closures by agents of the British Government, finding refuge in the cities of the United Kingdom didn't escape O'Brien. As with most refugee populations, they were discriminated against and vilified by their new hosts. Their religion was singled out by those fearful of popery and idolatry. Liverpool had been a Protestant city, siding in the Civil Wars with Cromwell. Taking the lead from the Scottish and Ulster Presbyterian church leaders they founded Orange and the Black Orange lodges in Liverpool to counter the wave of Catholic immigrants.

The city became divided on religious grounds. The Catholics gravitated along the northern banks of the Mersey from the city centre to the borough of Bootle, and inland, in slum heaped upon midden slum, up the slopes to the watershed of Netherfield Road where the Orange Protestant enclaves of Everton and Anfield held sway. To the south of the city centre, the Lodge had entrenched itself in parts of Toxteth, South Dingle and Garston. The divide was not clearly defined either. Parts of Bootle Village held Protestant enclaves; streets of Garston closer to the docks were staunchly Catholic. Within these districts of Liverpool acidic envy ate at the sweetness of the innocent; religious processions were attacked, families were burned out of their homes, riots of revenge initiated, mass meetings and mass beatings held and meted out, all in the name of the same Almighty God, worshipped as he was, for forgiveness and brotherly love.

As the Church founded the INP to preserve the Gaelic heritage and promote Home Rule in Ireland, the lodges aggressively strove to protect their own community. Work was given, housing allocated, contracts awarded, and jobs created by the taint of religious colouring. No city in the United Kingdom, other than Belfast, was divided more along a hard sectarian stripe than Liverpool. The craft unions were dominated by Protestants, membership of the lodge being a requirement. On the docks, woodworkers and joiners were Protestant, so much so that locally the 12th of July celebration, when the Orange Order marched to commemorate the English victory at the Battle of the Boyne, was called 'Carpenters' Day'. The Welsh Methodists tied up all of the building work. The bricklayers, builders, roofers, and labourers building the terraces of Walton, Everton, the Dingle, Toxteth Park and beyond into Allerton Vale were Welsh, brought in from North and Mid Wales and employed only if they were Chapel. That left the Irish only opportunities for what they were perceived to be good for: manual labour.

As the miasma of religious intolerance separated the worker, so did the allegiance to political parties. For the Protestant working classes, the lodge became the de facto Tory Party local office, wherein the lodge retained its massive influence. For the Catholic, the Church aligned itself to the INP, telling its congregations that they were Irish first and Liverpudlians second. The INP candidates were accordingly elected to council office and Rome retained its massive influence. The seething sectarian oratory from the Orange Lodge and Irish Nationalists were the reason why Labour struggled to get the working class vote in those areas.

Fitzsimons continued, "We are hoping that politics can be more of an interest to you. We, Mr Harford and myself and many of our colleagues, can see change is coming to our constituencies. Whereas before, the Church, our heritage and Ireland's future were the cause of the Irish Nationalist Party, now that the Home Rule question seems to have been answered, though admittedly not to the liking of all, we have to position ourselves where we think will be most beneficial to our voters. To this end, we wish to promote the Labour Party in the north end and the rest of Liverpool.

"We know there are parts of Liverpool where religious sectarianism make Labour an unpopular choice, but it is our belief that if we can get the Irish Catholic voters away from specific Irish nationalist causes in our strongholds, we stand a chance to influence the Labour Party to address our specific needs.

"Some quarters of the south end, Bootle and Anfield where the Orange Lodge have established their houses of hate, will take a little bit longer to civilise. The Orange and the Tories go foot on neck." He smiled to his companion, enjoying his own wit. He continued, the smile fading. "Aye, happen that the war has tempered some of the hatred, with Protestant and Catholic fighting together for 'Dear Old Blighty', and the strikes since 1911 have brought people together, but it's the men in the pulpits on both sides of the divide who have always poisoned the workers to fight each other rather than unite in their common cause."

Harford shifted his weight in his chair. A dark thought passed across his brow, but he remained silent. The light had faded in the room as Fitzsimons had spoken, yet his passion surrounded him in a dark aura that silenced the others. They breathed out slowly.

O'Brien thought it politic to speak and fill the foreshadowing silence. "Why would you think of me, a relative newcomer to Liverpool and someone without no experience in politics."

Harford spoke. "Labour are making headway to become the party that will represent all working class voters, ourselves, the Protestants and any Liberals in the suburbs. In spite of what I might say, and you will hear me say this publicly in support of the INP, if we want an organisation that fights the Tories then we will need to get our Irish Catholic vote away from the INP, to stop them thinking of the priests and the Church of the old country, and to start thinking of their own poverty and how we can unite to improve their lot and redistribute wealth. We need them to stop striking for Irish causes, for the release of the Irish internees from English prisons, and to think of Britain as their future. The current wave of strikes are disrupting trade and damaging Liverpool's good standing in the world as a port. The strikes are not well received amongst the non-Irish and are causing upset in the Labour movement. We need to be able to organise the workers to strike when we need them. We need a candidate to stand up and tell the current INP voters that the way forward for Ireland is with a peaceful accord with the British Government, and that Labour is the party that can bring this about. A candidate with strong support in his parish, fresh from dear old Dublin, with a strong character and good morals is what we need. And we are sure that candidate is you, O'Brien."

"But the strike is over the internment of the leaders of Sinn Fein and their soldiers," O'Brien said, his voice beginning to rise. "Whether it be for the so-called involvement of the Germans, or because men wore the auld IRB's uniform, you will have to be very wary of this if you want the Irish Catholic vote. The British Government have taken democratically elected Irish MPs and imprisoned them. They arrested de Valera himself, but with the aid of a cake he's escaped Lincoln Prison and is off, I've heard, dressed as a priest, to America. And the stupidity of the British Government is that they play right into the hands of the Sinn Feiners. The Irish love a saint and a martyr."

"As it may be," continued Harford, placing his palms flat on the table. "In conversation with the Labour Party I've beaten the drum louder than most for the nationalist cause and Home Rule. But there needs to be a change from the law of the gun. The time for involvement in Irish nationalism for those living here in Great Britain has come to an end. They must leave it to the politicians. After the Easter Rising and the martyrdom of its leaders, it is only a matter of time before we will be seeing an Irish State, free of the United Kingdom. As slow as it will be and with I daresay more, much more, bloodshed to come, it is inevitable. The tide has turned. The British Government will fight it, impose draconian laws and fight in every way they can, but they, whether they be Tory, Liberal or Labour, can't hold out forever. With the concession of forming an independent Irish Dail, the first crumbling block of the fabled British Empire will fall. Those fighting for an Irish cause are an immutable force. They are fighting for nationhood and that nationhood will be achieved. What comes after they achieve it and obtain autonomy remains to be seen. We are hopeful that there will be a similar Labour Party to that which has grown on this side of the divide."

He sat again and leant back in his chair, fixing O'Brien with his gaze. "Ireland's troubles are not our own, yet they can still be advantageous to us.

"If I can get an acceptable Irish candidate to stand as a Labour candidate, one who is sympathetic to the Church but not a puppet of the priests. One who supports the struggle of the Sinn Feiners in Ireland but won't let himself be distracted by their internal battles. Put that candidate in a safe seat like Scotland Road North or South, then Labour can start turning the tide against the Tories and Liberals. I have already asked the Catholic Herald to support me in asking for the Irish Catholic voters in the rest of the city where there is no INP candidate to vote Labour. We can gain a foothold there. We think you'll be the man to appeal to the Catholics and Nationalists in the North of the city and persuade many to vote for the Labour Party. What do you say?"

O'Brien stared at his hands folded in front of him, trying to look as if he was taking a moment to consider. "To be fair, I've always been surprised at the level of support the INP has. I know of Liverpool's large Irish contingent. In Dublin, every other man has a cousin or relation who is over here. Since I've been here, I've heard tell of the Liverpool Irish Volunteers' part in the uprising of 1916, and the Gaelic football games played, and of the funds raised by the different Irish societies, and I've even heard whispers that people in Liverpool played their part in getting Dev out of Lincoln Gaol and out to the USA, but your parochial politics are invisible to the life of the ordinary worker.

"Aye, it would sound to me that Labour would be the natural choice for any working man or woman. But my life in Ireland hasn't qualified me for the politics of Britain. I'd agree that you need to find a change; I'd differ in that I don't see me as the man for yourselves."

Fitzsimons stroked his chin and tilted his head quizzically. "Surely the politics of Ireland and Great Britain are intertwined, and the Labour Parties and the Catholic Church are both in the vanguard for Ireland's freedom."

"We have similarities," ventured O'Brien, "we work every day under the same class system you do. Aye, and the system is backed by the same powers of the establishment and religions. They may be Protestant or Church of Ireland and in the future, they may be Catholic, but the control will be the same.

"As for the Catholic Church being for Ireland and the Irish, what sleven told you that? Maybe the hedgerow priest or the odd radical clergyman would support the cause, but the Church are the establishment, and a conservative Church at that. The poor go hungry while the rich and the churches get richer; fine buildings and cathedrals are erected, and the poor live in squalor. And it doesn't matter whose hand is on the neck of the working man, it's always backed by the dog collar of religion.

"And here in Britain, you don't have to live under an occupying army. The people of Ireland are fighting a war against the British while you are worrying about your own parish politics."

As he delivered his words he watched as the rising stridency in his voice caused his audience to stiffen their posture. Had he over reached? He composed himself and laid his hands palms upwards on the table in a gesture of reconciliation.

"Are you a communist, O'Brien? To say that of the Church?" asked Fitzsimons.

"No more than you are. I am a proud Roman Catholic. But I stand for the virtues of what Christianity, if not most religions stand for, and not what a papal edict of some God forgotten Pope may say. I've been brought up to see that each of us only walks by God's grace, and to be thankful of it. But I also see the power of the Church, and its hypocrisy."

Fitzsimons raised himself in his chair, his cheeks beginning to enflame, and he squared his rounded shoulders. "I don't think you realise what the Church in Liverpool has done for the Irish people and in particular some of the families in your own parish. We have Gaelic Associations and Hibernian Clubs; our associations and charities fund the Catholic Institute, secondary and primary schools and educate the lower classes. We keep Irish tradition alive in Liverpool. We have members of our community involved in your struggle. Nor as a relative newcomer do you see the barbarity served out to the Catholic Irish in this city. The processions at Holy Cross of the Blessed Virgin attacked by Protestant mobs wielding swords; families in St Anthony's and All Souls' parish forced out of their homes in their thousands."

"Aye, don't you pontificate on my behalf" retorted O'Brien, his own temper beginning to rise in rubied colour. He stood, resting his knuckles on the mahogany table. "I know as an Irish Catholic exactly what the bigotry of religion has done in this city. I am, after all, one of those discriminated against in the docks and even in my current work. The times you speak of, the days of bigotry and prejudice served by violence, hopefully are gone. The war has changed attitudes, Orange Ulsterman and Green Dubliner fought in the trenches together. Even the General Strike of 1911 changed things. Protestant and Catholic worker alike were charged by the police and shot at by the army."

O'Brien sat down in his chair. He wiped the flecks of spittle from his lips.

"And with regard to what you've done for the Irish people, I think you mean 'what you've done for people in Liverpool from Ireland'. The ordinary man in Dublin or the people out in Limerick, Sligo or Donegal don't know about your good works, and frankly, care less. They are working, like ordinary people everywhere, with a pittance for pay, poor health and living like animals amongst their own dirt. I've seen some of the slums in Liverpool and they are bad, aye, but by the standards of Dublin they're ten times better than the tenements there. Some of the hovels are so bad you'd be ashamed to house your pigs in them. Though it's bad here, you're streets ahead of Ireland. And that's not because of the British rule in Ireland, as harsh and cruel as it has been, it's because of the economy based on agriculture, and the lack of opportunity. Ireland has the propensity to breed men who travel abroad. That's their major export. That's their industry. Working men.

"Ireland doesn't have coal or iron. Maybe in Ulster they've had an industrial revolution but the rest, no.

"Ireland exports its people. The best leave to find money and work to send home. They cling onto the Irish shamrock and cry into their whiskey for the auld 'Mountains of Mourne' and send money home for those who can't escape."

He looked at the faces. He could see the hurt beginning to register in Fitzsimons. He thought himself still Irish. A third-generation grandson of a Mayo tenant farmer chased from his land and still bitter at his grandfather's death.

O'Brien, though proud of his birth right, had adopted this city and was glad to call Liverpool home. He paused and lowered his voice and continued into the heavy still falling on the room.

"Do you not see? The Irish in Ireland, or over here for that matter, might think that an Irish government would be better for them but how will it be so? If that government has the same class-based, old school tie Conservative elite as now? What happens if the Labour Party rule in Ireland but turn on their socialist values, as yours has done here, in fear of the press, in order that they be accepted by the establishment? You ask me if I'm a communist and I'll tell ye no, emphatically not, but I am a pragmatist and I see what rules the world. In Dublin, Larkin and Connolly, the idealists have gone, and their trade unions are a shadow of what they had been; Sinn Fein and Labour tell us they are for the working man but that remains to be seen. The vacuum in the nationalist movement has been filled with those politicians seeking a career. Aye, and if you've a mind to seek a career then I'd wager that it'd be better for yerself that you're Conservative by nature."

He sat down, his passion spent. The light had ebbed from the room. Clouds had flooded the western sky, brought by the onshore winds from the Irish Sea, and the day was beginning to fade into night.

"So, let your Labour Party here fight for the cause of the common people, and your 'comrades' do the same in Ireland, and for that matter in France and America. Aye, take that fight to the dominions and colonies of the empire. Let Labour fight for universal suffrage, so all women's vote is equal to that of a man. Let it fight for equality and the common ownership of the land and redistribution of wealth. But to me the establishment is too powerful, the churches too rich and the landowners too wealthy to give it away readily. You might win small battles, but it won't let you have your way."

Harford clapped his hands into the following silence, the echo rebounding off the hard surfaces, and rose from his chair.

"You are right, O'Brien, and your eloquence and passion would suit a politician, and a Labour politician at that, however cynical you seem. I would even agree, if Mr Fitzsimons will allow me," he paused and put his hand on his colleague's shoulder, "that the Churches are too powerful. That is why I am trying to get the Labour Party elected in more parts of the city and asking you, in all your eloquence and passion, to stand in a Scotland Road ward."

His arms were open and spread towards O'Brien, his head tilted to one side. He stood a long moment while O'Brien slowed his breath and becalmed his heart.

"Thank you, Mr Harford" replied O'Brien, "but I am only interested in politics in the general sense. I can pontificate and pass my opinions but it's a game I don't think I have the stomach for, the intrigue and deceit that must be an everyday part of life. I haven't the appetite nor the ambition for it, not to be an MP or Lord Mayor or even an Alderman. I am ambitious for my family and, aye, for the people less fortunate than ourselves to make good their lives, but not in politics."

He waited to allow his words to register with them. "But," he continued with a canny smile, "I am ready to use that ambition to help you outside of the ballot box and with your scheming, in any way I can. If you have another role for a fellow traveller, who would like to walk at a slower, shall we say, pace and maybe outside of the limelight you politicians crave then I can be, if you wish, your man."

Harford stood for a moment, looking down the long mahogany table towards O'Brien as if weighing up the futility of pursuit against the benefit of further persuasion; decided, he looked at his watch and signalled to Fitzsimons.

"Thank you, Mr O'Brien, for your candour," said Fitzsimons, "would you give me and Mr Harford a moment?" With that Singer rose, and touching O'Brien on the shoulder, they left the room.

a ghostly paradigm of things

When O'Brien and Singer were summoned back to the room Harford had gone, disappeared through an adjoining door. Now Fitzsimons stood next to a priest. Once O'Brien and Singer had been seated Fitzsimons spoke.

"Mr Harford apologises for not saying goodbye. He is a busy man and has matters of great importance to attend to. He asked me to thank you, Mr O'Brien, for your views so frankly expressed. He agrees with you that you may not be ready to enter the political fray. Perhaps, he suggested, in the future you would reconsider. He told me he was sure your paths would cross again in such a small city. He was intrigued by your offer to help our cause in any other way and suggested that I speak with you of more commercial aspects of our affairs."

"This is Monseigneur Rose. He is organising a fraternal society. It is to be called the Knights of St Columba. Its motto is not so dissimilar to our own aims: 'Charity, Unity and Fraternity'."

He smiled, showing his small canine teeth.

"Its aims are to further the cause of Catholic businessmen. Myself and Mr Harford will be founder members. The society will be a self help group similar but not so clandestine as the Masons, secret yes, but not ritualistic. Mr Harford and I believe you, Mr O'Brien, and your ambitions will serve the Knights well. We and the Church are in a privileged position to help with advice to those included as Catholic brothers to the Knights. There will be opportunities for all of us, as they arise, and we will be perfectly placed to take advantage of them. For these opportunities we will pay a tithe to the Church and its charities.

It is the Church's charities that will directly help the poor.

"Because of its secret nature we must agree and swear to mutually benefit each other. Favours will be granted, and those favours in turn, returned and repaid. As the organisation grows then I believe the rewards to our communities will grow. We are offering you a leading part in our fraternity."

O'Brien leant forward in his chair, ignoring the priest, and looking directly at Fitzsimons.

"So, this would be different from the old Irish societies of Ribbonism, the White Boys and the Defenders?"

"Aye, it would. They were mainly farmers protecting themselves from Protestant landlords in the Irish countryside. We have no need to protect ourselves nor threaten, nor dig empty graves outside the homes of our enemies. Not in these days. We need to promote and further our business interests." Fitzsimons laid his hand on the priest's arm. "And of course, the interests and good works of the Holy See."

The priest smiled benignly.

"Give us an example of how I can be of help?" O'Brien asked.

Fitzsimons was prepared. "Ah, for instance, we know of two properties, business opportunities, a failed dairy and a public house in Walton that have become available and they will be offered to those in the Knights of St Columba. The bank manager is a friend of the Church, and therefore of the Knights, and will have prior knowledge of its sale. He is willing to assist our brothers in financing the ventures. We would be looking for someone with imagination and discretion that we can trust to enter the world of trade. We have also heard that Liverpool City Council are preparing large scale building projects in West Derby and the Dovecot areas of the city. Some of our associates sit on those committees and hold the balance of the vote with another friend, not of our religious persuasion, but of our political colour. If you understand?"

O'Brien understood. He himself rose from his chair and opened his arms.

"Mr Fitzsimons, I was thinking myself of soon leaving the Cotton Exchange and I'd like to pursue a career in the retail trade, like my father in law in Dublin, either in the provision of victuals or fine ales. Or both. I was also thinking of venturing into the building trade if I can find a silent partner or partners to help me with the funding and distribution of any profits."

Fitzsimons, lupine, smiled at the priest. "Yes, silent partners are a good idea.

"Discretion is everything, Mr O'Brien. We may have to speak to Mr Harford's brother who deals with these matters on his behalf."

After the meeting they left the building and O'Brien went to stand on the corner again. The particles of the night had atomised the day's light and settled on the dying sky. A band of blue, tinged with the last pink rays of the dying sun sat on the western horizon. The lights of the city glistened through the dirty moisture of the evening. Singer joined him, standing at his shoulder, just shy of his peripheral vision. "Well, Peter? Did it go as you thought?"

"Aye, sure. To be honest I was surprised. I thought they'd be asking me to work in the parish for them and with that for the INP. So, the offer of standing as a councillor for the Labour Party came from out of the blue. I had to refuse it. I couldn't commit to the extra work with the family nor, as I told Harford, am I a political animal."

"And the Knights and the offer of working with them to further commercial interests? Is that something you will be working towards?"

"Aye, it is." O'Brien rocked on the balls of his feet, his hands stuffed into his trouser pockets and smiling at the city scene laid before him. "I told Fitzsimons that I'm an ambitious man and there seems to be money to be made. He seems a 'cute hoor' that one, and I'll have to be careful in what business I take up with him; I'm not a greedy man but, right enough, I'll help myself to whatever small crumbs fall from their table."

Singer moved into O'Brien's line of vision. He swallowed as if he was hungry and salivating over unexpected food. "When those crumbs fall, especially if they are too large for you to use yourself, keep me in mind. My father and family are always interested in any business opportunity, especially if the opportunity involves corporation or government work. You'll find my father can be a good friend and he has the enthusiasm for any business that you can put his way."

O'Brien appraised his work colleague. His lips were red and almost smacked at the taste of prospect. He was so eager to be involved; transparent to the point where O'Brien could see right through to his other side, where friendship weakened and was replaced by an appetite whetted for the taste of profit. Aye, he thought, I bet he would. Where money is to be made, you'll always find the well to do businessmen. O'Brien smiled, and said 'of course', and shook his friend's hand.

But I'll choose who I'll use, thought O'Brien, and for the time being I'll keep the faith of the Knights of St Columba. I'll use my Catholic friends first and foremost, and if there happen to be those crumbs too big for me to swallow, then I'm sure there'll be powerful men of my own beliefs who'd happily help me carve them up so I can take a bite.

In the west, the last of the blue darkened and disappeared. As the sky faded, the lights of the city reflected in O'Brien's eyes, brightening them with rare expectation. Fitzsimons and his political friends could give him the star of hope to help steer his ship homewards and into port to deliver the cargo of security and reassurance he wanted for his family. Happy, he slapped his companion on the back with his open palm. "Come on, Isaac, let's get me home."

rough beast

Outside the children's ward there rose the voices of angered arguments. Male voices not often heard in this enclave of the gentler, stronger sex were bringing discord to the harmony of the hospital. The loud voice of the matron could be heard in response.

"Get these rough louts out of here. Call the police. I will not have this behaviour in this hospital. This is a place for all the children of Liverpool. You will not dictate to me through threats of violence."

Paddy strained to hear and see. His mum told him he was getting better. She'd said he was nearly back to the shiny new button that she loved. He was better in every way except his right leg which lay, wasted like a dead branch, under the sheets. He asked the kid next to him, whose leg was raised in elevation to knit back his broken femur, what was going on, but all the lad could do was to shrug from his pillow. Every boy and girl stretched their necks, craning to try and see round the corner of the doorway to the hospital's entrance lobby.

From outside the discordant sound of bells rang from an approaching police van and whistles were being blown by the beat constables as they rallied to the call. Sounds of a crowd, pushing and scuffles, shouts of anger and oppression, curses and blows, prayers and panic.

In the ward the excitement grew. The sound of breaking glass from a window put through was followed by a scurried procession of nurses into the ward. The matron bustled in behind them.

"Get back out there and tend to our patients," she shouted. "Do not forget your training, especially you, Sister Geraghty." With that she turned and left the ward.

Sister Geraghty, a stout glass of a woman followed her, straightening her head dress as she left and rattling her shoulders straight. She half turned at the door and said one word. "Nurses."

That settled the fluttering of the young nurses who had been designated the graveyard shift and like a line of penguins shuffled out.

It was nearly nine o'clock on a June evening, the sun was lowering itself to tomorrow after the long hours of the summer day. The sunlight slanted through the glass, criss-crossing the higher layers of the room, catching the escaping dust particles and locking them in powdered light. Normally the ward would have been hushed quiet and the children threatened and scolded to bed, if not to sleep. It was a time of the day when the young nurses exhaled in hope, expectant that their workload would diminish, and the matron would take herself away to her quarters and give herself, and everyone else a breath of time.

For the children on the ward it was a time when stories could be told between them, whispered between the beds, of high derring do, exaggerated bravery or simple tales of home and missed loved ones. A time to be brave as they were told to be, or to lapse into doubt and unhappiness and drop tears into patient pillows.

Tonight was different. The ward, the whole hospital, was electric whip sharp in anticipation. Paddy could feel the edge, hear it honing itself, dragging its blade across the whetstone of expectation. He tried to sit upright, his left strong leg finding purchase on the lower sheet of the tunnel his body was locked in. He dragged his thin limb up, forgetting in that moment his despair for it. He checked left and right, no nurses on the ward.

"What's going on?" he asked.

"Who's that?" came a voice Paddy couldn't see.

"Paddy Donoghue. Who's that? What's happening? I heard glass getting broke. Maybe a window put in."

The voice came back to Paddy whilst others in the ward began their own conversations, soft voiced, still afraid of discovery.

"I'm Jack. It's all going off outside. I only came in today. Fell off a wall watching a fight. Broke my bleeding leg. It's done up in plaster now and does it bloody hurt?"

"What's going off? What do you mean? Where was the fight?"

"Haven't you heard none of this? A massive mob of us went down into Toxteth Park. There was a fight in a pub a couple of days ago, and a black fella got done over by some Swedes on Jamaica Street. Got stabbed twenty times in the face but he got away."

"Go'way, twenty times?"

"Spit down, my buddy." He drew breath, the belt of tension pulled tighter.

"Anyway, next night he comes back all bandaged up like. But this time he's got about forty of his blammo mates with razors, cutlasses, swords and guns. Killed a couple of Swedish sailors. Next thing coppers have chased them back to their boarding house and some mad darkies slashed and shot the coppers."

He paused, enjoying his version of the story. Others had started to listen, and a pin drop quiet had fallen inside the ward.

"So, me dad and me, and our Charlie all go down there. So, we met up with the fellas me dad drinks with and it's like a madhouse. Men are shouting about sending them home on banana boats to Africa and others are saying lynch them there and then. Some old fella who must have served on the ships during the American War brings out an old Confederate flag and a bugle. He starts playing 'Dixie'." The boy stopped to laugh. The children who didn't know what the Confederate was or what Dixie looked like, let alone sounded like, embarrassed, joined in.

The noise of laughter, being a rare enough sound in a children's ward, bounced off the hard tiles and lifted the room in sad dark brilliance. It didn't dull the sharpened tension of the boy's story.

"So, off we march and as we pass The Grapes, they all come out and then the pubs, the Ol' Knob, the Peacock and the Snakepit, they come out to join us. All bevvied like. Seven sheets sailing to the wind.

"There must have been a thousand of us. We march down to this doss house at the bottom of the Dingle and one of the boons runs, like, and we chase him down to the Brunswick Dock. He's only young, like. Maybe a bit younger than twenty. He's quick, like, and he gets caught a few times, but he can fight. Knocks a few out. Like Jack Johnson, the boxer, big muscular and shiny black chocolate.

"Anyroad, he can't escape, and we get his self and throw him in the river. Tide's just on the turn. It'll pull him out to Liverpool Bar. But at the moment he's there. Treading water. He can't swim, black's bones too dense, you see. So, there he is. He's floundering. Goes under but pops up. He's there, his head bobbing up and down like a coconut."

The boy stops to laugh, but now he is laughing alone. The silence is a razor cut in the satin fabric of their innocence. He is older than the others by years of hard faced experience and his talk is scaring the others.

"So, what do we do next?" He asks and looks around his audience. A pantomime response, a small voice shouts back at the child-thug 'hit the coconut'.

You can hear the smile on his face. "Is right, my pal," he says, "so we all pick up stones and, boom, a brick gets him, splits his head to his brains, and he goes under. A massive cheer from the crowd. Doesn't come back up. We killed him. Blood in the water.

Loads of it."

He realises the depth of stillness that surrounds him. It isn't one of tense anticipation. It is of regret, shame and innocence lost. Now with his audience gone, he quietens himself. In a lower voice he carries on the tale of the big 'I am'.

"So, for the last few days we've been hunting them down."

Some of the kids drew their covers to their chins. Others hid their heads under the sheets, hiding from the hateful bigoted reality of the world.

The boy's voice gloated, nasty, into the uneasy quiet, dripping prejudice and blind hate. "Catching them, eeny, meeny, miny, mo. Giving them a beating and telling them to go home, back to Africa."

Paddy heard the child in the bed next to him say something low under his breath and bravely, turned his back on the boy. His hands made the sign of the cross.

The unseen voice continues, slower at each sentence.

"Leave our women and our jobs for us.

"Been a few of them burnt out.

"They deserve it."

The ward dropped stone back to silence and Paddy Donoghue, ashamed for his race, pushed himself back into the tunnel formed by the sheets over the frame that protected his poor leg. It's safe for a seven-year-old in there.

When the morning light came, burning the shadows of the window frame, like a cross, dark on the high wall of the ward opposite Paddy's bed, he realised the bed on his left, empty last night now, had a child, bandaged and quiet, lying in it.

Paddy turned to face him. The skin of the child under the stripes of bandage was ebony black. He was older than anyone else on this ward, including last night's unseen braggart.

Paddy had never spoken to a black person. Would he speak English? He watched. The boy sensed the stare and turned to his face towards Paddy.

"What, lad?"

Paddy was surprised. English and Scouse? And black?

"You alright? What happened to you?" Paddy spoke slowly.

"Mob came to ours. Put the windows in, dragged out me dad and chased him off. Women came in and tarred and feathered me mum. Me and me brothers got cut by the glass and stones. The police came and saved us. We got put in a Black Mariah and brought here late last night."

"Where are your brothers?"

"They're both younger than me. Our Gerrard is only a baby. They're in another ward. My mum's gone the grown-up ozzy. I don't know where that is. I hope me dad got away."

"Where are you from?"

"South end. By the Dingle."

"No, I mean what country?"

There was a pause.

"Dad's Nigerian. Me mum's from Toxteth. Fuck off, you prick." The lad turned away. Disgusted. His back a broad wall of angry silence.

Paddy shocked into naive ignorance and innate guilt, sat and waited for his breakfast and wondered.

the crime of death and birth

The priest had sat on the end of Paddy's bed, stale breath of old whiskey and cigarettes, fingers stained saffron yellow with nicotine, and told him that all men were created equal. But Paddy knew different. The boy with the broken leg had been moved out of the ward. As far as Paddy knew out, of the hospital. When he'd asked the nurse, he'd been told not to worry himself over it. The boy had gone to join his family. Paddy's question of 'where?' was met with a shrug and a 'hush now' look.

"But Father," Paddy said, "last night, a man was chased into the Mersey and drowned. From what I've heard it was because he was coloured and the men who did it were white. Christian men as well, Father."

"Ach. Well, I'm not so sure it's as simple as that. The police are investigating the matter. They'll get to the bottom of it and the men responsible will be punished. In this life and the next they will be punished, son. They carry that mortal sin on their soul for all eternity. There'll be no Heaven for them."

Paddy thought on the word 'punishment'. He tried to remember his father and the last years before he went off to the war. He had watched as Joe Donoghue hollowed out. The whole man became a husk. The news that came in the telegram from Dublin had taken his dignity; he had lost personal poise and pride, and it was replaced with bile and bitterness.

In those months that followed the terse message instructing Joe Donoghue he was not needed in Dublin, he had sat, dispirited, at the kitchen table and talked angrily at his wife. Acidic sullenness tainted his words. He railed against Connolly and the martyrs of the uprising, jealous at his exclusion. Death for a patriotic cause deemed better than the sensibility of life itself.

Paddy remembered in the rambling sourness of his speech that his Da' would sometimes talk of the plight of the Irish. He called them a race of ghosts. To his father the Irish weren't the rich and landed gentry, he saw them still as the foreign invaders, the estates they occupied taken from Gaelic chiefs and upstanding noble Catholic families. They were absent English landlords, cruel Protestant Scottish patriarchs rewarded for their part in the invading wars of the Normans, Henry Curtmantle and Cromwell, or the crushing of repeated revolt by Erin's island race.

To Joe Donoghue, 'his Irish', when he spoke, were to a man, Catholic, spiritually enriched by priests and guilt; a romantically impoverished people, starved and dehumanised by poverty, brave and desperately proud in their deprivation. In the countryside in his vision, they had occupied a whimsical green land where every thatched cottage had cotton wisps of white smoke from the fireplace and the press was full of rabbits and pheasants culled from an abundance in the countryside. Hedgerow teachers and priests taught the happy children of a God given right to freedom, of martyrs and beatification, saints and sinners, scholars and rogues, and the sacred heart of Our Lord, the Saviour and the blessed blood of the Gael. 'His Irish' had fallen foul of landlords and their agents, forced from the idyll by potato famine, their land cleared for beasts of toil, sorry victims of the Englishman's cruel injustice. They wandered the now grey land that once whispered charms and magic; starving spectres, green grass stains at their mouths, haunting the empty towns and villages in the wild reaches of Connemara.

When Joe Donoghue's 'Irish' left their land to cross the far oceans to new homes, the shadows of their hard station travelled with them. Haunted by scarce possibility, forced into labouring jobs, belittled and alienated, housed in squalor and filth, they became the easy target of the bigot. The feckless Irish, drink and drunks, priests and statues, poets and prayers, suffering and melancholy, songs and tears; looking backwards across the heaving seas to a tempest strewn island of bitter sweet dreams.

Engineered by a potato diet, they were said to be stronger than the English worker; fed a diet of beef stout and gravel, these strong animals built the railways, canals and roads but were still unwelcome visitors in the towns they built. No dogs, no blacks, no Irish. Like all immigrants they sought out the poorer quarters and huddled their masses together, collective strength in the old ways of porter on a Saturday night and sanctified worship on Sunday to hear the Church's promise of salvation in the next life. This life, a veil of sorrow, of tears and the early death of children, tender aged, asleep forever in the dirty wrapping of rags, of strife and hunger and the humiliation of no work, no food, no hope for their teeming families. The lost hopes of those left behind haunted the ghosts of the Irish everywhere.

To Joe Donoghue in the main, 'his Irish' excluded the Protestant. They were invisible in his delusion; drudge-like souls, slaves to capital or their Church, blind servants of the occupying establishment. But there were some, Tone, Russell, Parnell, the righteous who used their privilege, education and standing to help free Ireland; the Countess with the Russian sounding name, the officers of the British Army, doctors, lawyers and teachers, and though oh-so-different, those other Protestants, they all could be included in Joe Donoghue's prejudiced view of 'his Irish'.

Most special of these to Joe Donoghue was the poet William Butler Yeats. Born to the Protestant ascendancy, educated in both Dublin and London, conflicted by his parents' opposing political sympathies, he turned his back on the Church and wrapped himself in a Joseph cloak of metaphysical poetry weaved from the colours of nature and legend, of faeries and folk tales, of heroes of the Gael and a love for his country's romantic re-emergence from ancient shade.

To Joe Donoghue, Yeats was the mystical soul of an emancipated Ireland that spoke to him of the island's heroic past and the folklore heroes vital for the future. He revered Yeats above those others that were revered for their special selfless sacrifice to the cause of 'his Ireland'. Yeats was the Book of Kells illustration: the swirling ornate motif that allowed the rich and wealthy Protestant to overarch religion and belong, unexpectedly and absurdly, in the ranks of Joe Donoghue's 'Irish'.

And in listening to his father's wild eyed dour rant, fuelled by small glasses of cheap whiskey, the feelings of separation and difference landed square on the shoulders of Patrick Donoghue. They festered into his own distorted sense of national identity to a country he'd never visited. He had learnt from his father that they, 'the Irish', specifically the Catholic Irish, were underdogs, reviled by but grudgingly accepted by their English hosts.

So, Paddy thought as the priest smiled a hollow smile and lifted his well fed backside from the bed, how was it that the coloured and black, the Chinese and Malay, the Lascar and Singhalese were not the friends and allies of the downtrodden Irish in the fight against unseeing prejudice? Why was it that the sailors displaced from their homes across the world, the freed slaves of the Caribbean and Americas, the sons of African kings and princes, all settled in the dark towns in the south end of the city, were chased into the dirty waters of the river to drown, by people who shared their paucity of wealth, health and opportunity? How could those people with little hope so easily find others to blame for their exasperation at life's feeble gift? There was no monopoly in the diaspora; the ghostly white Irish had walked from their farms and holdings, from city streets infested with disease and want, they had boarded ships to leave their empty country. From more distant lands, others coloured by searing suns to various shades, others had also been forced by slavery, poverty and the hopelessness of possibility onto the coffin ships and landed on the same shore, and been treated with the same scorn and contempt.

"Father," Paddy called to the departing back of the priest as he was leaving the ward. The man turned and again came to his bedside, his benevolent face showing the sin of pride. The pride of his cloth and his conceited imagined standing across the divided classes of the city.

"I'm taught by me Ma that we are all equal in the sight of Our Lord. Is that right, Father?" The priest said it was. "So, we are all equal and should be treated as such. Is that right, Father?"

The priest sat again on the end of the bed. "I have to explain to you, son," he started in a low melodic voice, "that the ways of men and the ways of the Church sometimes can't follow the same path. The pressures of life on men to provide for family can put an untold weight on their souls. They can become blinded by bigotry and hate.

"Take this city; after the war ended, it gave refuge and shelter to many men who served this nation. They came from all quarters of the empire to fight for their mother country. Many decided to stay and ended up here in Liverpool where we have had districts, almost like colonies, of Chinese, Africans, and coloureds for many years. Since the war, there has been only so much work for men. The new arrivals were preferred by the employer as they will work for less wages. Jealousy and envy and the need to provide for families has driven a wedge between communities and races. It is my opinion that prejudice is a human condition and prevails across all people; I've heard that Chinamen think Black people are descended from apes; the Muslim despises the Sikh, the Sikh the Hindu. Within Islam there are factions and hatred, in the Indian population there are caste systems. A group so lowly that they are called 'Untouchable' and imagine my child, many of these are Christian.

The father shook his head slowly in disbelief.

"Prejudice exists, I believe, so one man may look down on another, and from that twisted perspective, he somehow perceives a feeling of superiority. In our own communities, working class Protestants fight Catholics, the Jew is universally questioned and mistrusted, the Irish reviled and shunned. Now we have other races and religions being added to that tinderbox of prejudice and more flammable fuel provided with the desperate need for work. One righteous man vying for another's job and his own livelihood and the wellbeing of his children. The spark of envy and perceived slight ignites this world and people are hurt and wounded.

"Do you understand, my child?"

Paddy nodded. The priest smiled and asked if Paddy wished to say a prayer to help the soul of the dead man drowned last night in the silty waters of the running tide.

Paddy lied and said that he would. As the Father closed his eyes and joined his hands in prayer, Paddy stared at him, his hands in his lap. He had spent the night thinking about last night's victim of hatred. He knew that the men responsible for his death prayed to this same God. If the priest was right and prejudice was a human condition, then it was man who meted out brutality and cruelty and the injustices of this world. Man would not be helped or forgiven by praying to any god. It was man who must answer for the sin of man.

dark cloths

The sisters met in the Kardomah Café in Dale Street in the city centre. The weather had sluiced the exterior with squalls of May rain earlier in the day, leaving the pavement outside clean and the street awash with the waste of straw and litter of the many horse drawn delivery wagons.

The interior was crisp linen and cake stands. Antimacassars draped the high backs of cushioned chairs and doilies underlined the fancies. The high ceilings were painted chocolate brown, with a picture rail of thick cream paint holding the long wires of hanging replica paintings of Alphonse Mucha's stylised women.

They had ordered tea and had sat like bookends at the table in the window. Yet one bookend was more faded than the other. The sharp defined clothes, shoes and make up belonged to Mary, the elder of the two sisters. Bridie's clothes, whilst pressed were soft-worn creased, a lighter veil of pale from their original shade. Beneath her hat, her face showed the careworn lines of worry that powder could not disguise.

Beneath both their coats, their different dresses stretched over their growing children.

Mary was pregnant with her fourth child; due in a week's time the doctor had told her. She was strong and wilful and despite her husband's wishes had caught the tram into town, struggling a little with her body's precious gem. Under the gaberdine mac she had borrowed from the dead old woman's wardrobe, her sister, Bridie, was just only beginning to show. She tried to hide the small swell of her stomach under a heavily pleated dress.

"Bridie, Patrick will be well again. He is through the worst of it. You said so yourself." Mary reached across the table and took her sister's hand. "But it is you I'm worrying after."

Bridie leant forward. What she was to speak of wasn't for others to hear.

"It's a terrible thing I've done. One child in hospital, the others fatherless and me a whore of a woman, pregnant with another man's child."

"Stop that now, Bridgid. The boy will be fine. It's not a punishment. It's a disease. It's come from America. My Peter says there's an epidemic. It's like the Spanish Flu. It's come over on the ships with their troops and stuff."

Bridie looked down at the cup and saucer in front of her.

"Now, the other thing, the other child," Mary started, not wanting to sin herself in even thinking the word bastard; "it's too late to do anything than go through with it, and I wouldn't expect anything else. It'd be a cardinal sin to do anything to the wee thing. So, we'll hear no more about it.'

Bridie's mouth opened and closed, her silence telling.

"What of this fella? The father? Is he single? Please tell me you didn't sin with a married man?"

Exasperated, she snapped. "No, alright, he's single and he's away with the army in Brindisi."

"Well, no doubt you've spoken to him and he knows, yes? He'll be sure to do the right thing."

"He knows, and he's sent money. Well, some. He says he'll sort it out when he gets back. He asked me to keep it quiet. It'll kill his mother if she finds out."

"And who is his mother when the cat's at home?"

"I don't know, to be honest. I know his surname is Prescott,

George Prescott, but I've asked around the 'Fields and talked to our priest, quietly of course, but the name isn't known. I don't think they are Catholic. He is due back on leave in a few months' time. He might be back for the baby's birth."

"But you aren't sure. Well, we'll have to make the best of it. Is there no way you can pass it off as Joe's?" Mary asked, already knowing the answer from her sister.

She hadn't expected tears. Bridie crumpled to the table. Her hands held in prayer in front of her, her shoulders folded to her chest and she wept for her foolishness.

Mary hushed her as other diners turned to watch. A gentleman came to her and kindly asked if she was alright. His proffered napkin was taken by Bridie but held still, inches from her eyes, forgotten as the tears streamed to the tip of her nose and fell, dampening the tablecloth in an ever widening rose of grey.

Mary was embarrassed. Her younger sister had made bad choices all through her life. The rush into marrying her first husband, Shelagh's father, impetuously romantic, without thinking. He was already a sickly man when she married him and he died, lungs inflamed with TB, six years later. Bridie was barely twenty two. Then she threw herself recklessly into a search for a new father for their child.

Joseph Donoghue, known firebrand across Dublin, had swept into her life and schooled her in the oppression of the imperial yoke that enslaved Ireland, and the struggle of the working men and women for universal suffrage. She proved a willing pupil, oft saying that the principles of Christianity were entwined with the principles of socialism. He had nodded patronisingly and asked her not to speak of such matters with his communist friends.

So, they married, and she fell pregnant. He busied himself at the union office and drilled the volunteers of the Citizen Army, carrying weapons of brushes and picks, and dressed in various odd bits of uniforms, as she prepared his tea at home. Then the call to Liverpool and the start of their own family. Paddy, born in a cellar, and Anthony and Young Bridie following a little later, in tune with the dance that Joe Donoghue stepped to.

Then, she had been beguiled from her moments of loneliness by another and fallen pregnant again. How would she have explained this to Joe, her husband, ironically gone to war for Ireland's oppressor, who had been due to return home to find his slattern of an unfaithful wife skewered by a British bayonet. Perhaps, Mary thought, Joe's death was for the best. How would Bridie have explained the immaculate conception to him, with him away in Germany?

"Come on now, will you stop this. You're making a show of yourself. You're crying for yourself and your stupidity, not for your dead husband, his orphaned children nor for the joy of the child you carry.

"It'll be fine. We are living in strange times with the war and the flu and all. My Peter and I will help you out where we can. I'll ask about you moving in with us. Even with the new baby I'm sure there is room in Orwell Road for the family, and that's what we are after all, family."

She leant across the table and held her sister's hand. "And there are new ventures ahead; nothing I can talk of now, but we may be moving into newer bigger premises. Peter is being offered new opportunities daily."

Bridie, using the napkin to dab at her eyes, left the black kohl of mascara on the cloth. She straightened herself with a deep draught of air and sought some composure. Tremors of involuntary shivers ran through her shoulders. She shook off the last of her sadness and, for the time being, set her face steady as she spoke. Her voice quivered on the first syllable but settled quickly.

"Thank you, Mary, and thank Peter as well. Your baby must come first. I think we will be alright in Gloucester Place for the minute. Shelagh is to start at Coopers Fabricators in a week or so. I have a small pension and the old lady lets us live rent free. The kids are settled, so we'll see what may be in the future but for the present we'll stay where we are."

"Well, alright then, but you know you only have to ask."

They finished their tea and talked of inconsequentialities, not letting sentiment raise the temperature between them again. They had covered it and hidden it under the dark stained napkin and wouldn't let those emotions escape to spoil their afternoon outing.

Later in the soothing calm of the front room in their home, Mary told her Peter of the sorrows that Bridie faced. She told him of her offer for them to stay. He didn't say anything, he hadn't expected anything less of his wife, but his mind was on a derelict dairy in Bedford Road and the Stuart Arms public house nearby.

a battle fought over again

In the elegant chambers of the Cotton Exchange on Old Hall Street, Peter O'Brien was thinking of his pint. Saturdays at the Exchange were a half day and a chance to dress in sports coat and slacks, leaving stiff suits and collars behind, redundant 'til Monday morning came around again. The morning was used to invoice and file bills and correspondence, reconciling ledger entries of volumes and prices and profits made, and losses lost. The afternoon was his. Mary was at home with the children and during the football season, he normally would finish work and would take a pint or two in Rigby's old coaching house before jumping on the tram to Goodison or Anfield to watch one of the local teams. He was a Blue as was his father before him but if necessary he'd go to the ground of Anfield, happy to be entertained and happier still if the Reds lost.

Today wasn't a normal day. Yesterday on the first day of August the policemen of Liverpool had gone on strike. Half of the city's force had taken the day off and taken their families away to the beaches at Crosby or Formby, leaving the city's properties unguarded. As darkness had fallen, the rats of the slums came from their nests, poorly fed and scruffily raggedy arsed; how could they not feast at the unattended table?

O'Brien watched the slow tock follow slow tick of the office clock as it hesitated its way to one. Two desks away, one of the partners of the firm was sitting on the edge of a desk talking in a loud voice. Phillip Smythe was a caricature. He was tall, thin and stooped at the shoulder, his chin was a weak wobble of flesh with mutton chop sideburns framing cheeks rosacea pink, veined and coloured with hypertension. He always worked Saturday mornings, allowing the other partners their religious freedom on their Sabbath. This favour to his colleagues permitted him to shirk his accountancy duties and he spent the morning with the clerks on the office floor.

"Of course, the police are riddled with the Irish and you know what the Irish are good for?" He raised his head and looked at O'Brien. "Not you of course, old boy. The rest of them. They can't wait to have a strike or stage a bloody riot. Paper here says only half the union members have gone on strike. Eh, O'Brien I'll give you five to one that most of those strikers are Paddies. Stands to reason. Anytime there's trouble in this city it's the bloody Irish. Eight years ago, the General Strike, wasn't it fermented by Irish communists? Am I right?"

No one answered his bluster.

"During the war, in the riots when the Lusitania was sunk. Who attacked the German shopkeepers? Every Dicky Sam. That's who. All the bloody Irish Catholic families whose children and fathers went down with the ship – though to be fair you can't bloody blame them. Isn't that right, O'Brien? Who burns out Catholic families from their homes? Who smashes religious statues, and who stones each other and fights at ancient historical parades? Ha. You're right again, O'Brien, the bloody Irish."

Peter O'Brien willed the clock hand forward. It jerked to a tick; it spasmed to a tock. Seconds passed where minutes were willed for.

"So, by my reckoning, and I'm not often wrong, the police union is full of half civilised men from the bogs who have left the city to be ransacked by the slummies and out of work navvies who sit next to them at Sunday Mass tomorrow. And the papist priests will say nothing. And you know why, O'Brien? Ah, it's because what they've looted from the shops will turn up in the collection plate or outside the priest's door in payment for absolution of their bloody bastard sins. Oh yes, O'Brien, a rotten lot." He looked around the room with the supercilious rictus grin of the entitled. He checked his fob watch and looked at O'Brien. "Obviously, present company excluded."

Smythe was referring to the walk out of the city's police force. A similar strike had been held last year in 1918 by the National Union of Police and Prison Officers who, having balloted their members, took strike action. It shocked the government into a pay rise, as well as increased pension rights to get the strikers back to work. A government committee was set up to look into the grievances of the strikers. Although the committee did address poor pay, the revenge of the establishment was to ban policemen from belonging to their union and to replace it with a police federation for all ranks. Striking by the police was outlawed. In protest at this the NUPPO called its members out again.

The minute hand reached the summit on the face of the dial and O'Brien sat still. All around him the nail scraping of chairs grated on the hardwood floor as the rest of the office rose to leave their Saturday duties.

Isaac Singer stood before him. "A pint, Peter?" he asked.

"Aye, a pint of plain to wash that shite from my ears," he replied and stood.

Standing at the bar in Rigby's, with his foot on the base rail and his hand surrounding his glass, O'Brien spoke. "To my mind," he started, "the police in this city have got a terrible hard job and I for one support them in this strike. It's done the right way; the union has balloted and it's a nationwide strike. If their employers, the City Watch, won't sit and listen to their grievances, then what else can they do but withdraw their labour. The numbers on strike from the London force aren't the figures of last year but we'll have to see what transpires."

"The trouble is that the strike in London has been pretty ineffectual. Hardly any of the bobbies down there went on strike," answered Singer, looking into the abyss of his empty glass as if searching for the answer. "Then you've got the local trade unions. After what happened at the transport strike years ago, there's no great sympathy amongst them for the police. You're not likely to down tools to help the same coppers who used batons on St George's piazza to beat you back to work." He signalled to the barman for refills.

"True, they were quick enough to be the government's lackies then. I suppose they think this is different. It's the Liverpool police union members who are carrying the torch for their rights. I'm wondering if things aren't so bad in the rest of the country. I've been told that here in Liverpool you pretty much have to fight your way back to the Bridewell if you catch a thief. In some districts, and you know which they are, Bootle, Everton, Scotland Road and Great Homer Street, the prisoner's family and neighbours will take it upon themselves to be the judge and jury, and free him if they have a mind to. The police force are like a regiment, you're marched to your beat by the sergeant, walking the same rounds for eight hours on your own with every slimy thief and bandit, burglar and robber, thug and bully boy against ye. With a whistle and a stick for protection and company. Aye, I'd be on bloody strike too if it were me." He took the fresh pint that sat on the bar and drank the first inch of dark mild liquid.

"The Watch committee pay them a pittance and insist they live in the better parts of town away from the low-lifes they are meant to police. They aren't on the same money as a dock labourer even, and with a harder job and all. Aye, never thought I'd hear me say this but pity the poor bobby."

"Well," Singer said, after a long pull on his pint, "I'll be locking my doors and barring the windows tonight, as we won't have a whistle or baton to protect our worldly goods."

"You'll be alright up there on Mossley Hill. Haven't you got your own police force up there? I'm sure all you landed gentry on the top of the hill have your own cocky watchmen, armed to the teeth that they are, with shotguns and pistols and cutlasses. No,

Isaac of the Singer family, born of the tribes of Judea, you and the estate and the family jewels will be safe tonight. You won't have to be after burying them in the garden just in case the Irish come looking for ye tonight.

"And while I'm thinking on it, how would the Irish gobshite looking to rob your silver get to Mossley Hill? Ah, of course he'd jump on the tram and then a cab, and him without a penny to his worthless name. Then the same all the way home to his hovel on Scotland Road to share his spoils with the thirteen children and his crone of a wife, and all his brothers and sisters and Ma' and Da' who all live together in said hovel, like sardines in a tin of shite. Oh, and according to that bugger, Smythe, have some to give the poor old priest at St. Anthony's."

Singer took the fob watch from his waistcoat pocket and checked the time. He smiled. "Yes, Peter O'Brien, Knight of the Holy Saint Columba, protector of your countrymen, you are probably right. But I think I'll still sleep with a cocked Webley under my pillow tonight."

"Aye, aye," Peter said with a grin, "right you are, ex-Lieutenant Singer, you be careful with your cocked Webley and all. More especially what you do with it, you won't want it going off and leaving the sheets of your single bed stained with spent seed, sure enough."

They finished their drinks and left to go their separate ways. The tram would take Peter down Scotland Road and onwards to home. Whilst he hadn't mentioned it to Singer, he knew little would have changed from what he had seen this morning. The route into work had taken him past burnt middens of rags and clothes heaped mindlessly in the street. The plate glass windows of shops had been crystallised into tiny gems bejewelling the pavements. Smoke from a lower floor tenement whispered into the early Saturday morning, a remnant of a curtain finger flapped weakly at its passing. Still drunk men, unshaven, unkempt and uncared for, the dignity of man undone by alcohol and its persistent nagging, sat on the kerbs alongside shoeless women, their dresses dirty and stained, the radiance of womanhood dulled by grinding poverty and clouded by the dearth of hope.

He was restless as he stood on the pavement and decided to walk up Dale Street. There was little to rush home for in today's climate of uncertainty.

They lived in a road in Kirkdale that had some of the larger houses in the area and were blessed by good neighbours and a strong community of successful people. People who had used their own wit to strive for the oxygen that had allowed them to prosper and grow from between the cracks of the hard pavements. Where some fell and lay barren in the moss and clay, these others had used what little nutrients could be garnered from that detritus to set their roots firmly in the dirt and flourish. Those roots that anchored them to their values allowed them to withstand the buffeting of ill fortuned winds that threatened them in the storms that swirled around the city. Because they had risen, albeit to low heights, they hadn't forgotten how to fight for or protect their own. O'Brien's immediate neighbour, Terrence Walsh, ran a set of hackney cabs which afforded him some of the comforts of life that his upbringing in Black Sod Bay on the furthest green margins of County Sligo never promised. The ease of his current station hadn't softened the hardness of his fists nor slowed the quickness of mind that made him a fearful enemy in a fight. Aye, O'Brien thought, there were a few handy men in Orwell Road to be relied upon in times like today. He made a mental note to visit them later in the day and organise them into their own Watch Committee.

That night, across the city, shops and homes burned. Looting of shops and businesses was widespread. Brave and getting braver, unrestrained by the absent police, gangs of men and women trickled into the city streets bringing poisonous vandalism with them. The city centre was protected for the most part, the strike breaking policemen, focused by their station's officers to protect the wealth of the few from the wanton need of the many. They were joined by a thousand quickly sworn in special constables, hired from the banks and business houses to specifically safeguard their temples of Mammon. Outside the centre, on the periphery of the city, along the many arterial roads, general anarchy ruled. London Road was described as looking like the French town of Ypres after shelling during the World War, such was the damage done to the fabric of the store fronts. Any establishment was fair game, and tales abounded of wardrobes and furniture being robbed and then abandoned, only yards away when they proved too heavy a burden for the looters. Displays of single right footed shoes were taken from shop windows, useless to everyone bar the one legged. Victuallers and grocers had windows smashed and were ransacked of every tin and box of food. The mob attacked any pub or hotel or licensed premises where liquor could be found to fuel the riots, but were often met by armed landlords and their regulars, intent on protecting their own. Between the looters, fights broke out between themselves; squabbles and disputes between families and neighbours, long simmering feuds found fuel in the absence of order and bloody revenge extracted. Like times before and like times to come, a heavy cloud of dark disillusionment and distrust settled over the city.

When Monday came and O'Brien took his starched collar and dark suit from their pegs and dressed for the office, he opened his newspaper and read from The Herald. It bemoaned the coverage from the national press. Much of it echoed the sentiments of Smythe, the senior partner at the brokerage firm O'Brien worked for, in blaming the feckless and the poor. Singled out for their misdemeanours were the Irish and in particular, the Catholic Irish. The Herald's editorial railed against this opinion and O'Brien read it with a look of resignation on his face. To him it seemed impossible to surmount the elevated attitude towards the Irish in the country he and his family were in the throes of adopting.

The policemen of Liverpool stayed out for a total of eight days. Again, the government's response to the problems on the streets of Liverpool was to send armed troops out onto the street and position British naval ships riding at anchor on the Mersey; their eight-inch guns aimed at the city, ready to shell their own countrymen. Eventually the strikers surrendered and in capitulation offered apologies to the Watch Committee. In venomous spite the Committee dismissed the gesture and ordered all striking policemen to be immediately sacked, and that each would forego their pensions.

Outside the Bridewells of Liverpool piles of blue serge jackets and trousers, high collared and silver buttoned, sergeant striped and plain, many with flashes of rainbow ribbon for bravery commendations and good conduct, began to be piled high as the officers returned their uniforms.

O'Brien, walking home by the Bridewell on Westminster Road, witnessed men distraught at the loss of their jobs and their dignity break down in tears. He wondered how the working man, organised or not, could ever defeat an entrenched and wilful government.

before a looking glass

"You'll have to hold still for it to relax your muscles," said the nurse, a large-hipped article in a white rubber apron and gloves. A frond of hair had escaped from the tight bun of her hair and hung, limp in the steam, across her face. She huffed it away.

The baths were unbearable. The cold ones he could just handle, his body more used to them from washing in the yard on frigid frosted mornings. This one, the hot water immersion, boiling to the point of invention, not so. The skin searing heat of the water was an alien notion to him. Previously washed in the lukewarm dirt of a shared bath on a Sunday night in front of the hearth, or a cold swill of the face, flannelled roughly clean on waking each day, was one thing. But thinking that this cauldron of steam and scalding could be beneficial to his health was considered with deep scepticism by Paddy.

"Let me be. I haven't done anything wrong. Tell her, I've done nothing."

"Tell who? Paddy?"

"The woman in the dark blue dress. The one who comes every day with the doctor. They look at me, he touches and prods me. She watches but says nothing."

As far as he could fathom, the water treatments were a punishment for unknown crimes against the matron. It was she and the doctor who appeared daily, to consider the chart clipped to the end of his bed, who meted out this retribution for his sins. The doctor who never spoke to him nor asked of his health. The matron who never spoke to him and only asked the nurses of his health. It was those two, the silent ones, who punished him with the regimen of water tortures. It was part of the only cure they had for the virus that had laid young Patrick Donoghue so low that his right leg stopped growing for a time. It seemed none of the waters he bathed in, steaming high temperature or iced cold, could make it grow again.

"Now don't you start. It's good for you. The heat expands your limb and the cold shrinks it back to normal size. It'll make your leg stronger."

So, by turns he was dropped into the cauldron and blanched, or immersed in frost bite cold and cooled frozen, in hope to cure his disability.

"I'll have you out in a minute, wrapped up in warm towels."

As good as her word, after the five minute clockwork timer had pinged his rescue, she lifted his shivering body from the cold bath; but the promised warmth was replaced by blister inducing heat. She placed him on the sweltering sheet of a white hot towel. Paddy's back arched to shield his tiny form from the unremitting heat. The only parts of his body touching the surface were his shoulders and the heel of his left leg. The nurse pushed his arching stomach down with an arm sheathed in heavy rubber gauntlets.

"Sweet Mary and Jesus, oh, Sacred Heart" shouted Paddy as his body was wrapped tightly, mummified into the unbearably hot towel.

The nurse was mortified. Such a foul mouth on a wee eejit of a child. Her face fixed grim, she tightened the shroud of a towel and clipped it fast.

The double doors swung hard on their hinges as she slammed her way out of the room.

"I can't breathe!" shouted Paddy, after her departing bustle.

He lay alone in the quiet. He was burning in the towel. He could only move his head to see the room. It was stark white, tiled to the ceiling in small, bricked shapes. Copper pipes ran across the walls framing an oversized clock whose second hand moved in agonisingly slow beats. A tock and a long pause; a tick and a long pause. Watched intently, it barely moved forward in time. Trolleys, pumps and buckets, and the two enamelled baths that stood on the floor. Above him a bright white lamp thrummed down on him. Glowering and dimming with the slightest pulse if he looked at it directly.

He called out until he grew scared and then he fell silent. The towels grew cold and contracted more tightly around his body, he breathed harder, a mild panic rising within his self. He began to cry but stopped. He wouldn't give them the satisfaction. They could find his murdered body and the nurse would be hung for the hateful bitch that she was, but he would die the proud innocent. Like Connolly, his namesake, a cripple martyred for the cause. No tears would stain his shroud. He closed his eyes and waited for death.

The nurse charged back through the doors and into the room with a smile on her face.

"Right, young Patrick Donoghue, there'll be no more of your blaspheming. Do you hear? And your mother and you, the good Catholics that you are. I won't have it on the ward and matron certainly won't have it in her hospital." She loosened his binds and stripped away the towel. "Now sit yerself up and put on your pyjamas and dressing gown."

He looked down at his body. White skin, puckered with moisture, crinkled and pallid. His legs mismatched, a piece of string aside a rope. His torso white and thin, muscles wasted from his bedridden gaol. He felt every part the enfeebled worm. His stubborn will left him, and he cried, a huge draught of breath followed by the sobbing despair of a child.

The nurse busied herself with the towels and basins, and turned a deaf ear to the youngster, her heart hardened by the sorrows of her work, her conscience knowing that the child at least would live.

At least once a week he was taken without a word to see the physiotherapist in the basement. The man, stone silent and thick armed, beat upon the maimed leg. He chopped and slapped, lifted and stretched the leg in vain attempt to lengthen its stride. The leg, stubborn to a fault, refused to catch up to its partner; it lagged behind in strength and size. His leg sought support in the canvas, leather and iron contraption that signalled to the world Patrick Donoghue was, and would remain for all his life, a cripple.

He was fitted with his leg-iron in a shed at the back of the hospital. He was pushed in his chair down tiled corridors of white and green. At each junction he looked to see into different wards. Some, when the doors were ajar showed him glimpses of other children, from infant to teenager. Some walked, wounded, and bandaged, some sat in bed listless and ill, others sat crowded around tables playing cards or building blocks. When the doors swung shut, the noise extinguished, and the only sound was the swish of the rubber wheels of his chair on the linoleum floor. Nurses passed each other with grave nods, sometimes with the tiniest of a smile touching their lips. If the matron was seen, then Paddy felt the tension in the grip of the handles of his chair. If a young handsome doctor passed by, the chair would slow, and a glint of seduction would spark, electric, unseen, through the air. Out past the rear entrance's double doors and into cold sunlight. Low grey cloud quilted the sky. It was early July but the summer had reneged on its promise and failed to arrive, leaving a tired sullen spring to provide what weather it could.

In the building adjacent to the hospital, across the yard, the engineer of false legs and hopes, grunted a greeting. Taking Paddy under the arms he was lifted until he stood upright. He was told to stand his crooked body up straight and hold tight onto the weathered poles of parallel bars. His left leg was measured and noted down. His right leg was measured, and the man gave a low whistle. The man turned away to the workbench. He took a screwdriver and adjusted the apparatus, then turned and offered it up against the boy's leg. He took the appliance away to the bench and made corrections to the length and width. He finally fitted the canvas straps over the boy's bare skin on his thigh and calf, and took his foot and introduced it to the clump of a leather boot.

Hanging scarecrow like from the bars, Paddy could shift his weight from his left to his right foot. The sensation shocked him. The thick sole of the boot and the torque that the calliper pressed on his leg made him feel as if he was standing again. He knew the feeling was false. If he moved, he would overbalance and fall. He looked at the man, who nodded and removed the boot and straps, sat the boy back into his chair and placed the gift of his future in his lap. The man ruffled his hair and then turned away. The nurse pushed him back to the ward.

He asked her what would happen next and if his mother would come to take him home.

The idea of home and his mother made him cry.

a sufficient end

The Donoghues still lived in the terraced house on Ferdean Street. Seven years on from the arrival of Paddy, the old woman remained alive in the bedroom to the right of the stairs, sounding her presence in coughing fits and starts so fierce that they worried the walls.

Her food was carried up the stairs by Shelagh, who would often sit with her while she ate and listen to her stories of a miserable life of poverty and starvation in the genocidal famines that blighted the west of Ireland in the 1840s. The poor life had emptied the land and spread the nation across the world, a good measure of the dispossessed staying in their first port of call, Liverpool, while many headed west to the Americas and away from oppression.

It was Shelagh who emptied the old woman's chamber pot and changed her bedding, struggling to sit the old woman, ricked back and all, in the chair in the corner whilst she did so. The short journeys from bed to chair and back again were followed by spasms of hacking coughs, and spits of gobbets of green phlegm caught in a handkerchief and entrusted to Shelagh to deal with. At times the old lady cried out in her dreams and it was Shelagh, alone, who came to sit with her and hold her blue veined claw.

The bed ridden woman was the object of curiosity and fear for the children who played in the street outside her window. Told of her spells and bewitchment, scared into believing she held powers from worlds beyond, the boys and girls would dare to creep over the front step. They held each other's breath on the way to her bedroom door, to try and steal a glance at the old witch. Fingers were crossed and Hail Marys incanted as they creaked tip toe unbidden, lip-bitten unwanted, up the top of the stairs. If their nerve held, they would reach the door and look in, before scaring themselves down the narrow stairway in a thunder of feet and shouts to run screaming into the street.

She would confide in Shelagh, with what passed as a smile on thin blue lips. "Aye, I'll hear the whispers of the young ones before they begin. I can hear the street becoming silent to the skipping songs and football games, the shouts of the small girls and boys. Then, I'd hear them on the stairs. I'd listen for the step on the tread, the creak of the riser, and you know, you can almost feel their little heartbeats as they get closer?"

The palpable tension would creep ahead of the children, and into her room, as they stole forward. "Then I can hear the wee cowards at the back, whispering 'will ye go on now' and 'be brave, you baby', encouraging the brave hearted at the front. I'd be holding the sheets to my mouth to stop myself laughing. Aye, the anticipation you could cut with a sharp knife. Then, before they had even got to the door, I'd set me face to a horrible grimace hoping to scare the pants off them, but they never get to the doorway."

She told Shelagh how she laughed aloud when the fragile children's nerve broke and they ran away, rumbling down the stairs with squeals of delight and fright, followed by the imagined nightmare cackling laugh of the bewitched. In telling her tale, her laughter turned to a wracking cough as she failed to find her hiding breath, but those small pleasures were a faint light, a radiance of promise in the rapid fading of her days.

As Shelagh grew older, the time spent with the old woman got shorter. Shelagh had left school at fourteen and was lucky to find work at a small factory off the London Road. Every working day for the past two years she had left early and had returned home late, exhausted from the grind of the canning line. She was paid each Thursday and would hand her penny wages over to her mother to put with the small army widow's pension that was paid to her.

Shelagh was small and dark, with hair that hung over her shoulders in skeins of caramel ringlets but had to be tied up and hidden under a turban of cloth for the work. Her eyes, black pearls in her rough farmgirl complexion, bore a sadness that often had the neighbours asking quietly what affected the girl. But those eyes belied her years, and she bore life's strains with innocent forbearance.

Her mother, on the other hand, would sit at night, candle lit to save the gas lamps of the kitchen, and using the same rosary beads that had escaped her son's grasp as he had fought the hot clamps of fever, prayed for her forgiveness.

It had been her weakness of flesh that had allowed the Devil to enter her soul and persuade her to sleep with the father of the child that lay within her. The sin stained her soul and the souls of her family. It had crept black hearted into her husband and her eldest son. Her sin had visited the influenza upon her Joseph, had entered his lungs and spirited him away, miles from nowhere. Her sin had crept into her son's forming spine and stifled the growth of his leg, leaving him unable to walk without support. Her sin had left her with child and with no excuses for the suspicious neighbours, that the growing child within her was fathered by someone other than her dead husband.

One late summer evening, after the younger children had been called in from the dimming light of the streets and had been fed a cold supper, and bedded down in the upper room that served as their bedroom, Bridie was sitting by candlelight and darning socks. The kettle sang from the range as Shelagh came into the room and took up the book she had been reading.

"She's gone back now. Asleep again, though how long she'll be out for, who knows. She's lost an awful lot of weight in the last few days. She was never carrying much to begin with."

"Aye, the cough's got worse as well. I was up there throughout the afternoon. I was back from the washhouse by one and all I could hear from down the street was her hawking and spitting into the bowl. When I went up there was blood in the bowl. Did she eat her tea?"

"No, Mam. Left it all. Not a drop. I put it back into the pan."

"We should be ready to call the priest. Put a few pennies to one side. Father Michael will come down, right enough. Do you think we should do it now?"

"Best ask Mrs Mac next door. She'll know. She's a friend to death, she's lost that many babbies and her mother last year, God rest her soul."

"Aye, true. I'm not after having the priest in the house for too long. Not in my condition. I'll go in the morning."

The house stirred the following morning at around 6:30 when Shelagh woke to stoke the kitchen range, banked overnight to keep the flame. The light of the fire breathing life could be seen through the grated door, the embers fed flames that spirited upwards, each one a reassurance to the day. Shelagh pulled her shawl around her. The sleep encrusted her eyes and she arched her body with fingers outstretched to the nascent hoped heat of the coming daylight.

She felt rarely rested. This morning, with the rising sun beginning to creep into the night, the thought came to her of how well she'd slept. There had been no calls or cries through the night. As it dawned on her, she took the wooden steps of the stair to the landing. There, standing at the door to the old woman's room, with her rosary beads' crucifix at her lips, was her mother. She shook her head in answer to the plea in Shelagh's dark eyes. "Go now, and fetch Father Michael."

uncertainty of setting forth

In his bed on the ward, idle save for the daily baths and massages, Patrick Donoghue was reading. Where once letters had failed to form words, a patient nurse had taken a primer from her own child and had sat, after her work had finished, to show the boy how the letters, rearranged, made sense. Happy to see such progress, he was wheeled to the hospital library by the nurse, seated at a small table and left to explore the volumes of Arthur Mee's Children's Encyclopaedia. He had seen books at school but had never come across the wealth of illustration and the abundance of new words. He read what he could, and asked questions of what he could not, and with patient coaching he soon was reading ahead of his years. The nurse, in mind of his withered leg, spoke to him of teaching and education and of a life where thought outvalued physical work, and Paddy started to dream of being a scholar.

It was after five months in the ward in Myrtle Street Hospital that he and his right leg, encased in its calliper, stood on the pavement and, taking his mother's hand, awkwardly stepped up onto the tram. He sat next to her, needing to feel close, but she pushed him away, protective as she was of the promise of the growing child inside her.

He had lost the summer. He had watched the light change of the seasons from his bed. The high windows of the ward let in the morning sun, painting white rectangles on the upper reaches of the walls. He watched them as they moved across, monitoring the slow pace of the day. When he awoke, they were sharp, shadow latticed and square on the wall opposite his solitary station. By late afternoon they'd become squinted and oblique on the wall above the door that led to the ward sister's office. It was late September, and the days were unusually warm and the light, to his starved senses, had a bewildering quality. The sun had a corona of sequined glister which touched the clouds, white and crystalline glass amongst intense back swashes of blues and greys.

He had turned eight while in his hospital bed and had missed the beginning of the school term. He was to be kept off until he gained strength, the doctor had told his mother. He stayed at home with his younger siblings and watched from the old lady's window as the empty streets filled with kids returning from their lessons.

Behind him, the room hadn't changed. The old woman's bed was now Shelagh's. The few coats and dresses that were in the wardrobe had been altered to fit Bridie. Those few belongings that couldn't be used in the house were sold in the pawnshop. Her dressing gown, nearly new, and now Shelagh's prideful possession, hung on the nail of the door. When he breathed in, the dust of the room carried the odour of the old woman and her stale last breaths.

From the dirty window, he watched as the boys kicked a ball of tied rags against the gable end of a house. A set of goalposts had been chalked on the bricks. He could hear their laughter through the thin glass. He recognised his friends from the time before his freedom was stolen and wanted to join them but, looking at his crippled leg, shamed himself into remaining a silent spectator. He took himself down to the kitchen and sat with his mother as she made the tea.

It was the next week before he headed across the terraced streets to the small primary school of the Sacred Heart Church on Low Hill. It was with an unhidden pity that the other kids looked on as he limped into the classroom. The teacher stopped in mid-sentence. She had been telling the class of their duties to the church, how and when they would attend, and how the year would proceed to its Holy conclusion. This year, being their Holy Communion year, they would become one with God and the Catholic church.

Mrs Gerrity, the teacher, was a widow. Like many, she had lost her husband in the brown shell ploughed fields of Flanders. The loss had weakened her. Her smile had diminished, her spirit worn threadbare and her heart as low as only a woman's heart can fall. She saw in the face of Patrick Donoghue someone similar to herself. She knew of his father's death and his own sudden failure to frailty. She saw in him another soul undermined by fate, not realising that his young years would provide a stouter shield to his fortunes than her own. She would fade with the years, the weight of her self-pity crushing her; he would grow and throw that weight off, replacing it with rank spite, or anger, not allowing himself to drown under the clouding waters of disappointment.

She fussed over Patrick, and to his eternal embarrassment, he was seated at the front. By already being able to read beyond his years he shone in those early lessons. But by the end of the first playtime, Paddy Donoghue had gone. Seeing his empty chair, Mrs Gerrity looked to the playground, but it was empty save for a small boy returning from the outside toilet block with a dark stain on his short grey pants.

At home, Bridie was kneeling at the front step. She was scrubbing the paving flag that surrounded the step, her fingers raw and red with cold water and soap, when her son threw himself around her waist crying.

"Paddy, son, what is it?" she said, as she righted herself. Looking at her son it was obvious. His left eye was bruised black and swollen shut; his left knee bloodied with scrape skin, rolled in tiny coils, cigarette paper thin; both elbows of his knitted jerkin were gone, wires of ripped wool left limp, and his scoured arms showed grazes of pink and white. She cried herself, to see his tears of shame and confusion.

"See what they did to me, Mam." He sobbed his heart away. "I did nothing. They called me spastic, a cripple and I couldn't fight them." His breath was heaving, sucked gasps of air, as he fought for consolation.

Bridie's neighbour, a soft sofa of a woman, covered in the black shawls and aprons of the widow or spinster, folded him into her arms. "Patrick James Connolly Donoghue, who did this to you? The bloody fecking cowards. You tell me and I'll teach the little bleeders. You and all, with your paradised leg.

"I have a stick I've been waiting to use on someone. Tell me who it is, and I promise on my mother's grave, they'll get it."

Her incandescent fury burned a way through his tears. The snot blew a bubble as he snorted a laugh through a sniffle. The woman was barely five foot and without a tooth in her mouth.

He smiled at her, as his tears funnelled on his lips and penetrated his mouth. The tears tasted salt, and the bitter vinegar of humiliation.

"I know them, Mrs Mac, I know them." He shucked the tears and running snot from his nose and swallowed. "It'll do no good you getting involved, and you a woman, and all."

"Well, me laddo, you're right and you'll have to get them yourself. You're right, it'll do you no good for me to do it for you. Aye, you'll maybe have to bide your time a while; but don't you forget this moment. Aye, keep those wee thugs in mind for a future day. You'll get stronger, me laddo, I know you will."

through summer and winter alone

In the back yard, forgotten under the tarpaulin that held fetid water pooled in its creases, and moss spotted with unsavoury spores of dampness, Paddy found the dismantled cart. He asked his mam where it came from and pestered by his insistence that night at the kitchen table, she told the story of how they came by the cart, the cellar and of his birth and rebirth.

The children fed with scouse and rough crusts of bread listened entranced. Apart from Shelagh, they had never heard their mother tell a story.

Paddy watched from under veiled eyes, as she held the baby on her knee. He wanted to see him as the new bastard child, James, named after his absent English bastard soldier father, but Paddy couldn't separate the love for his mum from the blind hate for the baby's father.

Bridie, bathed in the light of adoring upturned faces, began to tell the story. She used the lightest of her voices, the one she had saved for these occasions in the past, unused for years; a different voice to the flat monotone of drudgery, or the shrew shriek they heard reserved for scolding; this voice painted pictures with grace and drew them in towards the reverie of imagination.

With a wash of words, she laid the canvas background. The reasons, the poverty and inequities of a time past, still present; how the army with their horses and shining helmets moved into the parks and green space of Liverpool, how wicked Churchill sent the English navy to bombard the city into surrender, how the police and secret agents beat upon the innocents with cruel savagery. It was of these people and other people, of this city and other cities, of this country and other countries; universal brutality laid by the powerful upon the backs of the weak.

The role of her husband in the Great Strike was built with a heavy layer of bold paint, a central figure, brave and heroic. She portrayed him in the children's mind, a valiant standing against the foreign foe, behind him an unfurled red flag, full blown in the wind of change. In the foreground with filigreed lines she highlighted herself and Shelagh, shielding the unborn waif under a barricade far from the waging war beyond. Then they moved to the scene of her finding the cellar door through the dirt and flags, littered with the wounded and dying, and finally with the fine detail of a thin brushstroke, she painted a nativity picture, where Shelagh and the mother with the boy child between them lay amongst broken barrels, crates and flagons. On reverent knee before the crib, in loving pose was their loving, devoted, father; smaller, softer, a pastiche of what they slimly remembered.

"But what about the cart?"

Bridie was still in the throes of her own eloquence, remembering times before, when younger, in Dublin at home with her sister when they wrote and performed their own plays and poetry. A lifetime away.

"The cart, Mammy? How did the cart get in the backyard?" Paddy said, desperate to break the spell bound by the story.

She smiled, her eyes fond and loving in the circle of her family. "The cart? Oh, you mean the chariot. Under that old tarpaulin in the yard lies the very chariot that your father stole from the mad general in charge of the troops that charged the crowds that very same day. He was a man of stature, the general, but like most Englishmen, simply mad. He arrived at Lime Street on the train, with his chariot and horses mounted on a flatbed wagon. As the train arrived, he raised his whip to them and shouted, 'Onwards Hercules, on yer go Beelzebub'. With a leap they were off and away from the train station and around St George's Hall."

Shelagh was entranced by the change in her mother, watching as years fell from her tired eyes, now sparkling with life. Pushing her chair back from the table, Shelagh stood in the shadows, and smiled at the wide eyed faces, caught bright eyed with joy in the gaslight, all turned, captivated, towards Bridie.

"The general calls to the cavalry, all of them in scarlet tunics and on huge white horses, all with the ugly faces of Cromwell's soldiers, and he musters them forward. They raise their swords and ride headlong into the crowd, slashing and gnashing, flashing and crashing through the bodies of the men and women.

"Well, your father, the young Joseph Donoghue as he was, was having none of it. He stands and waits for them. He ducks the swords and spears and waits for the mad general. Well, the general is so angry that your Da' never ran away like the rest of the sots. He whips his horses and makes for your father.

"As the chariot passes, your Da', no word of a lie, jumps up between the horses and with the scissors he always carried, snips the traces from the horses. They gallop off and leave the mad general stranded. Like all bullies, he's a coward; all bluster and wind, and he tries to make off back to the station, but he is caught and held by the men. Well, the crowd just love the bones of your Da'. He gets carried around the square on their shoulders. Then the lord mayor comes out, chain and all and says 'Mr Donoghue, the people of Liverpool are in debt to you, sir. Have the treasure of the chariot and take it home with you. Hide it carefully though because every man jack will want it.'"

"So, your Da' says 'But Mr Mayor, I have a wee baby and a beautiful wife to take home and my darling daughter, Shelagh. How can I take the chariot?

"After a minute thinking the Mayor says 'We'll hitch the mad general to the front, and he can pull you up to Kensington Fields and home. And I'll give you a man to kick him up the jaxi if he slows'."

The children at the table howled at the use of such bad language by their mother. Hands covered mouths in shocked surprise and giggling looks were passed as if to question her cheeky impudence. Mammy said 'jaxi' their eyes said, alive and electric shocked.

"And that's how the chariot is hiding in our back yard. The paint may have been lost and the glory that was the mad general's faded, and we may call it a cart these days but at one time it was a chariot."

After their tea, Paddy went to uncover the cart. In the damp yard the stones were covered with a film of black slime, the algae encouraged by the shadows had bred unchecked for years. He pulled back the tarp exposing the arms of the cart. Underneath the canvas, moss had formed on the dismembered wheels and bed stacked against the wall. The arms, used to pull or push the cart, were angled upwards. Paddy placed his hands on each arm and pulled himself upwards. He felt the muscles contract in his chest and arms; he lowered himself until his elbows were bent and pushed up. The flow of blood drained his chest of air and he dropped to the floor, landing awkwardly on his weaker leg. His brother Anthony stood in the doorway with a cob of bread, gnawing away at the food. He had watched quietly, without comment. He smiled. With this tiny encouragement, Paddy took the arms of the cart again. He straightened his back and tucked his left leg under his body. Biting his lower lip, he forced himself to dip down to where his elbow bent to ninety degrees, then push himself vertical. He forced a second but failed on the third before landing back on the floor. "I'll do ten by tomorrow, Anthony," he promised and pulled the tarp back into place.

Paddy felt the pump of pride and adrenaline in his arms and

chest. If his leg was useless, he could be strong in other ways. With that strength he'd get the bullies who blacked his eye and tore the knees out of his kecks, who called him cripple. It might take a while, as Mrs Mac had said, but aye, they'd get their comeuppance. Shame and retribution is a strong motive. So every time he passed the cart on the way to the outhouse he would use the cart for his exercises. He quickly reached the promised ten and went further, driven as he was to change his body and reclaim his dignity. By kneeling under the cart's arms, he could pull himself up, feeling his back broaden with the effort.

At ten years of age he became wiry and supple, his chest, back and arms strong. It was a couple of years later, when the first hormonal effects of puberty took hold, shortly before his thirteenth birthday, that he began to appreciate the changes to his shape. With the encouragement of the chemicals in his bloodstream, his shoulders and arms started to thicken, his back and chest broaden. He used the suppleness of his childhood and the growing strength of his body to try new exercises. He started walking on his hands. Then in that upside down world, he began climbing the flight of stairs up to his mother's bedroom and back down again. His brothers and sisters laughed at the monkey man, the circus act, Paddy the acrobat; but whereas Paddy allowed himself to be a figure of fun for them, he would not accept ridicule from outsiders. On the street, there were no gymnastics or feats of strength, he still walked with the embarrassing gait of a cripple, avoiding other children when he could, not wishing to hear snide and hurtful laughter, and keeping his own vengeful counsel.

His press ups in that unnatural vertical pose grew his chest and back, his biceps and triceps; the caps of his shoulder muscles rounded solid and his neck thickened with roped sinews. He fed his body, absorbing the heavy meals cooked on the kitchen range: stews, scouse and hotpots, pea-whack, colcannon thick with vegetables and thin on meat. His body readily converted the nourishment into muscle and as he grew physically, so did his bitterness fuelled appetite and his greed for transformation.

As Patrick Donoghue grew into adolescence, other changes were made. The changes shaped his attitudes as the exercise sculpted his body. A woman left his life and others stepped forward to take her place. The childish thoughts and fantasies were put away and responsibilities landed, chipped, on his broadening shoulders.

But at ten he was still infant-close to his mother. They had grown inseparable in the years after polio had stolen into his life and robbed him of the two inches of his right leg, and carried off his balance into dim memory.

Before that day he was his father's delight and future hope, Joe Donoghue's darling. His Da' had told him, 'Patsy, you're a special lad; special and destined to outshine the stars'. Together they would sit on the step of the house or sometimes wander the area, looking for a way to get away from the dull street gas lights. His Da' would pick out the stars in the heavens of the plough and tell him stories of his own upbringing in north Dublin, and the hopes for his country, and colour it green with his envy for the power of the rich, white with his raw hatred of the English and gold for future dawns. Then Joe Donoghue, for all his Irish nationalist conceit, had left him. His Da' had gone to fight the war for the very same race he despised, leaving his very own Paddy confused and alone, a child holding his mother's hand.

She had been his constant, always there; the succour of life, a hand holding through first footsteps, a watered comb for his hair, a button on his shirt, a kiss for painful goodbyes and a hug of joy when he returned. His mother had been there when the thief stole into his life and came and took the use of his leg; she was there to whisper to him of life's mystery when his Da' died confused, not a brave soldier of the Irish Republic, but a victim to the raging diaspora germ of influenza, while still in his traitor uniform of the Crown. She'd nurtured Paddy and dried his eyes when he woke up from dreams he didn't understand. When he'd been bullied, she taught him at home. She gave him the rudimentary skills of arithmetic. He was a sharp pupil when any example of multiplication, division, adding, or subtraction involved money. He was ahead of his years enough in adding the pennies and farthings in her purse and tallying her daily shop. She took to trusting him to take her money and, after the other kids had gone to school, his stiff callipered leg to Dobson's shop on the corner. She could give him her list and he'd remember the prices and only take the sum that was needed. If Dobson put the prices up, young Donoghue would let out to the old biddies in the shop which articles had risen and by how much. Shamed, Dobson would let him have it for the money he had in his hand and the old women watching would nod their sour venom at the victualler for trying to rob the poor crippled child.

If he began a life-long appreciation of money at his mother's purse, it was going with her on her weekly trip to the public library that allowed the dreamer in Paddy to awaken. He'd seen the organised and the factual in the encyclopaedias in the hospital library; he'd learnt the words and the definitions, and nurtured the vision of a life in academia. But the books his mother put in front of him gave him the romance and promise of the stories of far-away adventure and undertakings. They fuelled his weakened body with the optimism of the whole and the audacity of the brave. He inhaled the words off the page, breathing in letters and the cadence of a sentence with a gusto that gave him a different life. He read, and in reading he day dreamed a new leg for himself, he became as tall as the tallest, as fast as the fastest, as nimble as Jack in jumping the candlestick. In the books he found a new imagination. He took this imagination and put it with the troubled dreams that still haunted his nights. He had learnt that they did him no harm. They, like the books he now read, told a story. A story where he was a part, but not a part; where he thought he was in the slow confused pages of the night, but not there. Oft times repeated or retold in different circumstance, in the shading of the light or a small detail embellished, but the story and his tenuous understanding of its meaning was constant. He was born another in a far off land where the entire arid countryside was a biscuit coloured wash faded by the sun. He lived even now a parallel life unknown; a simple life where the smell of dried cattle and goat's dung, acrid on the dry gravel of spent riverbeds was as common as the cart horse manure on the streets of this city. He foresaw a death that was another's but was also his own, an end to a life but a beginning of another. He saw tunnels that led down to the dark deep and onwards up to the cross-hatching of dust filled light; and he could see the past and the present and the future all at once but not remember the why, the wherefores, the which, the who, the form or the substance.

He had tried to tell first his father, then his mother, and then Shelagh, that he was there in the dream, and not there, but they sang the same studied song. Dreams disappear in the light of the day; they are of the dark and of the unknown and best left where they are. In the moment of waking, a fleeting remembrance of no value, soon lost.

But his dreams lived on, waiting in sleep's deep obscurity, to tell a tale of another time.

and flowed from shape to shape

The sheets of the bed had wrapped around his body while he slept.

Paralysed. Held by an unseen hand. His petrified limbs heavy marble, veined blue on alabaster white. The weight pressed down on his breathing. He sipped at the stale air, his mouth near full of dirt; he calmed a cough, stifling the gag reaction that would swallow the soil and begin to choke his lungs. He was drowning in earth. He pushed with his tongue, working the debris from his gums and teeth, giving him some respite from the sickening fear that rose in his heart. A fingertip pulsed life and he moved it in a slow circle, moving the weight away from his body. As the load lightened, his hand followed the finger, the arm followed the hand and the weight dissipated, rising off his body like mist coiling from hot summer pavements. The burden lifted, the soil falling away to the abyss below, he rose into a light. All around him he sensed the touch of others as they carried him onwards. His mind crackled with pale ignitions, snapping electric impulses behind his eyes fired sensations to his dormant brain. His eyes triggered opened and for a moment he was blinded. Then the forms around him began to morph into familiars. He knew their shape but they were not of this place. He was rising and they stood still. Beneath him, their arms reached for him and he shied away. He lost his footing and he began to fall. A hand held his arm and he turned to see the face of the man that always appeared in his dream. Paddy knew him in the moment. He read in his eyes the flatness of the land where he was born, the plains that rose to limestone cliffs, flecked with the drab green of desert plants. The smell of dried hay and rusted standpipes, fetid water lapped by stray dogs, acrid smoke from dung fires and the circle of the sun that span westward in the sky. The hand loosened and Paddy turned to look to him, to speak but found himself alone. He called out to the cold pressed sky and raised his head as rain drops began to fall. The bruised clouds simmered with discontent, never quite touching their boiling point; lightning bolts split the sky above the horizon and left bright wormcasts floating in his eyes. He heard the keening of gulls over a flat washed sea, the smell of seaweed on the high dock wall, and the westerly breeze coming off the river, calling out his name, in the form used only by his long dead father.

to trouble the living stream

Paddy awoke to the sound of rapid knocks on the front door. Someone out on the street was giving the old door a battering. A set of three knuckle splitting raps, followed by a few seconds of silence, then again. He could hear stifled movement from his mother's bedroom, the rustle of clothing and whispered talk between her and Shelagh. In his own room, Anthony and Young Bridie slept on, in the deep sleep of the innocent. As the first footfall sounded on the landing floorboards, the front door handle was turned. "Hold on, will yer, give me a minute!" shouted Shelagh, as she stamped down the wooden treads of the steep stairwell.

Anthony sat bolt upright; his eyes startled wide open and straight from his dream. "What the feck is going on?"

"Be quiet," said Paddy, climbing from the shared bed and finding his trousers from the heap on the floor, "and don't be using language like that at home, Mammy'll kill you."

The late autumn light from the netted curtains was filtered through a smoked brume of a fog that had settled heavy wet on the city overnight. Paddy had reached the top of the stairs and was looking over the head of his mother, still in her nightie, who was halfway down as the door opened. The latch had been lifted by Shelagh but before she could pull it open, it was pushed inwards as a man quickly entered. He had his fingers on his lips and closed the door behind him. He looked up the stairs, his eyes glaring white in the half gloom, full of frightened urgency, willing them all silent.

Minutes seemed to pass before the low threat of a car engine grumbled past the house. Silence. The man shrank as he relaxed. His shoulders dropped and he raised his hands and beckoned them all towards him. "Bridie Donoghue?" he whispered, in the low soft lilt of a Galway native. "Missus, I'm Kevin Boggan. I was a friend of your husband, Joe."

Bridie knew what it meant. "Ah, well now," was all she said. She bustled down the stairs, pulling her shawl tight around herself, as if the thin wool could shield and protect her. With a throw of her head, she motioned the man to follow her into the kitchen. He sat uninvited at the table and untying the belt, opened his coat, revealing his dangerous secret. Bridie stared. She handed him a towel and he wrapped it into a bundle, careful to ensure it was fully covered and hidden from sight.

Bridie took it and unbolted the back door, disappearing into the back yard. She opened the gate and went into the entry. She came back into the kitchen wiping her hands on the flannelette of her night gown, her feet wet from the yard with a tide mark of dirt on her toes.

"Shelagh, take Mr Boggan's coat. Make him a cup of tea and give him some bread and dripping. Paddy, close your mouth, you won't want to be catching flies now, would you?" A face peered around the door jamb, "and you, Anthony, you can go back to bed for a bit. I'll call you for Mass in a wee while."

Paddy came in and sat down. The stranger's foot was tapping on the kitchen tiles in uneasy pulsation. He looked up at Paddy and followed the boy's gaze as it settled on his leg. He reached down and placed his hand hard on his thigh to still the nervous tick. Paddy saw the knuckles of his hand, covered by a bloodied handkerchief. He was dark complected like Paddy but younger, maybe in his early twenties; a black beard and moustache, trimmed neatly, sat below a snub nose and tired black pearl eyes. His hair was wet from the hanging fog and a slow bead of moisture ran down his face. The tea was set before him and he thanked Shelagh.

Bridie sat down opposite him and took her mug of tea from her daughter. "You, Paddy, upstairs and get dressed." She waited for him to leave the room, sipping at her tea patiently. When the steps had receded and she heard the bedroom door close, she stopped and listened. A second later she called out "I mean it. Get to your room. I won't tell you again." Quiet whispers of footfall told her she'd been right, and she heard the door close softly as the child finally obeyed his mother.

"Mr Boggan, you'd better explain yourself and do it quickly. I've got four weans upstairs and no man. I can't afford trouble being brought to my doorstep."

"I know, Missus." He said, his head lowered in apology. "I was given a list of people who could help me. Not normally known to the company here in Liverpool. The first two wouldn't or couldn't help. Then I think I was tailed by the Special Branch for a bit, and I've ran all over the town to get here. The fog dropped down around four this morning and it's been a blessing that's hidden me from sight. I'm safe enough now. I wasn't followed here. I made sure of that. I waited a good ten minutes at the end of the street and there was nothing out there. Unless yer man is known to the police, and you've had visits recently, then I'd say we are safe enough now."

Shelagh stood, went to a drawer in the dresser and brought out a towel and gave it to the man. "Dry your hair now, or you'll catch your death of cold." She waited beside him as he tousled the damp from his hair, then ran his fingers back across his head so his fringe parted in the middle like curtains. He looked up and even in the pressing anxious atmosphere tried to put a smile into his black diamond eyes.

"You look too young to have known my husband," said Bridie, her eye cold to his charm.

"I knew him when I was only eleven or so. My family moved to Dublin and my Da' worked as a carter and then joined the union. That's where I first met Mr Donoghue. My dad signed up to the Citizen Army and I always went along to play soldiers with them."

"And are you still playing soldiers now, son?" said Bridie. He nodded, not sure to be proud or ashamed. "The blood on your hand? Does it need looking after?"

"No. It's just a graze. Bad enough to bleed but it'll heal soon enough." He peered under the cotton of the handkerchief, then looked up into her eyes. "Mr Donoghue kept in touch with us, you know. He wrote to us while he was serving in the British Army. He regretted signing up. He lost his way, after the rebellion, thought he was unwanted, but we contacted him again and brought him back into the fold. He was learning explosives; he told us he was coming back to Liverpool to take you and the kids back to Dublin. Back home."

This was the first time Bridie had heard this news. Her jaw dropped softly open to her chin. It shamed her more to think that she had been carrying the child of another man while her husband was planning a future for them.

"We could do with him now. There's a war for Ireland's independence being fought at home and we could do with every man who's served to be giving us a hand.

"I'm over here only because we were asked back in September to help the comrades here in Liverpool after that set of troubles at Balbriggan. Though to be honest, after Croagh Park with the bastard Black and Tans, I'd have come anyway just to give out to them on their own turf."

The hired ex-British soldiers who last year had hurriedly been signed up, mercenary like, to fight against the Irish nationalist cause were called the "Black and Tans". Their mixed uniform of the Irish constabulary's black with military khaki gave them a distinctive uniform and a feared reputation of dark killings and reprisals. Their response to murders and ambushes of their colleagues, in the guerrilla war being fought in the city streets and country hedgerows of the counties of Ireland, was to seek retribution.

Just a week before this stranger with the soft accent and beguiling eyes had fallen through the Donoghues' doorway, the Black and Tans had turned machine guns on the crowd of a Gaelic football match final in the National Stadium in Dublin, killing fourteen in the crowd and wounding scores more. Earlier that day, Michael Collins and his IRB had sought out the 'Cairo Gang', a group of British Army and intelligence officers, and had gone to their homes to shoot all twenty one of them.

"Aye, but to be fair, the boys and girls here don't need much of our help. They seem to have done well enough themselves. As we've been told, if you can't organise yourselves into a disciplined fighting force then make sure you disorganise the enemy. Hitting the docks here is striking a blow back home. As yer man told me, 'an eye for an eye.'"

The life and dreams of idealism and patriotism that Bridie had once shared with Joe Donoghue seemed a faraway world from the drudgery of keeping the household together, the family fed, clothed and educated.

Joe had been a troublemaker; she'd been warned about him but that had also been the charm of him. He saw injustice and acted upon it. He had never been afraid of taking a fight to where a fight had warranted it.

The decision by the leaders of the Dublin Uprising in 1916 to leave him in Liverpool had taken its toll on Joe Donoghue; some of his fire had been smothered but the ember of patriotism must have stayed alive. It had been rekindled in the army when he'd met fellow Irishmen who took the King's shilling but spat on the royal's silvered head as they put his coin away in their pocket. In small groups late at night, away from the listening English officers, standing stiff around a brazier lit to keep the cold and the rats at bay, they talked quietly about Ireland's future. They spoke in seditious tones of treason and plot, and their plans to return home to fight again, after the guns of the Great War had stopped. Each one willing to use the military training acquired at cost in the bloodied acres of Flanders and Ypres and take his skill back to the four green fields of Ireland. Joe Donoghue, for all his hope for a future independent Ireland, had never reached his homeland. It had been left to the others to carry his hope and pursue the possibilities of his dreams.

Bridie still occasionally would speak to friends of her dead husband and pick up snippets of news. She'd be at home and a knock on the door would be a union colleague of Joe's, or sometimes an Irish stranger of Joe's past slim acquaintance who would sit and sip at the tea, asking after her and the family's welfare. They'd fill her with the latest limp gossip from headquarters and she would listen, looking with deadened eyes into the low flames of the fire in the grate, until they realised her disinterest. Then, embarrassed by her indifference to their zeal, they would politely thank her and leave.

Sometimes she'd get a letter from home, her father not truly supportive of the actions of the Irish Republican Brotherhood, but quietly proud of his countrymen's fight for freedom. Newspaper reports told of the police and establishment spies being identified and murdered in the plain sight of the streets by bare cheeked gunmen. She had shaken her head and crossed herself, seeking a blessing for the dead; politicians and sympathisers, soldiers and civilians shot dead on their doorsteps by uniformed men. An eye for an eye seemed about right, in her estimation of what was happening, and she wondered how long the blind revulsion of Ireland's war of revenge and killing would continue. Perhaps, she thought, with that old sensation chilling her blood of heavy steps across a fresh dug grave, it would never have an end. As she took the ends of her shawl and pulled them to her to still that shiver of fear, she realised the man was staring at her.

"Missus, I said, would you mind if I stayed a day or two while the dust settles?"

Bridie nodded.

"Shelagh, get Paddy, Anthony and Young Bridie up and dressed, ready for Mass. Tell them, in no uncertain terms, not to speak to anyone of Mr Boggan. He's a friend of their father if anyone asks. After Mass, call in on Mrs Mac and ask her if you can sit in there. I'll come and get you in a little while. Bring the baby to me."

Bridie looked in the pan that stood in the larder cupboard, covered by a damp muslin cloth. She put it on the range and bent to stoke the flames. It warmed slowly and Bridie fussed at the counter, sawing bread into slices. When the pan started to boil, she spooned the remnants of last night's dinner into a bowl and passed it to the man. She sat with him at the table and took the man's hand and rested it in her lap while he spooned the thin gravy and soft vegetables into his mouth. The blood had blackened and congealed on the bandage, sticking the material to the flesh; the wound needed cleansing and dressing. While Bridie went about her work she asked, without catching the man's eye, "Will you tell me, son, why you are seeking a safe refuge. What is it you are running from?"

The man put the spoon down and wiped his chin with the back of his free hand. "I suppose you have every right to know, Missus, but I'm aware that if I tell you you're likely to be considered an accessory after the fact if the Special Branch or the Guards ever connect you to ourselves."

"Well," Bridie said, "with you and me being the only souls that know you're here, then I am sure they'll never find out. Don't you agree, Mr Boggan?"

"Kevin, please Missus. Mr Boggan is me father's name."

"Aye, alright Kevin. So long as you call me Bridie and not 'Missus.'" She looked up into his youthful face, his eyes cast older with the weight of weariness unspoken.

"Right so, Bridie," he answered, the smile that had been promised in his eyes, but suppressed by that unspoken weariness, making a fleeting appearance across his face. As she unwrapped the handkerchief, he started to tell his story.

The Wednesday before, he and three others had met in Birmingham. Each had come separately on the ferry boats across the sea, from Cork and Dun Laoghaire, landing at Swansea or Holyhead, and had found friends with sympathies to their cause to billet with. From Birmingham, a local haulier had offered safe passage to Liverpool where they met with the officer-in-command of the local battalion of the IRA.

The plans were set to bomb the docks; detailed maps had been drawn and trial runs had been undertaken. Paraffin and petrol sat in jerry cans, while tools to cut high tensile steel bolts were acquired from workshops and factories. They waited and kept their heads low, spending the daytime doing nothing, and in the evenings meticulously going over the plans.

Within the local group two sisters caught the eye. Pretty and slim blonde, a schoolteacher and a clerk, their pillow talk was of their people's rebellion, of romantic freedom, and they were more wanton and easy with their favours to the Irish freedom fighters than good Catholic girls should be. They smoked with the grace and ease of the stars from the silver screen. They bragged openly about their part in the acquisition of guns and ammunition, procured by favours given to smitten squaddies, and how they sourced readily available explosives from the cocky watchmen of mines and quarries in Lancashire. They laughed at their involvement in the smuggling of munitions to Ireland and on the return, gunmen to the mainland on the regular coal tenders that ranged the sea between Liverpool and Dublin. Men and guns hidden in the black cargoes with the captains and crew happy to turn the blind-eye while on a promise of a suggestion from the sisters.

It was the girls that had first showed the rest of the company an article in The Times that publicised the recent discovery, during a raid on Sinn Feiners in Dublin, of a plot to bomb the docks in Liverpool. The paper condescendingly dismissed the outrageous plans as pure fantasy. Together the conspirators shared their nervous laughter at nightmare thoughts that, prompted by the Special Branch, the newspaper was involved in a game of bluff and double bluff, and that armed officers could be waiting for them at the dock gates. To allay their rising fear, extra ammunition was ordered.

On the following Friday, a sortie was led by the O-I-C into the streets of warehouses that ran behind the river in Bootle. A padlock snapped open and a gateway unlocked. Shadowed figures entered the yard. One minded the nightwatchman as he sat by his smoking brazier outside his hut. The others prepared a fire amongst the timber yard. Rags soaked in paraffin tied around plank-ends in a wood pile. Once the rags took light, a low whistle signalled the men and women to leave. Concealed in the doorway of a nearby building, a silhouette of a man timed the arrival of the fire engines that would respond to the call. The smell of wood smoke carried on the wind alerted the nightwatchman to the danger. He raised the alarm and rang the brigade. By the calculations of the man hidden across the road from the timberyard, it took six minutes for the first fire tender to arrive in an excitement of bells.

On the Saturday night, the incendiary equipment the IRA arsonists carried was doubled. Twice the amount of petrol, paraffin and oil were loaded into covered vans and driven down to the docks. The two groups split; the van that departed earliest at seven sharp took its passengers down the Dock Road, southwards and into the city, passing along The Strand and out into the area behind the King's and Queen's Docks. This neighbourhood was a warren of streets filled with tall warehouses and small workshops converting industrial chemicals, lying in the shadow of the rising tower of the new cathedral. The other van left later - a shorter journey to the timber yards and silos in the north of the city in Bootle, on the river side of Derby Road. Each of the separate groups were accompanied by two IRA gunmen familiar and conversant with death. Kevin Boggan travelled in the first van.

The smoke from coal smothered hearths solidified the November river fog that rolled up the low lying streets into a carpet, covering the pavements damp and coating the roads oil slick black. The dank blanket covered the actions of the men and women as they split up and moved on their targets. Torches highlighted doors in circular beams. Locks were sheared by heavy bolt cutters. Hushed footsteps washed petrol and paraffin on the floor, soaking into the stacked goods piled inside the buildings. Small tins of oil were opened and placed on bales of cotton and inside the stands of timber. As the fire took hold, they would spill and their contents accelerate the flames. At eight thirty, a watch was checked, a match was struck and held to the mass of hand held soaked rags. Seconds of breath held patience passed, as the flames grew and then, as they threatened fingertips, were swung and thrown free to alight on the fuel. A second of wonderment reflected red in the eyes of the firebombers before they turned to escape.

Small spirits of flame danced in the yards and warehouses of Effingham, Rodney and Benbow Street in Bootle and in Jordan Street in the city, before feeding off the night air and growing in stature. Shango, the African god of fire, took hold of the hand-picked cotton, sacrificing it for the souls of a people enslaved by others. Logi, Norse god from the pine forests and Lansa, fire deity of the Brazilian rain forests, breathed destruction on the hopeful flame to kindle an inferno of revenge for the despoiling of nature. The gods wreaked devastation; the flames burned high into the fog of the night and embers flew on the dirty wind, carrying a spoiled message to man from the gods of man.

On St James Street, Kevin Boggan cradled his pistol in his arms and waited in the doorway for the rest of the gang to appear. He could see a faint glow of pink colour smudge the fog as the fires took hold. From the south, he saw a pair of policemen on their steady beat, walking slowly towards him. He pressed himself against the door, seeking the shadowed cloak of invisibility. Talking in low whispers, the other IRA gunman and one of the local men turned a corner and stopped dead, ten yards away from the police. Both turned on a quick heel and ran, heading in opposite directions, along Norfolk Street. The police shouted to stop. A blown whistle cut into the grey brume. The echo of heavy leather soles and hobnails bounced off the walls as the police began to chase after the men. A single shot rang out.

The bullet fired from the assassin's gun, aimed to kill an agent of the British government in revenge for past brutalities, rifled into an innocent victim. Returning from his Catholic church on Parliament Street, a young man of nineteen years unknowingly completed the old saying of 'being in the wrong place', his life a forfeit for the causes of a country he didn't care about. He died instantly on the wet pavement of his home city.

Kevin Boggan watched as the police disappeared from sight, chasing the gunmen. People came and knelt by the dead man. Boggan went and stood with them. Silent, he was part of the grief but only to hide himself in their pain, the better to make his escape. They said the dead man had only just left the church and they fetched his priest and prayed for his dead soul. Boggan mumbled learned, now half-forgotten, responses of a lost childhood and crossed himself at the proper time. No stranger to death, the outsider watched the tears flow and the people cry until he thought it safe for him to leave. Amidst the death and the fire and the smoke, he went to find a place to hide.

Bridie had bathed his hand, greased the wound with salve and wrapped it in clean rags. She had held it as he told her last night's news. Now she dropped his hand. He winced as it hit hard on the tabletop.

"A boy was killed?"

The man nodded and looked down. He pretended to be repentant for the tale and its telling. He needed somewhere safe and he thought he could play act his way into this household. A household of soft women, he thought, with no man and them by birth sympathetic to his cause. He had no shame for his actions or his fellow soldier. He was a soldier. He had killed before. English officers, agents and spies, broaching casual conversation with them in doorways or on the street of towns and cities in Ireland, then nonchalantly, indifferently, carelessly shooting them dead.

Bridie looked at the clock on the mantlepiece. It had been the old woman's. It was brought downstairs when she died. The clock had kept the time when the old woman's was done. What a time they now lived in.

"With my own children on their way back from Sunday Mass, you tell me your friend killed an innocent soul. A bystander."

"Not me, Bridie, I've never shot a gun in my life," he lied, "the gun I was carrying was another man's. That was my job, to hold onto the gun in case it was needed."

"Aye, needed to shoot someone else. To widow a man, to orphan a child, to leave a mother without her child." She sat stilled by thoughts of loss. "You can't stay. I can't have you in my home."

She rose and left the kitchen, returning with the bundle. "Take this and leave."

He shook his head. "I'm going nowhere.

"You, Bridie Donoghue, do you know what you are? A fecking hypocrite. That's what. What the feck do you think your Joe was up to? Training the volunteers; training them in what? Aye, drilling up and down with spades and hoes, pick axe handles for guns. But you know what, Bridie? When the shipments of munitions and weapons came in from America and Germany, they soon found themselves fighting with the real stuff. They died for the same cause that your Joe believed in. The cause I'm fighting for now. And who taught them to fight and die? Your precious Joe did."

Bridie was silent.

"And you are saying now that you won't help the same side that your Joe trained to fight and kill? And because a boy was shot? It was unfortunate but he's a casualty of war. Until now, for the best part, the war has been fought on Ireland's soil but we will bring it back here until you sign the treaty we want. I see you, Bridie Donoghue, and I know what you are."

He paused. His quiet anger powerful in the silence of the dead house.

"Do you remember this? 'In the name of God and of the dead generations from which she receives her old tradition of nationhood, Ireland, through us, summons her children to her flag and strikes for her freedom.' Your Joe did. He remembered. He quoted it to me in a letter, saying the words made him cry every time he thought of the lives sacrificed in Dublin back in 1916. Do ye know that the survivors of the post office were spat on by the people of Dublin as the English army walked them to their martyrdom. Can you imagine? And you with a stony heart and a dry eye, you're like those who wouldn't help raise the flag he served."

He stood and found his coat. Bridie remained seated, her hands in her lap as she looked down to the cot where her youngest child lay asleep.

He reached for the door handle but stopped. "I'm sorry, Missus. I had hoped you'd have helped a soldier of Ireland. I must have got you wrong. Still there's plenty of women in Liverpool who have been good to their faith and the cause. They've sheltered and fed, hidden and provided for any number of ourselves passing through here. It's a crying shame that you couldn't have done the same for the loving memory of your husband. So I'll take my leave of you, Missus, but I want you to remember this. When you return home to Dublin in the next few years and you enter a free Irish State, you remember how you played your part in the war. Don't be tempted to wrap yourself in the Tricolour and tell people how proud you are of the freedoms gained for yours by others. Aye, lean ar aghaidh. Think on, Missus, when the glasses get raised on St Paddy's night, that you could have helped the cause but chose not to."

He opened the parcel of the wrapped tea towel and took the pistol out. He dropped the towel on the floor where it lay fallen next to Bridie's wet and dirty feet. He casually checked the gun was loaded by flipping open the cylinder and then flicked his wrist to close it again, hiding it inside his coat pocket's lining.

Bridie sat stone faced silent as he opened the front door, checked both ways and slipped out, turning his collar up against the chillness of the November morning.

From outside, hidden in the mist of the Sunday morning just beginning to lift from the street, came the melancholic cry of seagulls as they sailed on the air, still carrying the ashes and smoke of the fires and the mourning grief of departed souls lost in the grey waters of the sky.

the sailing seven

After the man with the gun had gone, Bridie sat there for another while worrying if her betrayal of the ideals of her late husband was to join the shards of guilt that already pierced her sides; the bleeding spear wounds that stigmatised her shame. She had betrayed him on so many matters that this hardly warranted contrition. But her husband was dead, and she was to be with another man who would provide for her family. He was a stolid character, bereft of Joe Donoghue's hopeful romanticism, a man whose stock were yeoman farmers from Shropshire, middle England, with practicality at the fore and idealism a faraway fantasy. He would be a good, solid husband and father. Firstly, for their own child and herself, but ultimately, she thought she would make him be a father to all Joe Donoghue's children as well. She would make sure that her children were protected. That was her goal and happy gaol in life. The baby woke and started to cry, Bridie picked him up and for want of anything better to do, put her head to his and started weeping softly.

The children returned full of questions of the dark stranger who appeared and disappeared in the time that it took them to go to and from the church. He had melted in the lifting fog and Bridie took pains to vanish him from her children's memory.

It was Shelagh who showed her the photograph of the man in The Echo, two days later, who'd been captured for the shooting of the young churchgoer on that flame wracked Saturday night. His name wasn't given, as Boggan and his black beard had been shaved, leaving him looking as pale a youth as the young man, the eternally grey corpse that lay awaiting burial in the front room of his parents' house. Shelagh asked her mother if it was the same man. Bridie turned away and gave no reply.

As Bridie's silence stole away from the shadows of pain and the past, and from Joe Donoghue, seeking out a new pragmatic self, Shelagh turned into the light of realisation of her own character and how life had fashioned, moulded and made her. She sought out newspaper articles and began to educate herself on her Irish origins, and whilst her own mother shunned conversations of the old country, Shelagh found a ready ear and animated voice in her Aunty Mary. They say that the further you travel in time and miles away from Ireland, the more intense is your wish to belong. For Bridie, that wish had died with the birth of her new born Englishman's son; for Shelagh, the wish grew with the disappearance of the handsome bearded man that Sunday morning.

Whilst the war was being waged in Ireland, first between the British and those seeking freedom, and then perversely between the factions of the IRA who couldn't agree on the terms of that freedom, Shelagh sought an education in the shifting paradigms of Irish politics.

At her workplace she casually involved herself in the work of the union and its organisers, and quietly began to educate herself in the ways of a man's world and the women's suffragette movement. As she met the men who had known Joe Donoghue, both in the world of organised labour and organised struggle, she began to understand him more, and at the same time, less. Whilst Bridie's memories of Joe Donoghue were lost in the present with the man who was father to her new child, Shelagh started to understand a conflicted past that her adopted father had belonged to, and his vision of a becalmed future she wanted to be a part of. But Shelagh, as the hidden child of the family, kept this passion to herself.

On Saturday afternoons after work had finished, she would take a bus with Young Bridie and visit the '98 bookshop on

Scotland Road and speak with Mr Murphy. He showed her books and pamphlets and a version of history that centred on the Gael. He introduced her to Mrs McCarthy and she to others and quietly, as was her way, Shelagh signed up to the 'Cumann na mBan', the women's equivalent of the IRA. They trained her on excursions to quarries in Lancashire and the foothills of Snowdonia in guerrilla warcraft and taught her how to shoot, how to set incendiaries and the basics of explosives; how to pass messages and receive secret instructions; instruction in codes and ciphers within the small three man cell structure that kept the organisation safe. After her training, in the new year, she was asked to carry a small pistol on the tramways to give to an IRA gunman who was to target the owner of a house in Aintree. The owner of the house was known to be an officer serving in Ireland with the Black and Tans. In April she met with a man fresh from the Dublin ferry and played the role of his wife as he travelled onwards to Manchester. Days later, he was arrested and tried for conspiracy against the state. Worried that she might be known to the Special Branch through that association, the intelligence officer of the brigade asked her to go back to her life, laying low to avoid attention, bringing no interest to herself. There she remained, as instructed, a member of a radical group, having helped when requested, and now being held in discreet reserve for the time when they would have need of her again.

Bridie, oblivious to the slow turnings of Shelagh's world, did not see the change in her. Shelagh grew, strong and assertive and practical while Bridie faded, dreaming for the years to pass and for her soldier to return from the peace and provide for her.

Nor did the children recognise Shelagh's change; too young to comprehend, too distracted to see, Shelagh stayed the constant elder sister to them all. In the family, Paddy remained his mother's favourite. A special place in Bridie's broken realm for her crippled child.

On his eleventh birthday, Bridie gave her eldest son her dead husband's compendium of the poems of Yeats. He lost himself in the words and imagery, and the uneasy dreams that haunted him through his sleep lost their intensity in the daylight, and in the craft of the poet.

A year later, on Paddy's twelfth birthday, Bridie took her youngest child, her new husband's namesake, and left the house on Ferdean to live with him. Her new man had finally returned from active service and she willingly left the children with Shelagh, now just turned twenty years of age.

It would be many years later that Paddy would find out if Shelagh knew of their mother's intentions, but as Bridie closed the door to her old home and left her children behind, Shelagh became responsible as the surrogate parent to three children.

Paddy had sat at the kitchen table, having returned from the shops with a new loaf and the hopeful excitement of the smell of a freshly baked birthday cake. Instead he found himself alone in the cold room. He could hear Shelagh and his mother's filtered conversations, paired accusation and denial, plea and rebuttal from the bedroom above. Then the stair carpet stamp as his mother came down wearing a new green coat he'd never seen before, carrying a small suitcase and her new baby. Without a word said, she kissed Paddy and walked out. Confused, he didn't know if she'd gone for good until the others returned from school.

Shelagh sat them down and told them that their mother had left. She had taken the baby and had told her to say that she would come back and see them soon. They were to be brave and remember to say their prayers. Paddy sat and listened to his younger brother and sister cry. He fought to keep his eyes dry, swallowing that dry stone of hurt that lodged in his throat again and over again until he had straightened his tortuous thoughts into threads of silent anger. She had left him on his birthday. She had left all of them. He couldn't forgive her.

Now, all he had was Shelagh as his mother, and Young Bridie

and his little but whole brother, Anthony, aged nine. At twelve, he had become the last man of the house standing. The burden of that responsibility bowed his spine and bent his already weakened limb.

glory of changeless metal

The concrete floor was continually wet. The old enamel bath slopped cold water when the contents of hessian sacks of potatoes were dropped into it. The bath water, brown with mud, had a half inch of silt-sitting sediment stirred occasionally when a hand, red raw and chapped, fished for a prize. Having pulled the spud from the water, the man or woman, both sitting alone, hunched on stools at either end of the bath, would peel the skin between thumb and blade, eye the potato with a turn of the knife and drop it into a tin pail, swilling more water on the floor.

She was faster than the man; her hands dipped into the bath twice as often, skinned and blinded the spud in deft repetition and signalled her pail full by tapping her knife loudly on the side of the bath.

The man would then rise and carry the bucket, the bobbing potatoes rolling the water over the lip, across his raw hands and down his wellington boots. He would tip the contents into a large sink of salted water and return the bucket to the woman, and sit down again silently.

The division of labour suited both. He had just been started at the shop, through the intervention of a friend and the charity of the owner. He was told he'd start here in the back, and if he learned the ropes he would go to the shop, behind the counter to fry fish and cook chips for the customers.

The woman was happy in the back. The cold mattered not to her. The repetition less so, she was quick and accurate in her work. Once the hundredweight of potatoes were peeled for the morning, she would leave her stool and stand at the sink and feed the machine which was inset with a seven inch blade, honed and sharp, and that cut the chips to be fried later. She'd be finished by eleven and she would leave, more often than not with a piece of fish, sausage or pie for her and her man's dinner. She'd return, letting herself in through the back door, at around four in the afternoon to prepare the chips for the shop's evening hours.

The door opened and Peter O'Brien, dressed in a long white coat, backed in through the door with two large mugs of tea. The vapour from his breath and the steam from the tea kettled together in the air. The woman thanked him with an inflection of her head and told him to set her mug down on the floor while she finished her work. The man, pleased for the break in the monotony, stood up at once, dropping the potato he had in his hand back into the bath.

"Thank you, Mr O'Brien. It's a reet welcome sight." He took the tea and circled his chilblained fingers around the mug. He was a slight man, with a globe of a head, disproportionate to his body, and a shock wave of black hair. His nose and chin were sharp and contrived to meet each other when he smiled.

"How are you finding the work, Jack?"

"Dull and boring, cold on the fingers; it's not like us Yorkshire folk to complain but it's colder than a witch's tit in here."

"Aye, do as Mrs Reid does and wrap up warm. An extra layer never harmed anyone, and do you know her secret weapon? She keeps a small jar of hot water by her side to warm her hands whenever she needs it. Water soon goes cold mind, but it's a help."

He counted the pails of white chipped potatoes as they sat in a line by the sink. He nodded. He signalled to the pair that they had peeled enough potatoes for the dinner time clientele. Those who would drift in from the surrounding streets and small workshops that ran down Bedford Road towards the church. The fish he'd bought that morning from the fish market lay cut into sized fillets on the marble slab. There was no need for ice to keep them fresh in the chill of the room.

As Jack washed his hands in warm water, O'Brien told him that he could use him in the shop today and told him to follow him into the kitchen.

Jack Braddock was happy to leave the silent cold of what was little more than a lean-to at the back of the property. The cold from the concrete and the enduring water gnawed at his flesh and settled deep into his bones. It took him a while for warmth to return him to normal while his partner in the potato peeling shed seemed content and happy in the frigid Baltic conditions.

He was happy for any work at the moment. He had arrived in Liverpool from his hometown of Dewsbury during the war and had become enmeshed in local politics; he then married and became a member of the Communist Party. His politics and his dour east of the Pennines attitude made employers uncomfortable in employing him.

O'Brien had done his mentor Fitzsimons a favour in giving Braddock a job. A small favour in return for the past kindnesses shown and future help promised.

In the kitchen, Mary sat reading the Liverpool Catholic Herald. On the oil cloth covered table was an opened letter weighted down by a cup and saucer. On the floor by her feet, a small boy played with a wooden train. The sound of a piano came from the room further down the hall.

"Mary, this is Jack Braddock. He'll be working here for a few weeks."

"Are you married yourself, Jack?" said Mary.

"I am. A fine bonny lass called Bessie. As yet we haven't been blessed with any childer, but we keep trying, Mrs O'Brien." His gaze strayed to Mary's swollen belly.

"If it's not too rude, I see there's another on the way. We always said the Irish Catholics like a big family." He was suddenly aware that his Yorkshire lack of tact had left the room in a disturbed silence, with the O'Briens wondering if there was any veiled slur in Braddock's comment.

Before anything else was said, O'Brien ushered Braddock out of the room and down the hall to the shop. From a peg in the hall, Braddock was offered a white coverall to wear.

In the shop the range had been fired and the beef dripping added to the tanks, both of which were beginning to broil. An older woman, her hair tied up and wearing the same white coat as both men, was leaning against the counter. Her face was set stone, eyes marbled, looking away.

"This is Mrs. Nixon. She runs the ordering and the till. You'll be working with me, but you'll be listening to what she tells you to do. Understood?"

Braddock nodded and the old woman chiselled out a smile from hard set features.

O'Brien showed the Yorkshire man how to test the temperature with a chip or a piece of batter, describing the process of battering the fish only as the customers came in, to keep it fresh and standards high. The batter was made by Mary in the kitchen and brought through when required.

O'Brien said that the recipe for the batter would be a family secret that would remain with the O'Briens as long as the shop was open. He'd taken a version of his mother's mixture but had enhanced it by replacing one key ingredient that, he believed, made it superior. Time, he said, would tell; if the shop continued to be successful, then the proof would be in the profit.

Braddock was overwhelmed at his first shift in the shop. As soon as the door opened at noon the first customers appeared. Children from the local school, clerks and shopkeepers from

County Road, and drivers and carters passing by, would draw up and line in the street outside waiting their turn to order. A barked request by Mrs Nixon to the startled customer as they entered, "Did you want fish?" An answer of size and species, 'large cod', 'small haddock', 'two plaice' would send O'Brien into a dip, wipe, dip, wipe of the fish into the batter then into the golden oil. By the time the patient customer had paid, good things come to those that wait, the fish would be ready. Mrs. Nixon would flip newspaper, douse vinegar and spray salt, wrap into a package and take the coppers, threepenny bits and tanners, a shilling for a big order, a half crown for a feast of Cana proportions and, with a blessing of thanks to all, see the customer away happy and salivating.

By half two the shop was closed. The blinds were pulled down and the sign on the door turned to 'Shut', the paper fingers on its embossed clock set to half five.

Mrs. Nixon counted the change from the till; tallied it against the list of orders she kept and bagged the coins into the paper sacks from the bank, taking it to the kitchen for Mary O'Brien to place in the safe. They drank tea as the fat in the range cooled. When the fat was cold enough, O'Brien insisted that it was drained and sieved through muslin cloth to remove any impurities. He would then consider the colour of the fat and replace it if he thought it likely to taint the taste of the food he served. As he oversaw this process, Braddock was instructed to clean the shop. The tiles, the counter tops and the floor were washed and cleaned. What parts of the range could be dismantled were, and dropped into buckets of soapy water. The frame itself was scoured spotless, each surface gleamed fresh, and then the whole thing reassembled and the coals in the fires set for opening time.

They sat at the kitchen table while Mrs O'Brien went to the bank with the baby in the pushchair, and Mrs Nixon stood outside and smoked. From the covered yard in the back, they heard the old lady come in and start the process of restocking the pails of chips from the hessian sacks stacked against the far wall.

Braddock blotted vinegar from the pool on the plate of chips in front of him. O'Brien looked at the back of The Echo newspaper and, with a stub of a pencil taken from behind his ear, marked down some fancied horses from a meeting at Bangor on Dee. He looked around the table for something to write out his bets. He found the discarded envelope and flipped it over. On the back was the name and address of Bridie Donoghue, her address in Gloucester Place and the acronym, S.A.G., St Anthony Guide. He pushed the letter to one side and reached into his pocket and took out a roll of pound notes. He scribbled out Bridie's details on the envelope and wrote out a list of bets.

"Have you nearly finished, Jack?" Braddock was just polishing the plate with a crust of bread and he nodded, his mouth full. "Do us a favour? Nip down to County Road, go in the snug at the Harlech pub and ask the barman for George. Tell him Peter O'Brien sent you. Give him this and wait for his slip in return. Do you have that?"

"Aye, you want to put a bet on and I'm to run to the bookies for you?"

"Well. In a way, but you are. In fact, you're just giving my bet to the bookie's runner. He'll put the bet on for me. So, you're not too involved. I need it on by four for the last few races, so if you could put a shift on, it'd be appreciated."

After Braddock had left, O'Brien's eyes fell on the letter pages on the table. He scanned the words quickly. He didn't want to be party too much to the woman's problems. He didn't want to see anything that he couldn't later unsee. He found the paragraph which had troubled his wife so and stopped reading. He folded the pages and returned it to the table. He shook his head.

O'Brien was behind the counter when he saw Jack Braddock turn the corner and enter the door at the side of the house. In a minute, he came through the door into the shop and passed

O'Brien a piece of folded paper. He put on his white coat and buttoned it up to his chin.

Mary O'Brien had returned from the bank and had brought a tin bowl of freshly made batter and two mugs of thick brown tea for the men. The children, returned from school, were being fed. Blind Annie was playing the piano in the front room. A sister from the local convent had called and was enjoying a meal, while thanking Mrs O'Brien for the generosity of their weekly donation to the Order. Mrs Nixon had arrived and was nattering nonsense to the youngest O'Brien children in the kitchen.

"I want to say thank you for this job, Mr O'Brien."

O'Brien looked up from lighting the range. The paper flamed and the kindling started the smouldering of the coke they used.

"Well, I was in need of a hand, just at the minute. I can't say if it will go past month's end, but it will put a few shillings in your pocket and you'll go home with a belly full of chips at least. If you get your wife to pass by on her way home from her work, I daresay we can find a chipped spud for her as well."

Braddock was preparing the sheets of newspapers used to wrap the food, readying them for tonight's trade. He ripped the broadsheet pages in half and threaded them onto string attached to the counter.

"How did you get into this game? Mr Fitzsimons told me you were once a docker."

O'Brien leant on the range and folded his arms. He told Braddock of the meeting with Harford and Fitzsimons. He told him of the flattering offer of a political career and his reasons for its polite refusal. Since then, O'Brien had indeed left the Cotton Exchange and had served a six month apprenticeship in the frying arts at Openshaw's shop further along Rice Lane in Walton Vale.

He didn't mention to the Yorkshire man that the opportunity only arose as Openshaw was also a Knight of St Columba. Nor did he tell Braddock of the purchase of the Stuart Hotel nearby by a consortium from the Knights, including a friend of Fitzsimons, a prominent local politician's brother, and O'Brien himself. It was run by O'Brien's brother as licensee, not long returned from New York and only too happy to help.

The time at Openshaw's fish shop had been perfect preparation for O'Brien. He had waited years to purchase, with the help of a bank draft and favourable terms, the old dairy on the corner of Stuart Road and Cromwell Road. He had transformed it by the installation of a coal fired frying range and by converting the front section of the house into the chip shop they now stood in.

"So, friends in high places?" said Braddock.

O'Brien snapped a chip in half and threw it into the warming fat. It sank and then rose loudly sizzling its complaint.

"I'm not so sure about 'high places' but friends of a sort, I suppose. In any life there's a bit of back scratching. You scratch mine and I'll make sure you're repaid in kind. Aye, and maybe a bit more than that. But mark my words, you can become too beholden to these men. They can be your friends until they turn. Then they can be the flea on your back that makes you itch and neither you nor they can reach to scratch that particular itch."

O'Brien rescued the chip from the fat. Looking at the chip closely, he tipped it onto a piece of paper. He mushed it with his finger and tasted the content. He nodded his satisfaction with his product and checked the temperature gauge on the range. He tapped the dial with his forefinger twice.

Braddock was looking without seeing out through the shop window as he focussed on his thoughts and emotions. "Happen as may be, but it's the way of the world. Me and my Bessie are beginning to see that.

"You know we are involved with local politics? No doubt Fitzsimons has told you we have further ambitions. But we are already getting flummoxed by those we are supposed to be helping. D'you know of Bessie's mother, Mary Bamber? She's been involved in the council and the Independent Labour Party for years. She was there in 1911, the Great Unrest they called it, as was Bessie herself working in soup kitchens. Any road she's just got back from Russia.

"You know, me and Bessie are members of the Communist Party, but we respect her mother's opinion more than we do our own, and for a tyke like me, that's a lot to swallow."

O'Brien took a sip of his tea and shifted his feet.

"Anyways Mary, her mother, says there's nowt communist about the set up over there. It's not the people who are running things. It's the elite. A different elite but still an elite. And the elite are backed by the military and the secret police. And the people? Mary never got to meet many, but she saw the queues, she saw the poverty that doesn't look to have been changed at all; not in the least in the six years following the Revolution."

Braddock lifted the towel covering the batter and used the fork to give the liquid an unnecessary whisk.

"We've been at the forefront of the Party here in Liverpool. We've fought the fascists in Sheil Park, we've defended the Red Flag, literally and meta-bloody-phorically; we've defended and promoted communism, we even occupied the Walker Art Gallery, but we are starting to feel we've had the wool pulled over us eyes by the Party and the effing Comintern."

O'Brien took the bowl from Braddock, set it on the counter and covered it again. Braddock continued.

"It's meant to be for the people but doesn't listen to the people. Its aim was to redistribute wealth, but it seems the money is just ending up in the hands of the Party members. And you know, they won't take any dissent. They dictate to us from Russia with no idea of the lot of the working man in Liverpool or Manchester or wherever. They have a mainly agricultural economy and ours is so different. But one rule applies to all. You might think that the actions of the police and army in strike breaking here is bad, but I'll tell ye from what Mary has told us, it's at a different level there. It's not broken heads, it's so much more; people disappear and for good. Communism hasn't liberated the peasant, it's entrapped them."

O'Brien passed Braddock another set of newspapers to separate and spoke.

"I haven't got any real learning of the politics behind the Russian Revolution. I can tell you this, from my experience, all systems will be perverted by the people entrusted to run them. Someone told me that power is corrupting, and absolute power corrupts absolutely. I think therein lies the truth. It's the checks and balances that can be put in place to ensure the power isn't corrupted, that is the only hope of the poorer classes in society. We expect it of our democracy, but democracy is still in its infancy and remember, all women haven't been given the vote yet. We'll have to see what happens in a hundred years or so. To see if democracy and the will of the people can arrest what is happening today.

"I'll give you an example, you'll know of the Poor House on Mount Pleasant, above the town. Well, it's to be sold. It's a long time off and not common knowledge at the minute but I've been told that eventually it will be almost given away to the Catholic Church for buttons. They'll build a cathedral there, bigger and better than the Vatican itself.

"The reason for the sale is hidden in politicking, but my thought is that there's been favours asked and promises long given to the Irish Nationalist Party to ensure that it becomes so. Why else would a Tory-run council sell off its family jewels? Why would a council backed by the Orange Order think of selling to Catholics? And when it happens, you can bet your last shilling that the builders will be every man jack Catholic; unless of course, deals have already been done in the selling to ensure it's the Proddy dog craftsmen who are at the fore. So, you'll know as I do, Jack, with Ma' Bamber being on the council, she'll know exactly how things work and it's not a lot to do with democracy."

At this, Mrs Nixon came into the shop and cast a dark eye on the men as if they were conspiring wicked murder. She opened the serving hatch and went to the windows to lift the blinds. It was quarter to the hour and already a queue was forming. She stared at Braddock with contempt.

"Aye," Jack Braddock said to himself, as much as to anyone, as he tore the paper in half, "power corrupts."

At seven that evening, just before the blinds were drawn down for the day, a man in a large flat cap and oversized raincoat waited by the door. When O'Brien turned from the range, the man raised a finger and caught his attention. O'Brien hurried to the door and went out through the hall into the street. He returned with a smile that creased his face and crinkled his eyes and couldn't help himself but tell Braddock that all his horses had come in at Bangor and he'd won big today. He put a finger to his lips to ensure Braddock knew that this gem of news was in confidence. Braddock nodded. He got an extra sixpence in his wage packet that night.

crooked thing

Mary O'Brien stepped off the tram. It had taken her an hour to reach Kensington Fields from Walton.

The news had come in a letter from Shelagh, telling that her sister, Bridie, had left home. Mary carried her three year old in her arms and another child quietly in her womb. She had left the youngest born with her mother in law in the home in Cromwell Road. She set her son down on the pavement. In the gutter the litter of life pooled in dirty rainwater. A sudden rain shower had left the pavement wet clean and she walked poised in her new shoes, aware and proud of the purity of their unblemished soles.

Shelagh was standing on the doorstep as Mary led her son John, but called Jack after her own father, in slow steps down the long street.

"Hello, Aunty Mary" she said, coming towards her and holding her overly long in an embrace. "Thank you for coming. The others are at school, except for Patrick, he's inside, upstairs in his and Anthony's room, reading."

"Why is there no school for Patrick?"

"He's never been. Mammy kept him away after the illness and she taught him herself."

"Good God, how old is he now? Twelve? But the other two attend school, the Sacred Heart on Low Hill, don't they? And they go to Mass as well?"

"You'd better come inside."

They sat in the kitchen at the table. It was dark as little light came from the window that looked out on the yard, shadowed as it was by the hulk of the cart. Mary sat her boy at the table, noting that none of the four chairs matched and one had no spindles to its back and functioned as little more than a stool. By the range, wood from broken fruit crates and odd scraps of timber waited for their last burning. In readiness, a small pile of newspapers had been rolled and knotted, sitting ready on a bucket half full of wet coal. In the press, the larder as it was called, a loaf of bread and jars lay covered from the omnipresent flies by a muslin towel. A pint bottle of milk, half empty, half soured stood in a pan of cold water.

"When was it that your mother left?" said Mary. "Where has she gone and why?"

Shelagh sat with her small white hands folded in her lap, her little fingers turning small circles.

"Joseph's father came back from the army. He's served his time, and she upped and left with him. It was about a week after Paddy's birthday, a Friday night. She told me as she was leaving. She must have prepared for it.

"I'd just come back from work. I was to see Jim, Jimmy Keegan, a lad from the firm's accounts department, that very night. I was in fine spirits. Then she met me at the door, an old suitcase in the hall and a couple of parcels wrapped in brown paper. The baby was in his pram asleep, Paddy quietly reading upstairs. She waited for me to come in and sat me down."

The speech was delivered monotone, detached; Shelagh's tears had been spent and wasted in the time between then and now. She had no more emotions to put on show for her aunty.

"She said she'd write in time to tell us where she was, but she'd been told to leave things be for a while. To let things settle. She left a ten bob note for us. The soldier must have given her money to keep us and to buy our silence. Judas money."

Low bitterness was creeping into her voice like mustard gas into a trench.

"She left me, Young Bridie, our Tony and Paddy. I'm twenty years of age. I should be having my own children. Who will take me on now with these three to feed and look after? I've not been able to go back to work. I explained to the foreman but jobs are hard to come by. There's any number of people waiting for a good week's pay. So he finished me off there and then, gave my job to one of his family."

"Young Bridie, I mean Bridgid, cried herself to sleep the first three or four nights. Tony and Paddy won't speak of it, nor of her. Paddy went out and picked a fight with the cock of the street, Tommy McClelland, and came back with his arse kicked and loose teeth in his head."

Mary watched her son draw on the paper she had brought with her. She reached for his shoulder and placed a gentle hand on him. She drew a breath of a sigh and straightened herself in the hard backed Bentwood chair.

"Well now, practicalities first; then we will talk about what the hell your mother was thinking. Plainly the poor woman's had a crisis of some kind and can't be well.

"Is she under the doctor?"

Shelagh shook her head. She didn't know, nothing had been said. In empathy of ignorance, Mary shook her head as well.

"Now so, have you enough money for the wee ones? I can help. Your Uncle Peter is doing grand at the shop and we have the pub also, so that's not a problem. Do you want me to take wee Bridie with me? And Anthony for that matter?"

Mary hadn't asked about Paddy as she would first have to speak to her husband. Poor blind Annie was still at home with them and she wasn't sure if his Christian charity would stretch to this abandoned set of waifs and the crippled boy.

"No, Aunty Mary, she said that the family should stay together."

"She's a fine one to talk about staying together. No, Shelagh, this is your decision. Me and your Uncle Peter will support whichever way you go with it. But you deserve a life as well. You are in your prime and I'm surprised you aren't already wed and with a few babies of your own."

She leant forward, hooked her own little finger around her niece's and looked deeply into her eyes. "You're a good looking girl, Shelagh Donoghue."

At last a smile touched her lips and her spirit lifted as the shadow of a weight was cast off.

"I'd like to speak to them all when they get back. About going with you to yours. I'm not sure how they'll feel if I desert them as well.'

"You won't be deserting them. And don't be worrying about their feelings. They're children for the good lord's sake, they haven't lived long enough to have feelings."

Mary lifted her son onto her lap, shushing him when he made to complain. "What time will school finish? I imagine three if it's the same as St Francis de Sales. That'll become their new school."

"They'll come straight home and we can ask them then. I'll take them home in a cab, it'll be a rare expense, but it has to be done."

"What of me and Paddy?" asked Shelagh. "He's just turned twelve and if I can get a job he'll have to be here, left alone."

"Aye, well, if he returns to school we won't have that problem." She thought of her own son, Edward, turning eleven and already with a scholarship promised at the Catholic Institute, or St Edward's as it's to be renamed, in Everton Valley.

"That's where Paddy should be now, in school, not idle in his room, reading. Then, if he can get some sort of job at fourteen when he leaves, he can stand on his own two feet."

Paddy was listening at the foot of the stairs, having shuffled down step by step on his backside to silence his lumbering descent.

He sat there as Shelagh and his Aunty Mary discussed the whereabouts of his mother and what must have happened to make her do such a thing.

Paddy had already decided what had happened. It had become too much for her. A lost husband, a cripple for a son, a bleak lonely existence. It had been made easy for her; a promise of a new life if she turned her back on the old. A new life, a new man, a new child, and a new future. Easy for her to turn her back on the old. Too easy, and in that moment he hated her for just how easy it was.

He opened the door and slipped out into the street and sway walked towards the school.

human dignity

Outside the red brick building a few women stood together, uniformly dressed in grey gabardine coats, their hair turbaned from the drizzle that had swept in from the sea, dampening the end of the day a wet grey. A man on the far side of the road watched, idle from no work, leaning against a lamp post, drawing smoke hollow cheeked into long-ruined lungs from the last inch of a roll-up.

If you'd had your ear pressed against the large wooden door of the school, you might have heard the voices of the children as they incanted the 'Our Father' in prayer, eyes closed and fingers templed in front of them. They blessed themselves in the name of the Father, the Son and the Holy Ghost, and then a barked command from the sisters, the nuns who taught them: "Chairs on desks". There was a collective scraping and bumps and bangs as the chairs were lifted up, allowing the cleaners to later sweep the wooden floors. Then in pairs, two by two, they left the classroom in quiet procession under the stern frown of the head mistress, sour and grey.

Once on the street they grouped into gangs; those juniors with infants in the lower classes would find them and begin the walk home together. Two boys started to argue. One swung a fist. A woman stepped in. "Eh. Eh. Stop that George McKenna. I'll tell your mother. You're making a show of her," and slapped him on the head. The boy contrite and embarrassed red faced, walked off. The woman shrugged herself back into respectful repose, arms folded across maternal chest.

Paddy found Tony and then Bridgid talking to their friends. "Come on, youse," he said. He turned and they followed. As he turned, the woman nodded to her friend. In unison they blessed themselves in quiet prayer that none of their own would be blighted with infirmity and disability.

Paddy couldn't manage to hold Bridgid's hand as they crossed the road. His gait that used his shoulder for momentum wouldn't allow it. Tony held his sister's hand and Paddy took the lead. He walked out in front of the oncoming traffic, a scowl of lowered brows enough to halt their progress and allow them to all cross together.

Once on the safe pavement that would allow them uninterrupted passage home, Paddy told them.

"I've seen Mam. She sends her love. She's missing you loads. She'll be gone for a while, but she'll come back. She's told me that Shelagh is to be our mum while she's gone. But she said we have to stay together whatever happens. Are you with me?"

Tony and his sister stopped. A hundred questions forming in their heads. But Paddy continued, "She's told me to keep this a secret between ourselves. We can tell Shelagh later, but no one else is to know."

He looked into their eyes. "You promise? Spit down? Not a word."

He could see they were excited, but he had them. "Good lad. Good girl, Bridgid."

She skipped a few steps, then came back and stood between them and offered them both her hands. "Swing me" she said. Between the easy movement of her brother Tony and the fixed form of Paddy, they swung her body forward and back, her delight coming in high squeals of joy.

After the carefree moment, Paddy settled the little girl.

"Now, Aunty Mary has come over to see us. She'll ask us if we want to go and live with her. She lives miles away and Mum's told me she's close to home. So, I think we should stay here. What do you two think?"

"Stay, and we can see Mum" said Tony.

"Yes, stay" echoed Bridgid. "Swing me."

"Grand," smiled Paddy, "but remember we can't tell Aunty Mary about Mammy, can we? It's a secret."

Both children nodded their agreement.

"Right, so," Paddy said. "And I have a couple of pennies to spend on sweets on the way home."

As they came from the shop two boys stood in their way.

"Giz us a sweet," one said, reaching forward uninvited. Bridgid covered the paper bag with her arms and turned into the safety of her big brother's body.

The boy's head was cropped short of hair and his Adam's apple stood from his neck, an un-swallowed lump of gristle. His friend was shorter and weasel thin. Both were taller than Paddy.

"No, you can do one," said Paddy, cradling Bridgid's head with one hand while the other wrapped itself around Tony's shoulder.

The weasel nipped forward and swiped the bag away from Bridgid's hand. "You can do one yourself, you crippled fecker."

Paddy pushed his brother and sister behind him and lunged forward. His callipered leg anchored him to the ground and his hands snatched at the empty air in front of the boys. He overbalanced and stumbled forward. The boys danced out of his reach.

"You fucking spaz," shouted one, his Adam's apple a sliding cube in his gullet as he necked sweets straight from the bag. He spat a sweet at Paddy and jumped to one side.

"What are you going to do about it?" he teased. The boy weasel circled at Paddy's back. Tony moved forward to his brother's side, but Paddy's arm held him back. The weasel stole in from the blind side and aimed a kick at Paddy's leg. It bent the crippled leg inwards and Paddy leant heavily to one side. He righted himself and took a step forward. The boys moved in front of him raising their fists like prize fighters and Paddy retreated into the shop front. From behind him there was a flash of black as the owner of the shop rushed out. Her black shawl fell from her shoulders as she swung a broom at the boys.

"Go on, the pair of you. Get yourself home." The swish of the broom caught the weasel on the arm, but he stood his ground and openly laughed at her. "You can feck off as well, yer old bitch," he shouted, then grabbing his mate ran into the dark of the street.

Bridgid was still crying when they reached the house. Shelagh and the neighbour, Mrs MacDonald, were sitting at the range. Between them, Tony and Bridgid told the story while Paddy sat in sullen brooding silence. When she rose to leave, Mrs Mac laid her hands onto Paddy's shoulder and looked into his eyes. The touch of her hand was more than reassurance. In the briefest moment of contact it seemed to Paddy that she measured the breadth of his strength and questioned the spirit that lay within. The slight smile in her eye and the faintest ask on her silent lips called questioningly to Paddy's pride. By the time she had released him from her spell, he knew what he had to do.

On Monday, he rose and left the house early. Tony and Bridgid were washed and dressed and eating their breakfast when he ghosted down the stairs and through the front door. On the step, he strapped to his leg the metal and leather contraption and, with his characteristic uneven tread, he disappeared into the gloom.

Paddy waited in the entry to the jigger that ran behind the houses of Warburton Street, just off Hall Lane. He was taking short shallow breaths. His mind was concentrating on the hurt he had felt. Not just on the previous Friday, but every time a whispered remark, a barely hidden smirk or a guileless pointed finger had made Paddy aware of his deformity. The time in the playground when he had stood up to the bullies but found he was a dancing bear to a pack of barking dogs that circled him. He lumbered while they darted in and out, sniping and cutting with taunt or tease. He had caught one of the circling dogs, clawing at him when he had strayed too close. But he had been staggered off balance and another boy had rushed in and punched Paddy crying to the ground. He remembered the hurt and humiliation but now he was stronger. Now, he wouldn't let the pack circle around him. Now he would wait, a bear at a salmon run and wait for his opening.

His hand rested in his pocket and his twitching fingers traced the outline of a heavy weapon he had fashioned from a short length of hollowed out wood and a lump of lead. It was smooth to his touch, even soothing in the few minutes of calm, the tight grain of hard wood sleek with a patina of violent promise. The weasel turned the corner. Paddy had asked around and knew his name now. "Charlie," he shouted, making the boy turn into the left arm that Paddy shot out at the boy. His fist grabbed at the neck of the sweater the boy wore, tearing the worn wool of hand-me-down thin threads. As the thin face of the boy came towards him, Paddy pulled the weapon from his pocket and hit the boy. It skimmed the flesh on the side of the boy's forehead leaving a small red welt, but the dull blunt object left Paddy's fingers and clattered on into the street. Paddy bunched his fingers into a fist and punched the boy, holding him away, as a snot of blood ran from the boy's nose. The boy's arms had instinctively raised his hands and held Paddy's thickened forearms tightly, his weak fingers trying to prize Paddy's off his grip.

"Aye Charlie, not so fecking brave now, are we?" Charlie started to cry. Paddy pulled him closer, "Now go and feck off to school.

And don't turn round and look back."

Charlie disappeared, round shouldered and head lowered, wiping his nose on his sleeve as he shambled onto the main road.

Paddy picked up the wood and lead sap and placed it in his pocket. He peered around the corner, looking up the rows of houses waiting for the boy with the Adam's apple to appear. He moved himself to a better vantage point to view his target, now not hiding in the recess of the alley but standing proud of the darkness. He pulled at the brim of his cap to shadow his eyes and waited.

Soon enough the boy came from his house and hurried down the street, late as he was for school. His eyes were downcast, tired from a poor night's sleep and a poor life's diet. When he heard his name called, the tired eyes looked up and met Paddy's with a dark light of recognition. The shadow of fear dimmed his newly washed face and his eyes shuttled in a loom of disbelief when a strong arm pulled him into the entrance of the alleyway.

As Paddy walked home, he touched the slight bruising over his left eye. He looked down at the puckered skin on his knuckles, saw how the skin had rolled into white whorls and exposed the bloody flesh below. He raised his hand to his mouth and sucked at his fist. He didn't feel scared of who he was any more.

take the roses

A year or so later, and although still shy of the age of fourteen by a few months, Paddy's upper body had developed to a young man's. Unfortunately, the strength of his torso was still mismatched by the weakness of his diseased right leg. Whilst he could exercise his left, and push the development of his thighs and calves, his right trousered leg couldn't be tailored or altered into anything else than what it was; a reminder of the childhood disease that had blighted and fashioned his formative years. It had stayed stubbornly years behind; a drain piped shadow of its full cut partner.

He was broad shouldered slimming, inverted v-shape, down to his hips. His hair a thick curl of black brushed to the side, over the piercing blue eyes akin to his father's. His skin was the colour of milked tea, he was quick to tan in the sun, quick to pale in the winter. On his upper lip and cheeks a down of darkening hairs had shadowed his passage to manhood. On finding a razor upstairs he had shaved them away, leaving the faintest coal smudges of maturity that made him look older than his years.

His mother had told him tales of his ancestry, of Spanish galleons blown off course around the British Isles at the time of the Armada. Wrecked ships with dark handsome Latin sailors coupling with the Irish women of whiskey auburn hair, colouring the complexions of their babies a shade or two darker than the white of a cut potato, adding romance to the drudgery of their souls and black velvet to their eyes.

His mother also told another story, one that depended on the listening audience. It was only told to those closest, lest she shame her own name. She was one of the 'Black Hayes' clan. A far off distant son of the Hayes' ancestors had travelled west, over the sea to North Carolina, founded a plantation, and had returned his shamed daughter to Dublin with a boy child born from a dangerous liaison with a slave worker. The stigma lost in time, the mother dead, the boy grown, subsumed into Irish blood; he became the father to many a Hayes boy and girl, all coloured with the milk whitened wash of black tea and an arrangement of features that favoured the family's children, their children and so on through the years gone by.

Whichever tale of mixed blood was to be believed, within it there was an infection. It carried through the first born male and lay dormant, until in puberty it was awoken by enraged slight. The infection was vengeance and it affected Paddy in the same way it did his father. The feeling came quickly like the shadow of a cloud on the wind, but stayed until slaked by restitution. As his hormones altered with his years, his tolerance to insult weakened and his reaction to it became more violent.

Sitting as he did in the quiet shadows of the library, others who considered the handsome child only saw what they could see. His maimed leg remained hidden from view beneath the table on which he leaned. On its surface, a book was propped up and Paddy laid his chin on his crossed arms and read. A minute would pass, and his idle arm would move to flick a page forward; sometimes he would turn back to another passage, to study, compare and contrast before returning to his place. His eyes moved through the words, covetously letting the ideas form, the speeches talk, and the story flow.

"We'll be closing soon," said a young woman's voice from behind him.

Paddy looked up to the clock on the far wall, realising that the afternoon's gloom had fallen slowly on the day's light as he had read. He stretched.

"If you want to take it with you, you'll have to come to the desk now. As I said, we are closing."

Paddy turned. Behind him with a small trolley of books was a woman wearing a pin striped dress. He stopped breathing. Around her thin white wrists, a helix of trinkets and adornments, around a pale swan neck a single thread of pearls. Her auburn hair, thick, piled up and pinned into a bun, loose ringlets framed the radiance of her skin and made him think of a half-remembered turn of word, 'I am looped in the loops of her hair.'

"Excuse me?" she said, her face turning to a half frown, old currency, but still legal tender at that time. "You are looped in what?"

"No, miss." Paddy sighed in embarrassment. "I'll not be taking it home. I like to come here to read."

"But you said something." The voice tired, terse with impatience.

He looked up at her and saw her eyes and was smitten. He felt the blood in his face ripen.

He knew beauty, he lived with it daily. His mother was said to be beautiful, although he wouldn't allow himself to see it in her these days, preferring to be blinded by disappointments; likewise, his Aunty Mary and his own sisters were said to be rare beautiful, sharing as they did the same Hayes' genes inherited from intoxicating romantic tales. But he considered their beauty differently to that of his mother. Nothing stained beauty as much as selfishness or mean spirit.

Nothing radiated beauty as much as clear human kindness.

Paddy's hand and arm floundered behind him, seeking the book's anchor on the shelf, as he stared at the librarian.

"It doesn't belong there," she said.

"I know, I keep it there so no one else will find it. Then it'll be here for me when I come back."

She raised her hand to her mouth to stifle her smile.

"The idea is that you take it home to read. Then you can bring it back when you've finished."

Paddy breathed. He recovered. Slightly. "I will then." He held the book to his chest, covering the beat of his expectant heart. "Will you be here tomorrow?"

"No, tomorrow we are closed. We have been told to close because of the strike. We have been told to stay at home in case there is trouble."

"Strike? But it's Tuesday tomorrow."

"Please, we are closing. Do you want this book to take home?" The fatigue and impatience had returned to her tone of her voice, the sound of tired footsteps on the long flight of stairs to bed.

Paddy nodded and gave the girl the book. She looked at the spine. A Tale of Two Cities. The best of times and the worst of times, she thought. He followed her to the counter where she stamped the book and handed it to him. When he walked away from the counter towards the Gothic oak doors of the exit, she noticed his swaying limp. As if touched on the shoulder by her gaze he turned, catching her eye in the half turn as she looked away, her head down, ashamed of herself by the pity she felt in that moment. A realisation that her estimation of the handsome boy in front of her had been shaken by her lack of grace and charity.

The evenings in early May were beginning to stretch towards summertime. It was still light with sunshine when the staff at the library started to leave the building. Two women, bookends in dark hats and coats, umbrella handles curved into their elbows, came through the doors and walked away together. A solitary man exited and hustled away to the nearest pub, glancing at the fob watch that strained time on its fake gold chain.

Then the young woman, now wearing a dark coat, came through the door. She looked at him and again smiled.

Paddy didn't step forward. He remained on the other side of the street. He wanted to move to take that awkward step of possibility, but faltered; nervous for its outcome, Paddy's body refused to move. His confidence hadn't grown beyond his knowledge that he was a child speaking to a woman. She may think him older than his years, but Paddy knew the difference. He also knew the difference between his disability and his background, and the upbringing of this young lady. He wanted to walk away but was held in stifled check by the thought of how his ungainly gait would look to the girl.

He was captured in uncertainty.

She looked away for a moment.

Paddy sought the fastest route that would take him out of her sight. Trying to hold his weakness in check, he turned the corner, relieved, angered and ashamed in equal part.

As he turned onto the main road, he lifted his eyes from the cracks of the pavement and met the blameless stare of a man coming in the opposite direction. Paddy stopped dead in his tracks, squared his shoulders and swung his arms free of his pockets. "What the fuck are you looking at?" threatened Paddy. In answer the man stepped into the gutter to avoid the latent intent of brooding violence rising from the boy before him. With his hand holding the brim of his hat low on his eyes, he hurried past. He stopped yards further up the street and looked behind him at the broad back of the grotesque. He slowly shook his head to dispel the humiliation that now replaced his trembling shock.

Once home with his mood and anger subsided, he picked up the

Evening Echo and read it in the kitchen while Shelagh busied herself at the table preparing the tea.

"Did you know about the strike?" asked Paddy.

"The trams and buses are out of service tomorrow. There's been a strike in the coal mines these last few days. The unions have called for a general strike. Uncle Peter was talking about it when I visited theirs last week. He's getting himself involved in the political side. Though I don't really know how much."

"Will it be like the day of the national strike? You know, when I was born?"

Shelagh put the bread knife down and sat, thoughtful slow, to take a moment to remember.

"I don't think so. From what Jimmy says of his talks with his shop steward, this is more organised, and as far as I know, there aren't the soldiers in the city like there were that time.

"Then again, they probably aren't needed, we know how the police will react themselves. They were bad enough back then. They did their master's bidding and look at the thanks they got. As soon as their own unions went on strike, to a man they were sacked, and the new crowd employed. They have become a rougher crew altogether. The Peelers, for sure, will have no mercy for the strikers and give out loads of it for the scabs. The truth being that they have, to a man, that scab mentality; recruited to replace the sacked striking policemen. Aye, we know whose side they'll be on."

Paddy was planning to take himself down to the docks the next day to have a look himself. He would get up early and walk down the London Road and into the plaza in front of St George's Hall. He didn't often venture out and certainly not that far. He could remember long ago trips, with his dad, on the ferry to New Brighton where the short crossing over the sand coloured river ended with a shudder of docking engines. At the landing stage, cushioned by worn tyres, the gantry would swing into place over water rainbowed with slicks of oil. Kids would run sandal-slap up the inclined platform. Then after a day of ice cream, pink rock and sunburn, the tired trip back to the Pier Head and the grandeur of the skyline of the 'Three Graces' and the wonderment of the floating road that took passenger and cargo to the waiting ships at the Prince's landing stage. But, since his leg had withered, those past adventures were lost. Now he kept himself within a short limp home.

He read the paper's front pages and the bold editorial which asked the ordinary people to keep commerce and business running by volunteering to work on public transport. He grew bored and turned to the sports pages on the back of The Echo. Paddy's team, Everton, had just bought a new centre forward from Tranmere, a local lad called William Dean. Paddy idly wondered if he'd be any good for his team.

He put the paper down and went to the yard. He rolled up his sleeves and jumped up to the arms of the barrow. He dipped his chest low, his arms at right angles and felt the strength pulse into his veins. He pushed hard until his muscles burned. Then for the slightest of a moment he thought of the girl at the library.

He blushed. With his face reddened from the exertion of the exercise, he dropped to the floor of the yard and went back into the kitchen for his tea.

When Paddy left the house the next morning, the sun was struggling to breach the banks of coal smoke that layered the streets. It sat low in the sky, a pale button of warmth unable to chase the chill of the early spring morning away. Paddy turned his coat collar up and pulled his sleeves down, gripping them with his thumbs to keep his hands warmer. It hadn't rained during the night, but the pavement slabs were rosed with condensation. The streets were beginning to wake, though there was an unusual quiet to the day. The carts and vans of milk and bread normally delivering early breakfast necessities were absent. Doors remained closed and workers and their families asleep. He had almost reached the end of Gloucester Place when he heard his name being called. He turned and two boys of his age were running towards him. "Paddy! Paddy Donoghue."

He dropped his cuffs and balled his fists ready. They stopped within yards and looked at him. They saw his closed fists and laughed.

"Paddy, mate, we aren't after you, we just wanted to stop you."

His name was Michael Sweeney and Paddy knew only that he lived further up the road where it crossed Albany. He was the same age as Paddy but thinner and taller by a head. His hair was bowl cropped ginger. His nose was flat against his face and his eyes were piercing blue. Paddy knew his mate as well. Terry Conroy was from a big family, all hard knocks but all known for acts of kindness. He smiled, to show a row of teeth stained by tea and tobacco.

"Where are you off to?"

Paddy kept his hands clenched. He didn't trust any of the kids. He didn't trust anyone any more.

"Going into town to see the strike," he muttered. He looked over their heads to see if they were going to be joined by any of the other lads, older and bigger, that they knocked around with. The street was empty. A few doors were being opened and men shuffled out and stood in groups idle, wondering how to spend their day without work.

"Was going to walk down Prescott Street and get into town. See if anything's happening, like."

Terry looked to his friend and said "We are as well. Come on, we'll all go together. Safety in numbers."

Paddy was quiet. The boys fell in alongside him, adjusting their steps to keep in time with Paddy.

"Slow down, fella," said Sweeney, "we've got all day and see what I've got?"

He was right. Paddy had been pushing hard, swinging his ribboned leg to follow his good one, forcing a pace he could never keep. He slowed. The others, either side of him on the wide pavement kept his stride. At lamp posts, one or the other gave way to allow Paddy free way ahead. He began to relax. Just a tiny bit, still waiting for the joke at his expense.

"What have you got have then, Michael?" asked Terry Conroy.

Sweeney showed him a silver threepenny bit. He held it as a pirate would hold treasure, to the sunlight, as if it would glint and glister with the wealth of other worlds.

"Get in, me laddo." said Terry and nudged Paddy with his elbow. Paddy bristled. "Sorry Paddy," he added quickly. "Didn't mean nowt."

Paddy breathed.

"It's alright, Terry," said Sweeney, "no offence meant, no offence taken. Isn't that right Paddy?"

Patrick Donoghue had to concede it was. He nodded and smiled an apology to the pair.

They carried on over Low Hill and down Prescott Street, turning right at Moss Lane to stay close to the university buildings. Sweeney had taken the role of lead, suggesting that they steer clear of Islington and the rough arse mobs of kids that ran those squares.

Under the sandstone tower of the university on Brownlow Hill, Paddy started to like the feeling. He had always kept his own company. He had heard the skits and snide comments thrown his way by boys, bigger and stronger, and had wanted to fight them all. After a few good knocks to his head, he had decided that he'd abide by the advice given to him years ago by his neighbour and that his time would come. With these two at his side, his shoulders dwarfing their growth starved frames, his arms beginning to be heavy with muscle, he wondered if that time approached.

They stopped at the Adelphi Hotel and looked to the right to see what was happening on St George's plaza. They could see crowds forming, knots of men, some speaking to themselves, others listening to union reps.

Sweeney led the way. On the pavement of the hotel whose cellars had been his birthplace, Paddy, now assured that his disability didn't always bring instant cruelty, told them the story of his birth and the chariot, as he'd been told by his mother and further embellished by Shelagh, his sister. Sweeney found a woman who'd set up a barrow selling hot sweet tea and the boys comrades in adventure sat on the statues of lions in front of the hall, sipping tea from glass jam jars and watching.

catch-cries of the clown

"Well, I'd say that was the biggest bag of shite I've heard today." Sweeney was drawing down the grey smoke of a cigarette. A new vice for young Paddy Donoghue. But manliness questioned is manliness answered and he sucked the foul taste of ash and smoke into his lungs and enjoyed the disorientation that fuddled his brain. Light headed, he sat still, and focussed.

They had been listening to different leaders of the different unions holding forth.

"But isn't it all a bag of shite?" Paddy answered. "Who is in charge? And really, are those who are in charge going to give into a ragged trousered set of no marks. I mean look at the rip of them. They're not in work, so why dress in your overalls? D'you want to look like the beasts of your own burden?"

Sweeney swivelled on the arse of his pants and looked askance at him. Then in pantomime mime, he looked towards Conroy and rolled his eyes.

Paddy saw it. "I mean, if you want to be in charge, look like you want to be in fecking charge."

Conroy turned on him. "You're missing the point, me laddo; they don't want to be in charge, my dad told me. They want to be told what to do, when to do it and how. They can't be arsed taking all the worries of the owner. But they want their shilling in return for making those who are in charge rich. And they want to do it in safety; doesn't sound unreasonable, does it? If you're working in a coal mine making money for the company you're working for, then it makes sense to do it safely. They look after the horses, on some jobs, better than the men who work them."

"So, there is no ambition for getting better conditions; they're just a beast wanting a better bale of hay at the end of his day?"

"Paddy, me laddo - they aren't beasts; they are men. And so are we – what's fought and gained today will affect us all. Me dad says the power of the union is the unity of the workers. Without that, yer right, they are a bunch of useless feckers. If one goes back on the job to scab against his mates, it all falls apart.

"And, by the way, why wouldn't you want the very best bale of hay to feed your family with?"

Paddy pressed on "So, what does your dad think about why this strike will work and others before it didn't?"

Terry Conroy had to think to remember, and in the pause Sweeney butted in.

"Well, my dad told me," he started in mimicry of his best mate, but was soon shut up by a sly dig to the ribs from a quick jab by Conroy.

"It'll be because we get more organised. He said before they were just random walkouts by hotheads, but now they've got all the unions together and formed an organisation to make collective decisions. That's what he called them, collective. So they'll all stick together. United we stand, divided we fall."

"Well, my dad told me," said Sweeney, "that the unions wouldn't know not to take the shitty end of a stick if it was offered to them." He punctuated his sentence with a nod of wisdom. Paddy and Conroy looked at each other, grins crinkle touching their eyes.

"And why wouldn't they know the shitty end of a stick? Do they have no smell nor common sense?"

Sweeney leant forward patiently. "I know it's not simple but try and follow. As much as the union wants to be for the men, they have bigger fish to fry. They have to be taken seriously if they want to have a future say in the way the world is run. To do that you have to play the game. Do you know chess?"

Paddy and Conroy shook their heads. "No? Draughts then?"

They nodded. Sweeney went on to explain in naïve terms how sacrifices had to be made sometimes to win the game; give up a piece if it would lead you to be crowned. Let a pawn be taken if it gave you the advantage. Did they see? His dad called it the long game.

"Well, how long is this bloody long game to go on for?" said Conroy. "If me dad hasn't enough to feed us now, how long will we have to wait? And you'd best know that my Ma' isn't the patient type."

Paddy spoke. "What you're missing is that there's another set of players. If your dad and the unions want to play the 'long game' that's fine but they're up against people who have been at it for an even longer time. I'm reading a book at the minute, 'A Tale of Two Cities'. I haven't finished it yet, but there's terrible poverty in both London and Paris, but it's Paris that rises up in revolution. There are two sets, those being the people in power and those who aren't. One side has all the power; the other none. But the mob in Paris overthrow the ones with power and start executing them.

"The thing is, the peasants and workers are just a mob, even if they do have some leaders; but those in power, the ones they are fighting against, have centuries of experience of doing this. They have the police, the army, the law and the judges, and they have the money. Look at all the kings and queens and all the countries in the empire. How do you think they got their lands and titles? It's not a God given right to be a king. They took it from someone.

"And then there is all the banks and the politicians and the like. The shipowners and the people who own the docks and the factories, the tobacco and the sugar mills, right down to those who own the carts and lorries and vans. They've got power and money. Do youse two reckon they'll give it up because we ask them to? On their home turf because a group of scruffy workers hold a strike?"

"But you said the mob in the book won the revolution," said Conroy, "so, what's to stop us doing the same?"

"Because the ones in power learnt a lot from that revolution and they've seen what's happened in Russia, and they are petrified of losing all the fine things they've got over the years. These are different times, and I don't think they'll give up or share very much at all. If any at all."

"Is that what you do all the time? Read?" said Sweeney. "Nah, this time it'll be different. Me dad said it might just be so. If the unions can hold their nerve and remember who they are meant to be representing, they'll win."

Sweeney cast his arm open to introduce the growing crowd. Men and women were filing into the plaza and some had formed up, military fashion, ready to march through the town to the docks. At their front, young boys struggled to keep the banners of the unions upright. Some had been paired to boys who shared the weight. Others had the ends of single flagpoles placed in a holder embedded in a thick leather harness. Behind them the trio could see flashes of the sunlight as band members from nearby Lancashire collieries tuned up their brass instruments. Periodically a bass drum would boom to announce a practice swing and a rattle of side drums would answer back.

The boys smoked as they took turns to sit astride the sleeping stone lions. Sweeney and Conroy shouted out to mates they spotted in the crowd. A few came over to speak but left, wary eyes on Paddy, a stranger and therefore mistrusted. There was no room for them or anyone else on the backs of the icons of empire.

The colliery bands took shape. The Lambeg drum painted with the mine's name, and the other smaller snares in front, shadowed by cymbals and other noisy percussion traps. Then the fat brass, the euphoniums and tubas, the lean trombones and finally, the slender trumpets. The banners, embroidered with crests and with words of fidelity and solidarity, held high with pride, snapped in the breeze.

At the front, three men were holding a rope to contain the ranks. Watches were being checked. A flag was waved, and a semaphored message relayed. The heavy drum of the bass thumped. It lay down the beat. It pulsed through the air. Cheers were heard from the crowd and the lines of men, queued up in the sunshine, marched on their spot to the tempo of the beat.

The drum echoed through the air. A long roll on the snare drums gave way to a line of trumpets and trombones in practiced precision. The Internationale started. The crowd cheered. And the procession moved off.

The three boys slipped off the grey green backs of the lions, Sweeney starting to turn to help Paddy was warned away by a glowering look from under his dark eyebrows.

"I'm not a fucking cripple, you know."

Sweeney raised his eyebrows and dropped his chin.

They watched the lines of men walk behind the banners and bands as they and their fathers, friends, brothers and cousins had marched away to war a few years before. Then they joined in with the gangs of lads who had hung around the fringes of the assembly and along with them they followed the march down the miles of docks that veined the Mersey. At times, the bands would stop, and the faint voices of speeches would be heard by the boys as an unseen official spoke to the men. Then the band would strike up and the procession would start again. They travelled south as far as the Brunswick Dock where the Overhead Railway that ran the length of the docks terminated after a steep climb to the Dingle. There, the procession turned back and headed northwards along Sefton Street.

The boys took the stairs to the Overhead Railway station and found the platforms deserted. A notice placed at the head of the stairs told them there were no services today. Conroy jumped on the track. "Come on, we can use this to get back into town, the 'lecky's been turned off because of the strike."

"Are you sure?" asked Sweeney. But before he had been answered, he'd followed his mate onto the cinders.

"It's the middle rail that's electrocuted," said Conroy, "me dad says it'll kill you if it's live. But it won't be on today."

Paddy couldn't trust himself to jump. He lowered himself to the edge of the platform and slipped himself further down until both uneven feet were on the wooden sleeper beneath.

From the iron causeway they could get to march in time with the band as it progressed along the Strand back to the finale orchestrated for the Pier Head. The boys' high vantage point showed Liverpool's docks, the wharf sides, and the warehouses. The ships lay idle in the water, some sailors stretched in undershirts on their decks, others busy with menial chores, attending to washing, mending and cleaning.

On the docks, timber piles and stones stacked high, cargo waiting to be stowed away or dispersed throughout the country. Carts and barrows, sleds and pallets, cranes and capstans, like the waters within the docks, all stood unnervingly still. The bonded warehouses were locked and secured by armed guards who stood as passive sentries to the fortunes inside. On the boys' left, as they walked the solitary track back into the city, were the high domes of the Custom House. This oversized symbol, together with the opulence of embassies and consulates, shipping offices and banks, marked the reliance of the city on its trade with the world.

Just before the Pier Head, from the platforms ahead of them, three men in dark uniforms were shouting at the boys and running towards them.

"Bizzies. Let's go over the top," said Sweeney. "D'you reckon we can make it?"

"Just do it, me laddo. Come on Paddy whacker. Let's go."

On one side, the rooves of the sheds that held the small gauge railway stock that worked the heavy loads on the dock: on the other, the protesting strikers. A small railing separated the tracks from a heady drop to the road.

"Be-fucking-Jesus" said Conroy. "That's a long way down."

"Get down there as fast as youse can, lad, the pol-is are nearly here. A night in the Bridewell and a smack off me arl' fella is not something I want to contemplate at the minute."

"It's miles down. The jump will kill us."

Paddy went over the rails. He gripped the lowest rail with all the strength he held in one hand. He looked down and whistled through his teeth. A man standing on the side of the band looked up. He tapped his mate on his shoulder and walked over. Others stopped to watch. They could see the drama unfold. The police were thirty yards away, slowing as they hopped over the cinders, finding firmer footing on the sleepers.

"Jump lad" they shouted to Paddy. He didn't. He reached for Sweeney with his free hand and told him to take his arm. He gripped it tight and pulled Sweeney. Paddy swung him down in an arc, to where Sweeney's feet could just be grasped by the crowd.

Above him, Conroy climbed over the rail, ready to jump.

"Wait, mate" shouted Paddy. He pulled himself up on one arm, the dead weight of his body lightened by every tensed muscle and sinew. Holding himself steady again, he reached for his new friend. Conroy hesitated and the police were on him. A hand lay on his shoulder. Paddy snatched at Conroy's hand. He pulled him over the edge and Conroy fell. Paddy's grip slipped free and he felt the rip of tendons in his shoulders as the weight of the boy suddenly released. Paddy felt his own fingers being prised off the rail by the policemen. One thumping downwards mashed his nails flat while another wheedled away at his fingertips.

Conroy landed in the upstretched arms of the crowd.

Paddy looked down on a sea of pink, upturned o-shaped mouths.

"Jump lad" they shouted to Paddy. "Don't let dem bastards take yer.'"

He let go and fell. The air, cool in the moment of release.

A man with broader shoulders and thicker knotted arms than Paddy's caught him, easy as, and put Paddy down in a graceful movement of strength. In a second, he had stood Paddy up and had turned snarling invective on the police above them.

The backs of the boys were slapped to stinging as the crowd surrounded them, then soon forgotten, they continued shouting at the police. A stone and then another, were thrown, a bottle spiralling ale as it sailed through the sky, broke on the rails and with a cheer from the huddled masses the police retreated away. "Go 'ed, yer fuckers" a man screamed at their backs.

He bent down to Paddy, spittle stringing his lips and kissed him on the forehead. Paddy shrugged him off and wiped his head.

The brass band struck up, the Lambeg drum hollow boomed down the road. The trumpets flared and with a cheer the crowd moved on. Drink in bottles of whiskey and rum were being passed, sleeves swiping excess from grimaced faces. A man carried a small keg of ale on his back with his friend selling jam jars of the warm liquid for a penny a go. On every corner women sold roasted pigs' feet and water cress, cobs of bread and potatoes black from the ashes and hand juggling hot. For every marching man there were a dozen children, dressed in rags or the charitably donated 'police clothes' of dirt brown rough cloth, stamped with a marker to stop them being pawned. Nearly all were shoeless, matt cherry black unpolished uppers and soles from years of buffing by the gravel and grime of the street.

Their faces were touched by the brushes of filthy smoke that swept through the city air. Coal and coke, ashes, and charcoal minstrelled their eyes making the whites, jaundiced by poor diet and hopelessness, appear bright and lively, when in life they reflected the spectre of beckoning death. The boys' heads, universally shaved to short bristles or less, gave no haven for lice or fleas though scabs and scars mapped the itch of wars long fought against the night time enemy.

The children were feral and fearless. The product of their parents and poverty. They came from the courts and the squares of Kirkdale, Vauxhall and Islington, some from the chained terraced streets of the Dingle or Kensington. The courts stacked people together, back to back in single brick dwellings, a bucket toilet shared between twelve families, slopped out for the soil man each day, not a sink or tap to be had for clean water, little or no privacy, and filth at every hopeless breath. The squares, built in Victorian times by the council, housed two thousand people in four storey high blocks of flats around a single communal square. A child's hold on life was as tenuous as a fraying rope on the highest drop; it made for a callous contempt for pain, pity or weakness. These weren't children who fought a fight to bloody an eye or leave a nose broken with hardened black blood snot clogging its efforts to find air. A fight between children or their parents could leave the loser kicked or stamped to death, thrown though plate glass, strung Christ like on railings of fencing or being found, failing air, in the waters of the brown canals of docks. Brutality was ever there, a stone's throw away, empathy a word barely known in that world of cold disinterest.

shy in the gloom

On the bar in front of Peter, the Daily Post was dated from yesterday, Monday 3rd May 1926, and the half pint glass of mild was ten minutes flat.

The barman, Thomas, his brother, was getting ready to open the pub and was closing the cellar door hatch after checking on the barrels and firkins of ales and stouts. He spoke to the barmaid and she took a long spill from behind the bar, lit it with a match and went through the lounge to the bar area and the snug to light the gas lamps and turn them low.

The phone rang behind the bar. It was answered almost immediately. "Peter, it's for yerself, are ye here?"

O'Brien hefted his seat off the chair and extended his arm to the outstretched handpiece.

"Hello." He looked up at the clock. It was ticking with the certainty of time towards five. He would have to leave and get back to the shop. Strike or no strike they would be busy tonight. He was more relaxed in leaving the shop to be opened up by Mrs Nixon, but still wanted to be a presence behind the counter. All manner of news and gossip would be talked of by the customers in the queue and many an opportunity arose from that talk.

"O'Brien, it's Fitzsimons. I tried you at your shop, but I was told you'd be here. Have you got a minute to talk?"

"I have, a small minute at that and getting smaller. What is it I can be doing for you?" Peter drained his glass and stood moving down the bar closer to the door.

"I know there was a meeting of the Knights yesterday and I was trying to solicit their opinions of the strike actions called today. How the Catholic businessmen and the others see it, in respect of their own affairs."

O'Brien knew that Fitzsimons would have already spoken to others present at the meeting and was trying to wheedle from him his own views. Those would be salted away by his political mind in ever growing mental filing cabinets to be used at later times for his advantage. The voice from the phone continued as O'Brien looked to the clock.

"Well, you'd know this city better than most, but the Knights do give another representation that, I can see, you'd be interested in. There are many a man like meself, that would naturally lean towards the left wing, but there are others from different parishes who, shall we say, take a more traditionalist view. Of them in the southern end of the city, you'll know who I mean, there is a majority feeling that the Trades Council have gone too far. That it will push the government into action, and it will end up being bad for what they care of most. Profit.

"For me, personally it's a show of strength from the TUC. It's posturing, a bit of arm flexing. The trouble is, especially in this city, if that posturing is questioned by the authorities, then it'll turn to confrontation."

"Mr MacDonald is set against the strike and is cautioning the TUC to be reasonable. They have, he admits, legitimate grievance and the mine owners have been callous and entrenched. But he can't let it harm the party. He's desperate to show that Labour are not a threat to the establishment. He's afraid of a label of Bolshevism being attached to the party. He's spitting feathers at the print union for stopping the Daily Mail's editorial about how unpatriotic the strike is. Ramsay MacDonald is arguing, rightly in my mind, that it will give the press the ammunition they need to demonise the Labour movement as a whole. We can't be seen to be a party of radicals and fanatics; how would the middle classes ever vote for us?"

O'Brien blew out his cheeks but remained silent. Fitzsimons continued.

"Of course, they are marching in the city centre and I haven't heard of any unrest as yet. As far as my local knowledge goes, both Green and Orange workers are being united in their support. Have you heard anything different?"

"No. In the past week or so we have had meetings in the upstairs room of the pub by some of the local unions, the local ILP itself, as you know, and the Irish Nationalists and they are all one hundred per cent behind it. We've also had a few fundraising nights for the miners which were well attended and raised money too for your own concerns."

"So, no talk amongst your customers about who they feel is right in the matter? No conspiratorial whispers I should be kept abreast of?"

"It's early days for that. No one's been affected yet, apart from the miners, so at the moment it's a day or two off work and not that much disruption. The shop is fine, we stocked up on potatoes and we have been told that fish will still be in the markets tomorrow. As far as your interests are concerned, the pub's got more than enough ale, stouts, and porter to last a week or two. We are expecting a few bumper nights through the week to be honest, so far from takings being down I can see a good week for all of us."

"Aye, excellent," Fitzsimons replied in the flat Lancastrian tones that O'Brien disliked. He sensed the man wanted to say more and waited. He eyed the clock. It was five minutes after the hour, he couldn't wait long.

"Well, the strike won't last much more than a week, I'm sure," Fitzsimons added, "there is more news which could be to our mutual advantage."

Fitzsimons paused for a moment or two as if collecting thoughts that eluded his recall and finally said, "I was with Mr Harford when I met Sir Archibald Salvidge in the Municipal Buildings on Dale Street last Friday. Do you know Mr Harford? He is the leader of the INP and destined for high places. He introduced me to Sir Archibald. Do you know he likes to be referred to as the 'King of Liverpool'? Tory fool."

He and I had an interesting conversation regarding the tunnel under the Mersey to Birkenhead. You'll know that they started last year on the pilot tunnel, a sort of dress rehearsal if you would. It is moving along nicely, he told me, but the interesting thing to me and some of my colleagues, is that they will have to find a huge number of labourers to dig the main tunnel.

"And where do you think he was proposing to find them? Ireland, of course. Land of men, thick of arm and thick of head."

O'Brien's lips pursed shut. This is how the English saw us. He said nothing.

"Which means an influx of Irish Catholics and a substantial increase in the Labour Catholic voting base. It means that we should start to have some real power. The old INP councillors will move into Labour and they will promote the needs of the Catholic Church and community first and foremost.

"The next question on your lips is, I know, where we will house all these people? So, we have to think about a round of corporation house building with, if we can swing it, the usual construction companies being contracted to complete them. If the proposals are new estates outside of Queens Drive, say Fazakerley or West Derby village, then we begin to get a higher proportion of Labour voters in Liverpool. The by-product of this is that if our friends get the contracts then it becomes mutually beneficial to us all. We all profit."

O'Brien finally looked at the clock above the bar and told Fitzsimons that he had to leave to attend to his customers. He promised Fitzsimons he would keep him abreast of any news that came his way and placed the phone's receiver on the bar. He walked to the other side and hung it up on its cradle. He looked at the bottle of scotch sitting on the shelf and, in that moment, wanted to wash the acid taste he had in his mouth away.

The pub had filled quietly whilst he spoke to Fitzsimons, and his brother and his staff were busy filling pints, pulled from the pumps with long strokes and laughing with the early evening customers. He watched as the pennies were exchanged and mined away in the till. He was still thinking of Fitzsimons and the unpleasant company that he kept when he opened the door to the chip shop and pulled on his white coat.

the leaves grow on the tree

Having been set on the floor by the docker, Paddy looked around him. Above the Overhead Railway opposite him was the Baltic Fleet pub, behind him the dock wall. Under his feet he could feel a tremble, indeterminable on the Richter scale but movement all the same. He looked up to see Conroy's face questioning him. "You alright, Paddy? You going to be sick?"

He shook his head. He pushed his right leg away from himself and he felt the change in the magnetic force beneath his body. As the crowd moved down the Wapping part of the road that ran along the docks, Paddy tapped his way across to the front of the pub. He stopped outside the boarded up window. He looked at Conroy and Sweeney who had followed him through the people milling along the road. He could feel the void beneath him. He couldn't say anything, his voice caught in the lump of his throat. He followed the pull of the vacuum beneath and stepped back onto the street. It wasn't a hole; it was a tunnel. It led somewhere. He traced the emptiness across the tarmac and pavement, ending at the dock wall. He knew it continued onto a place further, but he was stopped there by the density of the grey granite.

He looked back to where his friends were watching him. He shook his head and beckoned them over. He hadn't said anything, he had regained colour and told them they'd better leave. It was as they walked with the crowd towards the Pier Head that he told them.

"Youse are going to think me a complete head-the-ball," he said in a low voice "but I know there's a tunnel beneath the road. I can feel it. It starts at the pub and runs under the road and into the dockyards."

Sweeney stared hard at his face. "You're not kidding us are you, Paddy. I don't know you that well, but I don't reckon you're a mad one. You and me dad told me that there are tunnels everywhere in Liverpool. Summat to do with the sandstone the city's built on. Easy to dig, like."

"Like, those not far from us on Grinfield Street and Paddington, there was an old quarry," Conroy added. "Some posh fella hired loads of people coming back from some war with Napoleon and started digging holes. Then he filled them in, and he eventually just let them dig under the whole of Liverpool. They didn't stop until he came to the river. Lots of them have been filled with stones and stuff but there's no doubt they are there. It could be one of them."

"We should try and find out if there's one there." Sweeney was excited. "Be great to find a tunnel, wouldn't it? Could be a secret hiding place?"

"So how do you know it's there, Paddy?"

Paddy shook his head. "Honest, I haven't got a jam jar. I know going back some, when I was a kid, I felt a bit funny when I walked across a grating. Not just a cellar or the pipes under the road but proper tunnels. Sometimes I went a bit peculiar when I walked down Crown Street near ours, but me mum said it was just because of the vibrations of the trains running out of Lime Street Station. She said it was funny strange, not funny peculiar."

Conroy was laughing. "Aye, a gift of no fecking use to anyone. Go on, you blert." He reached up to ruffle Paddy's hair. Paddy shied away at the contact.

"Fecking useful if you want to break in somewhere though," Sweeney countered. "If that leads into the dock warehouses, I wonder what you could bring out with you? What about all the ones as you said on Edge Hill? Imagine if they lead into people's yards or the cellars of big houses? Fecking dead useful."

A moment's silence to imagine descended on the trio.

Paddy shook his head. That's not the way he was brought up.

The three boys, deep in their own thoughts, made their way back towards the Pier Head following the band and the crowd. At the bottom of James Street, they crossed The Strand from the Sailor's Employment Exchange building and stood in the arches of the Goree Piazza warehouse. It towered red brick five storey high above The Strand and the boys were able to find a drink of water in the fountains beyond, on the corner by St Nicholas' church.

The boys stood in the shadows made by the arches of the building scalloping the light, as the processions of bands and banners and striking workers massed under the high walls of the Liver Building. They turned when they heard the shout of the crowd rise above the clank of the tramline as a line of three trolleys crossed to their terminus on Mann Island. In the windows of the trams they could see the faces of men dressed uniformly in black, their faces snarled into a rage of unheard curses at the strikers on the pavements in front of them. At the doors to the trams, pairs of helmeted policemen guarded the conductor and driver.

The cry of 'Scab' was raised and soon echoed from a thousand voices of the striking workers. The trams weren't stopping. They were there purely as provocation, to show the city that the government wouldn't be cowed by demonstration. They ploughed on their metal furrows through the field of protestors. The police shouted for all to stand clear; those that didn't were pushed aside in fear of losing life or limb under the electric wheels. Men jumped at the sides of the tram, striking the windows with their fists and hurling invective at the occupants. The first stone was followed by another, and then bottles and half bricks, and then full bricks began to bounce off the tin walls and through the windows of glass. The men in black inside, brave before, cowered at the onslaught. Whistles of police reinforcements echoed in the concrete canyons between the Three Graces buildings. They came running from the city streets, batons ready, and were met by the resolution not to yield by the striking men and women. Bruises and beatings were being given and taken in equal measure, fights contused the road and the pavements with ugly colours bleeding to red.

The three boys caught at the rear watched as two of the trams rattled and shook their way free of the enveloping crowd, and unnerved headed back into the safety of the city. The third was stopped. The rails clogged by debris, the tracks hidden under masonry and glass. The policemen left shielding the driver and conductor, leaving the phalanx of hard men in black to decide whether they would fight or flight.

Paddy watched as the conductress, half hidden by the cape of a policeman, was struck on the head by a stone. She fell and in doing so turned her blood drained face towards him. He felt his backbone melt into his legs and would have fallen, except for the artificial strength of his calliper. It was the girl from the library. Her eyes, fluttering like the wings of a moth at a lamp, looked into the abyss of unconsciousness and fell, closed. Her body, lifeless save for a trembling arm, was surrounded by police and dragged away.

Still shocked, Paddy and the boys walked up the London Road homewards, past pubs full of men. They did not see any other trams, nor buses, nor hear any trains lyrically set the night on fire. The roads were empty, except for the police vans, studiously quiet and unthreatening and the small groups of men loudly claiming a pyrrhic victory.

Sweeney talked most of the way home, still excited by the day. They continued along the Prescott Road and turned on to Albany, still listening to him, laughing as he talked of imagined fighting he'd witnessed. He danced across the road, exaggerating the battles with swirling dervish fists and feet. When they had arrived at the junction of Albany and Gloucester Place the sky was beginning to darken, and the night chill started to fall upon them.

"Come on down to mine," pleaded Sweeney, "there's no one in except my sister. Both me mum and dad will be out. Go on, will ya, the pair of youse?"

Paddy wasn't sure. He should tell Shelagh. Let her know he was safe and sound, but the pull of new friendships was greater. And by the way, he told himself, he was fourteen, going on fifteen and nearly a man.

"Oh no, Paddy boy," said Terry Conroy, "you're going to meet 'Dirty Undercarriage'". He laughed and skipped away from Sweeney who aimed a kick at him from behind.

"Go'ed Michael, are you going to introduce Paddy to her?" he called from the other side of the street.

"Who's Dirty Undercarriage?" asked Paddy.

Sweeney chased Conroy, calling after him names that would have shamed a docker, until he caught him and punched the hunched laughing figure, huge thumps on his back. His anger left him, dissolved in companionship, and he turned calm and the mates both sat down on the pavement laughing together, arms around each other's shoulders.

It was a new experience for Paddy. He swayed towards them and stood over them, desperate for inclusion, and asked what the joke was. "You'll see," they both answered and disintegrated into bits, tears of hysteria beginning to form in their eyes.

When they reached Sweeney's terraced house, Paddy was amazed to see how neat and tidy it was. The front room was shown to him, Sweeney proudly holding the door, but not allowing them to enter. They were shown into the kitchen, spick and span spotless, a bowl with fruit on the table and a vase of flowers set on the window sill. The walls were clear of the black satin stains of damp that disfigured the plaster in the kitchen of Gloucester Place. The floor, tiled in cardinal polish red, was cleaner than the rough table top that Paddy and his family ate from.

Sweeney told them to sit down. He moved a chair towards the Welsh dresser of darkly stained oak and standing on the seat, he reached beyond the highest shelf. From behind the scrolled fascia at the top of the dresser he brought a small bottle. It was clear glass, holding a liquid the colour of weak black tea.

"Be-fucking-Jesus," said Conroy, "are you after drinking your dad's potcheen? There'll be holy blue bloody murder if you're found out."

"Leave it, lad," Sweeney answered, big man talk, "he won't mind. He's given me a drink before. I'm fifteen so it won't be long before I'm on the ale with him.

"What about you, Paddy me-laddo? Will ye have a wee dram?" he asked, in a cod Scottish accent.

Paddy nodded, unsure, and taking the flask took a draught. The fire of the rough brew burnt his throat, but he kept his face fixed, impassive, steadfast to any doubting questions of his manliness. He passed it to Conroy as the dizziness released from the liquid woozed across the palette of his senses. The bottle did another round of the boys and Paddy found himself smiling at nothing, in a daft oblivion where his mind felt a long second behind his thoughts.

Sweeney started telling a story about the owner at his dad's work whose nickname was 'the Priest'. He asked them to guess why that was? Neither a stupefied Paddy nor Conroy could come up with an answer. Sweeney, impatient for his own joke to finish, told them. "It's because he comes into the factory and starts every speech to the workers with 'Ah, men'." All the boys laughed. In the moment it was hilarious.

Paddy asked to use the toilet. He rose from the chair and felt the rush of confusion wash over his brain. He held the chair's Bentwood back while the sediment of balance settled, then moved cautiously through the kitchen and into the yard. After he'd finished and was shakily adjusting his trousers, he opened the door. Standing in front of him was a girl.

It was a while after ten o'clock before Paddy opened his front door. Shelagh called after him, from the kitchen, as he stumbled up the stairs. He said something to her, unintelligible, the words gibberish to himself. He was a mess.

Jimmy, Shelagh's boyfriend, appeared at the doorway, took one look at Paddy's face and retreated into the kitchen. A whispered conversation followed by low laughter was the last Paddy heard. He fell, fully clothed, on the bed. He felt hands roll him over onto his back and fingers fumble with the leather straps to remove his calliper. Then he tumbled into the deep well of sleep, dark and welcoming; his stomach turning, ever slow, so slowly, as he sank weightlessly slow to the bottom.

dreading and hoping

A vein pulsed on his forehead. In his ears he could feel his heartbeat against the pillow. He couldn't move. He couldn't speak, his tongue too thick for his mouth. Green bile lay in his chest below his throat. It rose and fell like the tide trying to breach his glottis and retch, swirling, from his mouth.

He lay still and his dreams, mist light, formed into banks of clouds with electric synapses of light firing within, and he began to remember.

A light in the dark, far away, getting larger as he moved forward. His fingers touched the red sides of the shaft, chisel marks in stone, the chalk dust stained his fingers. He looked at them and they were red, and the stains became liquid and ran down between his fingers. A voice spoke to him in a language he didn't understand. Sweeney's face appeared at his side and then he was before him, looking back and beckoning him forward with an inclination of his head. The light shone on them and they came into a room. Under the vaulted ceilings of brick glittered with diamante, chests of wood, brass bound and open mouthed, displayed their pirate treasure of pearls and doubloons that spilled to the ground. He turned to Sweeney, but he had gone, he had metamorphosed into a man in uniform, his face featureless under a peakless dark blue cap with a bright red star in its centre. Paddy looked at him, then became him, and was looking at himself. He watched as a girl in a stained slip, fat cream legs rosetted with pink, her breasts conical and nipple sharp, open her mouth and inside was rotten, mildewed with green rust. She pushed the body of Paddy to the ground and wheeled her fat legs over him. The body of Paddy was pinned to the ground, as Paddy in his other self, watched. She had his calliper in her hands and moved on top of him as Paddy became the body of Paddy and felt her weight suffocating him. He held up his hands and pushed her away, but as he pushed, she became grossly porcine and grew bigger, her nose as a snout inches from his face, her breath feral and wet on his cheek. He couldn't stop her. He came. He closed his eyes ashamed and wished himself far away.

He heard a voice and turned to see his mother. He felt a hot tear form in his eye, blinked it away and forced himself away from her arms and back into the tunnel. The light reappeared brighter than before, and he ran towards it on good legs. No limp, no swinging gait, no crippled excuse. He reached the light.

He stopped and looked down. He had no legs. They were lost in a mist. His phallus was engorged, elephantine and swollen colossal. It burst. Filth and sewage smut spewed forth from its eye and coated the floor in bedlam.

Conroy and Sweeney appeared dressed as altar boys, both kneeling in the waste, hands joined in prayer. They spoke in unison. "In nomine Patris, et Filii, et Spiritus Sancti" and crossed themselves reverently. Then holding each other, as they did last night on the pavement, and laughing together, said "Amen".

He lay still, the memory so alive it was like the dream itself, and he was unsure if he was asleep or awake.

He rolled onto his side and unscrewed his eyes, turn by turn, to the gathering light. Across from his bed he could see his brother, angelic at peace, asleep and untroubled by dreams of chaos and madness.

Paddy lifted himself on his elbow. A white enamel shaving bowl and a mug of water was at the side of his bed. He drank and then lay back and stared at the window, the light of dawn filtering grey on the dust en-grimed curtains.

The dream: his muddled mind floundered for its meaning. The soldier, the tunnels, and their red dust, the chests open to him with glory and treasure, the man with his voice, foreign and strange. He shook his head clear to find pain, pin sharp, at the back of his eyes.

When it had faded, he forced his arm to move and reached to feel under the blankets. His trousers were still on, the buttons on his fly done up wrong, mismatched to each hole, and underneath in his underpants there was a dry tackiness whose source he knew and recognised. He smiled.

"Dirty Undercarriage" he said to himself and returned to sleep.

wither into the truth

"I'm away to see Sweeney," he shouted out to Shelagh, "I'll be back in time to get the kids from school."

Her voice telling him to be careful was lost in the pulling to of the door. He left the house with a swagger to his faltering step. The day was oppressively warm for mid May. The previous days a heat wave had washed in from the south, a plume of hot air feathering warm wind across the land from southern Europe. The temperature had turned into a humid overnight heat, making sleep difficult and rest testing.

The pavements were wet with a rain that had fallen as the sun came up. Paddy looked to the skies to see towering thunder clouds rising from the west, bruised at their base in the lightest of blues and purples.

He had come out in shirt sleeves, rolled high up on his arms to show off the definition of musculature in his arms. His round collar was open to display the deepening between his chest muscles and the early show of small down hairs growing there. He breathed deeply and took a step out into a changed world.

As he walked down the street, his shoulders squared set, he raised his head from counting the cracks of the pavement when he heard the spank of thin leather coming towards him. Conroy was waving his arms as he came down the street.

He grabbed Paddy, pulling him off balance and threw an arm around his shoulder. "You dirty little boy," he said. He knuckled the top of Paddy's head. Despite Paddy thinking it had been a silent and secretive affair, Sweeney and Conroy had listened to every threat and demand given by Sweeney's sister, and viewed her assault on poor wee Patrick Donoghue through a jar in the door. She had forced herself on Paddy and he had gone unwilling to his maker. Suffer the little children. While she wiped her thighs and legs down with a rag, she had demanded a threepenny bit from poor Paddy. When he couldn't find nothing but a button and fluff in his pockets, Sweeney and Conroy rolled three pennies into the kitchen. Paddy, still lying on the flags, drunk and sated, was quickened by their laughter as he tussled to pull up and belt his pants.

Paddy shrugged instinctively, trying to push away this closeness but found himself, almost against his nature, latching his arm conspiratorially over his mate's shoulder.

They walked towards the house of the Dirty Undercarriage, but Paddy stopped at the lamp post. Conroy took in his face and read it plain. "I don't blame you neither," he said, and went to the door and rapped on it loudly. A round white face appeared at the upstairs window and then hid back into the room.

Sweeney left the house still buttoning his shirt and tucking it into his trousers. His bootlaces were undone and in his hand was a flat cap of his dad's. When he had sorted himself, he shook the cap open and placed it at an angle on his head.

Conroy caught the look thrown by Paddy and both fought hard to drop the rising laughter that threatened to undo them. "That's a rake of a hat you've got there, Michael." Conroy spoke, his eye threatening to tear up and betray his straight face.

"Aye, boy," answered the cocksure Sweeney, "it's one of me dad's and he said I'd cut a dash in it." He walked ahead of them with a bluster of a walk. The two fell in behind him, neither with the courage nor the charity to tell him it was sizes too big and balanced on, rather than fitting, Sweeney's peanut of a head.

All three of them walking astride as equals, the others' pace relaxed to fit Paddy's lumbering gait, shamble marched to the corner of the street where two or three other lads had already gathered.

Tommy McClelland, a boy who Paddy knew from the past, had his arm around the lamp post and was swinging in sweeping wide arcs. He was dressed in a dark suit, shined at the seat and elbows by the polish of age, and he wore a grey worn black trilby; its original sheen disappeared from countless soiled fingers pinching its crown. An unlit cigarette was welded to his lip. He stopped and sized up the group.

A cold trickle of sweat came from nowhere and ran the full length of Paddy's spine and disappeared into the crack of his arse. Sweeney leaned into him, shoulder to shoulder, bolstering support to his new mate.

"Patrick Donoghue?" asked McClelland, "And why would you be wanting to keep our company? All of a sudden, like?

"Have you stopped playing with your dolls in your mammy's bedroom? And by the looks of ye, you've done a wee bit of growing up since we last saw each other. What is it that yer after?"

Paddy's tongue tied a knot that strangled his words. Sweeney stepped in, with Conroy a close second, their own words colliding and entangling their meaning. Tommy McClelland raised the palm of his calloused hand, its knuckles white with scar tissue. He nodded at Sweeney who spoke.

"Tommy, me boy, he's sound as. Take our word for it. He's a fine fella to have in a scrape and he's got something for you and the rest of the 'Rip'." Sweeney prodded Paddy with his elbow and whispered, "The tunnel, you fucking eejit," when Paddy's head turned to him with questioning eyes.

Paddy shook his head, eyes wild in denial, his brow furrowed in silent reply to Sweeney's urging.

"What is it you've got for us, Donoghue. We're waiting now, and we haven't got all day."

Paddy took a few of McClelland's precious moments to formulate his response.

"Well, I've got this sort of thing where I can tell youse where a tunnel is. I don't mean like a sewer or summit, but like a proper tunnel. Maybe something a man can go through. Don't ask me how, I don't honestly know, but me mam said it's both a gift and a curse." Tommy McClelland stopped him as he began to accelerate his words into a mix of babbling incoherency.

He beckoned to a lad standing next to him, who sparked a match and, shielding it with his hand, offered the light to McClelland's cigarette. As smoke escaped his lips, he nodded his thanks and said. "This miracle of a gift that ye have will help us how, young Paddy Donoghue, boy?"

Sweeney spoke. "We are sure that there is a tunnel we know of into the docks, into the warehouses themselves." He let the words lie, allowing the potential to be realised. "It might not be something we can do ourselves but I'm sure, Tommy, you'll know who can."

McClelland primped his shoulders back at the flattery that furtively touched his ego. He sat down on the kerb and struck a Rodin pose, purposeful and intense, and let his innate intelligence filter through the thickness of his wit. He flicked the butt of the cigarette away.

"It'll have to be proved, boy. We can't be going to the men and telling them of this unless we are absolutely sure of ourselves." His head bobbed as he sought and found agreement with his self. "Yep. That's right," he decided. "We'll have to do a sortie. A trial effort and see if yer man, Donoghue, can be trusted. I have a place where we can test these magical powers, see if it's so that the man is a witch." The boys around him laughed and off they marched.

There was no mercy given on behalf of Paddy's disabled leg. He and Conroy and Sweeney brought up the rear while the older boys of the Low Hill Rip moved onwards apace.

"What the feck are we doing with this gang of no-marks?" asked Paddy, "And why would you tell them about the tunnel?"

"You want to have mates, don't you?" hissed Sweeney, "You want to survive in 'the Fields' then you'd best be on their side."

"I don't want anything to do with being a thief or a robber and, if you listen to me, nor do you Michael Sweeney. What would yer dad say?"

"It's a bit late for that, isn't it?" huffed Sweeney, "You're walking with the Low Hill Rip."

The gang of the Low Hill Rip were all from Kenny Fields. 'Kenny' was the shortened version of Kensington, the name of the area where the boys lived. It should not be confused with the Kensington Borough of London. Whereas the London borough was wealthy beyond compare, most of the mean streets in this area up the brough from the city centre's eastern margin were thin walled terraces, damp washed tenements and squares of decrepit homes for the poor and disavowed. A man was lucky to work; a wife lucky not to be beaten; a baby lucky to survive into childhood. A child beyond infancy would enter into a hard life of hunger and strife.

They got their name from the 'High Rip'. A Victorian gang of the Vauxhall Road area of the city; along with the Cornermen, the Dead Rabbits and the Logwood gang, they terrorised Liverpool at the turn of the century. Callous and casually brutal, they beat docker and sailor, ran amok through the north end of the city, robbing shopkeeper and publican alike. The police and magistrates struggled against them but finally, using ruthless violence and retribution, managed to force open their violent grip on the city.

The Low Hill Rip were bantam weight in comparison to the belted fist and bare knuckle brutality of their earlier namesakes. Nevertheless, they ruled their domain of smaller street based gangs in the area. The structure of the feral packs that dogged the people living in the triangle made up of Kensington Road, Low Hill, and Edge Lane was like a fiefdom. Smaller gangs based on local courtyards or squares were controlled by individual street gangs. These in turn were allowed to carry on with their own indiscretions with the permission of the Low Hill Rip. At times of battle with the gangs that surrounded their neighbourhood, they would form up together like the peasants in a medieval dukedom and pledge silent allegiance. Ready to go to war for their sire lord.

All of them were beholden to the hidden men. The older criminal element. The hard case men who carried soft smiles, wielding violence easily and readily. In the case of Kensington, it was the family of the Maddoxes. If there was major thievery to be done or minor disputes to be resolved, a word was passed to the Maddoxes and the brothers would come to visit. Victor and Bobby Maddox were the rising stars, eclipsing their ailing uncle, as he conceded his influence and his life to TB. They were the links in the criminal chain that tied and weighted the Liverpool underworld together. It was the Maddoxes that Tommy McClelland would report to if Patrick Donoghue passed his test.

The group passed along Low Hill, past the tram terminal and crossed Edge Lane. As they did so, the group naturally closed their ranks to a tighter band, allowing Paddy and his weak leg to catch up to the group. Without saying anything, they compelled Paddy into the middle of their circle.

"Eyes peeled. If there's any begrudgery then we'll tell them we are just gallivanting through, and we mean no trouble. If it's a fight they're after, then we'll have to oblige. But we all get back to the Fields together. Is that understood?" There were grunts of agreement and Paddy noticed the eyes were cast towards him, questioningly, and then shiftily away.

"Away then," said McClelland and the column moved on. It was expected that they'd meet another gang on their route. It all depended on who was around at that particular time. If the gang that were the cocks of that particular walk, the Crown Street Urchins, were about then they could expect trouble. More likely a few of the smaller lads would be out. If they didn't report back to their seniors, then the Low Hill Rip would be about their business and gone.

They saw no one. Which isn't the same as no one saw them. The areas were protected, and dues paid for the protection. No one wanted another gang robbing and abusing their home turf. Today the Low Hill Rip were quiet and in their quietness their luck held. They arrived at Mason Street, the site of the tunnel.

"So, Paddy Donoghue, I'd get me wizard's hat on if I were you and walk the pavement," McClelland said. "I know there's a tunnel in this street because me cousin lives over here. It goes into their cellar. They can walk about twenty yards and then it's collapsed, and they can go no more. It's somewhere down there." He pointed. "Go and find it for us."

McClelland folded his arms.

Paddy's hands leaked sweat into his palms and he rubbed them dry on his pants. With an unsure foot he stepped forward. Each step was tentative in probing further, hoping that the sensation he felt when he walked over the railway tunnels that ran from Lime Street eastwards under Brownlow Hill would appear again. He moved onwards. Behind him the group of lads followed slow motion. Paddy stopped and closed his eyes. It was a tingle, on the edge of a tremor, nothing more. He inched his boot forward. It was there. He moved the leg back and the vibration lessened to a quiver and then he lost it. Forward. Definitely, Paddy thought. It was there. He stepped both feet on the spot. His leg-iron shuddered, sparking electrically up through his nervous system to the base of his spine, coupled with the impulses from his other limb and sparking to his brain. He opened his eyes. He turned at ninety degrees and followed the sensations he felt from the underground energy. It took him across the road and right to the grating in front of number 158 Mason Street.

He looked to the group of boys whose eyes had followed his journey. Their gaze turned to Tommy McClelland, who stood still, eyes awide and said one word. "Feck."

Conroy and Sweeney crossed and stood either side of Paddy, their prize exhibit. "You did it, boy," whispered Conroy. "Aye, shove that in yer pipe, yer sap, Tommy McClelland," side-mouthed Sweeney.

As McClelland approached, Sweeney smiled broadly. "I told youse he could."

"Fair enough," McClelland allowed, "let's just walk up the street to see if there are more. The place is meant to be riddled with them. Go on, Paddy, lad." He gave Paddy a push in the back.

Paddy was flushed with his success and being at the centre of the boys' attentions. He moved down the street repeating the process. He walked slowly, with both his good and bad legs up the road towards Shimmin Street. Before the junction he stopped. He felt the quiver and the pressure that ran through his legs. "Here," he said. The group of lads following stopped. He was in front of a building that housed a small joinery factory. Inside they could see men in brown coats plane, saw and chisel pieces of wood into chairs and sundry furniture. Paddy's eyes turned across the road. On the opposite pavement was a manhole cover. He walked to it along the line of the force he felt from the tunnel. When he got there, he beckoned to McClelland.

"There's a grid," he said quietly, his eyes downcast.

"Aye, it's an ancient one and that's no sewer grid. Look at the name," said McClelland, reading from the grating, "J Williamson Esquire." His eyes ran back across the street and sized up the shop opposite, just as a van was loading up with an oak dining table and six chairs. The new owner stood on the worn step to the shop and handed the workshop proprietor white five pound notes. As the rest of the Low Hill Rip moved to his side, through the window McClelland watched the man open a small safe and put the money inside.

Later that afternoon after they had returned to the streets of Kensington, Paddy took his leave of the gang.

Before, McClelland had kept his arm around Paddy's shoulder all the way back to home turf. Excitedly, he talked of a plan to use the tunnel to break into the woodworking shop. Paddy remained silent, sullenly nodding only when he felt it necessary. When he reached the gang's street corner, he made his excuses and went home straight to the bedroom he shared with his brother. He collapsed his body on the stuffed mattress; coils of horsehair escaping from its broken seams.

He lay there blind, before his eyes focussed on the spine of the book that lay on the fruit box that served as a cabinet alongside his bed. The girl in the library. The bus, the stone thrown hitting her and her body still in the arms of the police as they carried her away. He filed away his worries about Tommy McClelland and the Low Hill Rip gang, picked up the book and went downstairs and out the front door. He checked both ways to see if his departure would be seen by McClelland and his boys. All clear. He took the back entry that ran behind the terraces and kicked his way through the debris of poverty, hearing the rats' claws scratching on the setts as they retreated from his approaching step.

On opening the door to the library, the vacuum of the musty smell of books and erudition drew him in. Behind him the noise from the street faded, cutting off the cry from the vendor of the early edition of The Echo and the rail rattle of the trams and clopped hooves of drawn carts. As the door brush sealed set, it hushed the silence. He went to the desk where a woman, hair severe in a tight bun and face sharp behind pince-nez spectacles, was stamping books. He waited. She looked up and held him in a pitying stare before her eyes went back down, her hands flipping open books and marking them returned with an angry thud. Paddy, too shy of authority to disturb her, started to move away.

"Can I help you?"

Paddy turned, awkward on his callipered leg. Her gaze took in the encased limb. She stiffened, reinforced in her will to be of the least help she could be to this street urchin. Paddy stood, his hands before him folded on the book he carried.

"I was here a week or so ago. There was a young lady who was kind to me. I thought I saw her on a tram during the strike. I wanted to know if she was well."

She peered down at him. The levels of contempt in her face immeasurable. "You saw her on the tram, did you? So, you weren't on the tram, were you. You were in the street with the mob?"

Paddy's throat tindered dry. He nodded.

She slammed the cover of a book closed. She stood; the elevation of the reception area made her taller, her lips twisted with the disdain of the imagined superior.

"You ask of Miss Schreiber. She was hurt by your crowd of ruffians. She suffered a head wound. Her father took her home to Allerton. She has not been back to work since. I, personally, do not expect to see her here again."

Paddy turned to leave. Her voice pierced his ears with spite. "Is that what you and your communist friends wished for?"

He placed the book, Dicken's masterpiece on divided worlds, on the table by the door, shamed by the last word she spat at his back. "Scum."

Paddy looked at the woman, his face a mirror of calm, pale ignitions firing behind his eyes. He left the building and crossed the road. He picked up a half brick from the gutter. His breath smoked into the night air as he went to the double doors of the library. He drew his arm back and threw the brick through the stained glass windows. The coloured butterfly wing shards radiated across the entrance hall as the brick slewed across the floor to rest at the feet of the old woman.

one by one we drop away

"Put another drop of tea in the cup, would you, Mary, my Cushla Machree."

O'Brien had returned from the fish market early, in fine mood for such a sullen damp day. He had afforded himself the luxury of a taxi back to the shop. It was still early in the day, but late in the year. The clocks would go back soon, making dark the journey home from town.

The daily trip outward to St John's Market, in Parker Street, meant he rose at five, dressed and walked to Spellow Lane to catch a tram into the top end of town and Great Charlotte Street. The market was open at six o'clock and he was normally through the doors first. It was usually a quick affair. He used tried and trusted sources, who after these last three years knew what O'Brien's chippy needed. They would deliver it by nine when he and Mrs Reid would fillet the fish and ice it for use later in the day.

They had delivered the daily local paper, the Post and the Manchester Guardian. He also regularly bought two copies of the Catholic Herald from the parish priest and the nuns, who called at different times of the week for a free fish supper.

The papers, folded crisp and clean, lay in front of him as Mary fussed at the range with a skillet of eggs and bacon. There was also promise of a treat of bubble and squeak, made from left over vegetables from Sunday's lunch, and fried to a shard in beef dripping. He sat back contented.

The days had run into each other; time bled into weeks and pooled in months gone by with anniversaries and birthdays marked. They celebrated each Saturday, after the shop was cleaned and the accounts totalled, with a family tea. In the summer, Peter would take them out and treat them at small tea houses, fashioned on Lyon's State Café. As the summer ended and the football season began, Peter and his brother Thomas would take their sons to Goodison Park to watch Everton. It had been the team that he and his family had followed, the Catholic team in the city so closely linked to Dublin. There was still the air of sectarianism between the clubs, the founder of Liverpool being associated with the Orange Lodge and the Anfield district being a Protestant stronghold, it became natural for the Liverpool Irish in the lower lying districts of the north end to follow 'the blues'. On the return from the match, Peter O'Brien usually took over a small room upstairs in the Stuart Hotel. His brother would provide a meal of pies and mashed potatoes, with cakes and pastries for a dessert.

While the family ate, Peter would be called away to speak to different friends and associates in his ever widening circle of influence. A glad hand there, a passed whisper of gratitude for a favour given or returned, a handshake for an unspoken deal. All was done quietly and amongst friends.

That particular morning when he'd finished his breakfast and before the tea was poured, his wife Mary asked if everything was well in their world.

"It is indeed," answered O'Brien. "We have the fish ordered, the spuds to be peeled and we have the newspapers to wrap them in."

Mary smiled. "You know what I mean, Peter. The books look fine for the shop; the pub is doing well, and the bank account is healthy. But they are the only things I know about and I have a feeling that there is more going on than I'm knowing."

"I have a few irons in the fire which I'll tell you about later. But for the most part you know my business. I've told you about the interest we bought in the two building firms, Power is one. You've met the owner, Vincent Power, and the other is Longford's, who you haven't. One is Catholic and the other Protestant. So, we are hedging our bets with the work that will be coming our way from the council. There's talk that because of this we might be able to get on the list for the new houses being built. Winslade Road has been mentioned. We should maybe go over and see it. It'd be rented from the council but it's bigger than here.

"Apart from that, I've been looking at houses on Nixon Street, further down Bedford Road. The bank manager has told me the current landlord is to go bankrupt shortly. So, the gossip is he has five houses rented out. We could be in the right place to pick them up for the proverbial song. It would be extra income for the household and in time there'd be a home for each of the children." He smiled up at her, his dark eyes catching the light from the window.

"Peter O'Brien," she said coyly, "we only have four children". He winked.

"Well, we will have to see about a fifth."

She smiled and lightly slapped his shoulder with the tea towel in her hand.

She left the room to see to the children and send them off to school. O'Brien sipped at his tea. Before she returned, he glanced at the door as he opened the paper to the racing pages and quickly noted his fancied horses. He found a scrap of paper on the table and wrote the racecourse, time, and their names for later. He tucked the paper into his waistcoat pocket and turned to the front page.

The General Strike as forecast had run for several days before the TUC put a stop to it. It didn't serve their aims to be seen by the powers of the land as a disruptive force. O'Brien thought himself pragmatic and judged, with a degree of pomposity, that the unions had acted prudently. With the media, the orchestra of the establishment, firmly entrenched on the right, the TUC danced to its tune. Instead of improvising, according to the tempo of the times, they took their lead from the dogma of their more experienced partner. Faltering slow steps of social revolution rather than a bold move to the centre of the political stage.

O'Brien didn't see social revolution as a volte face, a complete circle of change, but a gradual reform of the old ways by influence and persuasion. The strike had achieved little; the promise from the government to set up the usual ineffectual commission to look into the conditions of the miners. With that vacuous promise the unions claimed victory. They had asked for a promise that the workers wouldn't be victimised and the government, with a sigh of lies, said it was their understanding that the mine owners would be sympathetic to the strikers. The unions sent their men back to the mines and thousands were turned away, never to be employed in the pits again.

O'Brien heard the door open and close in the back room as Mrs Reid started her shift. He listened as the tap filled buckets of water, hard potatoes tumbled into the bath and she settled down to eye and peel them ready for frying later.

With the kids sent off to school, Mary came and sat with him. She was still smiling.

"Ted's playing rugby for the school this afternoon. Three thirty at the pavilion. Will you be able to get over to the playing fields to watch him?"

O'Brien knew the second of his bets ran at three thirty at Chepstow.

"That's harsh. I can't make the start, but I'll try and get over for the second half. The Christian Brothers say he's doing well academically; he'll pass his matriculation and be a candidate for university."

"Aye, he's a bright lad." She got up to make a fresh pot of tea. She leant into the back room and asked Mrs Reid if she wanted a cup.

Folding the paper, O'Brien leaned back in the chair. "Have you spoken to your father recently? What's the feeling at home, with de Valera leaving Sinn Fein and Fianna Fail? Will he take the oath? And your uncles in Carlow, are they still up to their rebel ways?"

Mary stirred the pot. "Dada is for him but says his brothers on the farm see Dev taking his seat as another sell out. And by the way, Peter, they weren't rebels; patriots is what I'd call them, and they paid the price for the stand they took. I think it's right that they reap some of the benefits for their sacrifice even if it's purely political. They can see the death of their wish for a socialist republic; the bishops and the government are seeing communists on every corner. There are lots of powerful men making money in the new Dail who never lifted a finger for the Free State."

"As it will always be," sighed O'Brien, "there's corruption everywhere."

He didn't see his wife's question mark of a raised eyebrow as it punctuated her face, but she remained conspiratorially silent.

She smoothed her pinny and sat down. "I've been meaning to ask you if you'd thought any more about the nephews and nieces. If we could help them out at all. With the houses being built in Walton Hall Park, and the houses you're thinking of buying in Nixon Street, would it be better to bring them closer? Away from Kensington and Edge Lane, and bring them over here. My sister's been gone nearly three years now and though they've fended for themselves, it'd be better for them to be nearer family."

O'Brien hastily folded the paper and slapped it onto the table. He drew a breath, "They're doing fine over there. That's their home. I'm not sure why you want to be involved?"

"Family, Peter O'Brien." Her hand came down hard in a slap on the paper in front of him. "Simple Christian charity. You'll remember, doing something good for someone out of the goodness of your heart. Aye, and not for profit, maybe."

O'Brien felt himself flinch. A raw nerve touched. He looked down at the table searching for words hidden in his own selfishness. His wife reached over and took his hand.

"Shelagh should be married and with children of her own. She's been courting for three years now. The boys are getting older. Paddy could help in the shop, at least with the spuds if nothing else. He'd be a pal for Ted, they could go to the match together, and then there is Anthony and Young Bridie. They'd be friends for the younger ones as well. Please, Peter."

When he looked up, he felt as he did all those years ago at the wedding reception in Dublin when they first met. He'd told her then, with equal parts glistering Irish charm and boldness, that she'd do for him. She'd looked him in the eye and told him that she'd be more than that. And so she had proven after all those years, so much more than a measure for his dreams. He touched her fingers, turning the gold wedding band, and leant over and with gentle lips kissed her quiet.

nobody wise enough

The clouds of the summer had sailed through the blue, slowly pulling time with them. Paddy hadn't told Sweeney or Conroy of his family's plan to move away from the area. He saw them every day and spent time with them, leaving at breakfast and not returning until the man lighting the gas lamps visited their road. They traversed the safe parts of the city centre, the areas where the shoppers congregated, and the policemen were on every corner watchful and quick with their truncheons, ready to deliver retribution to those street kids who lifted purses or robbed the stores.

The boys rode the ferries to New Brighton and Seacombe. Paddy sat and watched, swinging his good leg on the sea wall, as Sweeney and Conroy swam on the beaches with holidaymakers from Manchester and Birmingham. Paddy would strip his shirt off and let the sun bronze his thick arms and broad back. Girls walking past would slow and talk quietly amongst themselves, whispering dares and dreams until Paddy turned and his leg was seen. Their lips reddened by ice cream would shape into the letter 'O' before they shuffled away laughing, elbows fluttering, rib digging each other at their foolishness. Paddy would flush with anger and embarrassment, and turn his gaze back to the blind sea.

To that end, to hide his fluster, Paddy started wearing long trousers, the baggier the better. He also discovered something else. He found that if he put his hands digging deep into his pockets, it worked to offset the imbalance of his legs. It straightened the crookedness. It re-aligned the twisted. He still swayed like a sailing ship caught in a cross wind, but it was more controlled. Less of a roll, more of a swell. His new walk tired him, but it was worth it to be seen, even for a short time, as ordinary, as human.

In the afternoons, on their return from the ferry, sometimes they would linger, hanging around at the Pier Head, watching as ships unloaded passengers, and the carts and vans used the floating roadway to bring goods ashore. Later as the sun dropped and the offices emptied, they mingled on the pavements with the clerks and officials leaving at work's end. As the city emptied, they would walk through town and back up the London Road homeward bound, happily tired.

In this way Paddy avoided Tommy McClelland. One day he had told Sweeney, while waiting for the sun to dry his pale skinned body after a swim, that he wanted no part in any robbery from ordinary people. He was happy to be a small part of the Low Hill Rip gang, but he said he couldn't be involved in thieving from his own. He had heard of the plan to rob the joinery works; to wait until the weekly wages were due to be paid and the safe would be heavy with coins and notes before they used the tunnel to break in. He'd said it wasn't for him, his Ma' and Da' would die of shame. Nor should it be for Sweeney or Conroy, he added. It would bring disgrace on their families and worse, fold them into a blanket of criminality from which there would be no escape. It would end up suffocating the life out of them.

"Are yer scared of Tommy McClelland?" asked Sweeney. "He's a fucker of a hard knock. Seen him fight and he's a nasty piece of work."

Paddy considered his answer. He knew McClelland from old. He had bullied Paddy and beaten him when he was small. Not so small now, he thought, and I'll have my time. As his neighbour Mrs Mac had told him 'every dog has his day'.

He knew he wasn't scared. Fear didn't factor. Embarrassment did. If he wasn't in control of any confrontation, he knew he would be humiliated. Anyone with any sense would stand toe-to-toe with Paddy, sure footed and nimble against the clumsy moves of the top heavy body. They'd jab and weave, in and out, avoiding the haymakers and upper-cuts that Paddy's muscle heavy arms threw their way; they'd dance and spin .When his crooked legs failed to move quickly enough, they'd see the advantage. In they'd dart, snake fast, and strike before he could react. His frustration would boil his blood, his simmering annoyance would explode, and he'd lurch forward in exasperation. Off balance, they could circle like sharks and nip in to take small bites from his pride until his temper was spent and he surrendered to shamed defeat.

But if he could get hold of them, off-guard and unsuspecting, and lay one tight grip on their body, they wouldn't escape his strength. His upper body square and set, compared to his cock-eyed and skewed withered leg, would hold them fast. His arms would lock around their neck, python strong, and choke the air from their lungs, or he'd ham his hands, broad and flattened, into a massive fist and pound submission from them.

He wasn't sure if he was strong enough, just yet, to hold McClelland. He was a slippery and vengeful bastard, Paddy thought. He laughed to himself as he recognised his own traits in his foe.

"Am I fuck scared of that gobshite," said Paddy.

Then later, when the days began to shorten, tumbling like dead leaves towards Bonfire Night, came the day when returning home with his two best mates, McClelland stepped in front of them. They'd been happily talking of the hero, Dixie Dean, who was scoring goals even with a metal plate put in his head after a motor bike accident. Sweeney was acting the goat and the boys were still laughing when they turned the corner.

"The Maddoxes want to see you." He pointed at Paddy and turned away. At the end of the street, he half turned and looked at Paddy, jerking his thumb over his shoulder in clear message for the boy to follow.

Just before the corner of Walnut Street and Peach Street, at the mid-point away from the Mount Pleasant workhouse, they arrived at the end of a Georgian terrace, blackened with soot and grime. The pavement was lined, careworn, with cracks and gaps, and loose flags rocked underfoot. Once with a grand façade, the pub's face now mirrored the hardships and deprivations of the area, the tiled walls reflecting the oil-black puddles in the street gutters, and the paint flaked and broken.

The name of the brewery, Robley, and the ales they sold were written in faded gold letters on a faded purple board that ran the length of the building and etched into the glass of the lower windows. Even at that time in the afternoon, Paddy could see the backs of drinkers standing at the bar through the windows. There was an equality in their uniform; flat caps and rough cotton jackets of harsh serge over heavy twill trousers, patched and mended, and the sole-worn work boots of the dock and factory worker. McClelland knocked on a side door and as it was opened, they were ushered in and shown up the stairs. On each step, over wooden uncarpeted treads, Paddy's heavy leather boot repeatedly hit the riser, setting a slow metronomic thud echoing into the space as they climbed upstairs.

In a room at the top of the stairs, two men sat at a table. The older sat in a singlet vest, the braces of his pin stripe trousers hanging loose, his feet in shined leather brogues. On the back of the chair a suit jacket was part covered by a white linen shirt and silk tie. In front of him a cup of tea and a short glass of whiskey. Across from him sat a younger man with a broad fixed face, thin-moustached and smiling, wide grinning at naught in particular. On the table before him was a wide brimmed fedora. Both were looking to the door as the final thud of Paddy's heavy boot faded and he shuffled his debilitated body through the entrance.

The old man coughed and swallowed his phlegm, his Adam's

apple bobbing a curtsy at its passage. His face was whiskered white, rosacea pink pimpled his cheeks, and the plump folds of skin beneath his eyes were the colour of damsons, underlining shining wet blue eyes.

"Is this the wee fella you were telling me of, Bobby?" The man's voice was soft Scots lowland. His gaze dropped to Paddy's calliper. "Polio? Wee man."

Paddy pulled himself to his full height, squared his shoulders and brought his hands to rest in front of him. He nodded.

"Aye. But you're not such a small lad, are you? You've got some heft on ye. I bet you're as strong as any of your compatriots in your shoulders and arms. Am I right?"

The stiffness left Paddy and he relaxed, accepting the compliment for what it was.

The younger man, Bobby, turned to McClelland and asked him about the tunnel on Mason Street. As the story was told, he watched Paddy, the smile never fading but never quite reaching his eyes.

"Well, my wee friend," he said, mimicking the older man, "that is an unusual gift indeed. Can you guarantee the tunnel leads to the cellar?"

Paddy shook his head. "No, sir. I can guarantee it runs from the manhole cover to the building, but I can't say if it goes into the cellar of the workshop."

"As I thought." Bobby turned to McClelland. "You fucking useless article. Did you not think to check this fact before you came here to waste my time? Go on and get yerself down that tunnel and see where it leads. Do it tonight and bring me your news tomorrow. Do you hear?"

McClelland turned to leave, and Paddy started to follow.

"Not you, young man," the old man barked, "you can stay a while. Find a seat. I've got a few questions for ye."

Paddy found a seat at the table. "What do you know of the tunnels in that area around Mason Street?" the man asked, then interrupted himself, "By the way what's your name? Nobody was polite enough to introduce us."

"Sir, I'm Paddy Donoghue. I'm from Gloucester Place, off the Low Hill."

"Are you a Fenian, Patrick Donoghue?" asked Bobby, the smile still fixed, nailed in place.

The old man waved the remark away and leant forward on his elbows; too close. Paddy could see the wire hairs of his eyebrows, long and wayward, and the first signs of tendril hairs sprouting from his ears and nose. White gobs of spit stretched in the corner of his lips. He glared at Paddy. Then slapped the table hard. Paddy jumped.

"Ach, it's no matter to me if yer are or yer not, nor should it you, Bobby," he decided, "What of this strange knowledge you have of the tunnels?"

He smiled, a mercurial change in mood that left Paddy doubtful and confused. "Do you know of Williamson? The man who started men home from the war and paid them to dig holes one day and fill them in the next? Do you ken of him? Well, he must have had the notion one day to carry on the digging and started making tunnels of the holes. He must have been quite mad. D'ye not think? He's got tunnels all over. I've been in some of them. Vaulted ceilings and arches, passageways to nowhere and back again. And for what?"

The Old Man's question was thrown hard at Paddy who could only shrug it off. "Because he was mad?"

"No, not mad. He was an altruist. Do you know what that is?"

While Paddy wrestled for the answer, the old man took in the patched and raggedy hemmed trousers and the oversized shirt, darned at the elbows, that Paddy wore and changed tack. "Well, my lad, an altruist is someone who does good for others."

He added softly, "It doesn't look like anyone has done you much good in a while. Would that be true?"

Paddy blushed, not in shame but in growing anger. "What would you know of my life?" A tear formed in the corner of his eye, but he willed it still. He tilted his head slightly to fix it steady and not allow the tear to betray his pride. "I have my sister and brothers and family who have stood by me, and I by them. We don't need pity or altruism from anyone."

The old man opened his palms and sat back in silence. He spoke quietly. "Patrick Donoghue, I meant no offence. I've come from nothing myself and now have a modicum of wealth. The journey's been dour and hard, sometimes without food and shelter, without a penny, but on that journey, I've always kept some dignity. I see that dignity in you, wee man. That quality isn't present in a lot of the people I come across."

Paddy relaxed his hands and unclenched his fists. He felt the tear in his eye shift, ready to trail a wash through the dirt on his cheek. He thought he was fast enough to capture it with the end of his finger and wipe it away. The old man saw it but kept silent.

After a moment he spoke. "I'm Robert Maddox. And this is my nephew. Also Robert Maddox. We call him Bobby. Tell me then, Patrick, what is your life like?"

Paddy half-bowed to the younger man whose rictus smile barely masked the diamond hardness of his eyes.

Paddy told them of his birth and of his father's death, and his mother's departure. He told them of his withered leg and Yeats; the dreams he dreamt and the draw of the subterranean paths that pulled him downwards, and the fragile knowledge of a life lost and forgotten but yet to be lived.

The old man had leant back in his chair and closed his eyes as he listened to the tale. His son, the fixed grin still in place, had put his fingers to his lips halfway through and rose from the table, leaving the room. Paddy finished speaking and sat thinking of his story and where it might take him, in the company of the silence of the old man.

"Ach, lad. It's a story of sadness; yet there is hope and salvation there. I can feel it." Maddox still had his eyes shut. "I never knew my father, nor my mother. My brother and I were left as foundlings in Dumfries. Taken in by a farmer out in the country, Ecclefechan town, who wanted labourers to work his land. Worked us hard, as well. Like beasts we were to him. When we were old enough to leave, we took off one night. We left for Carlisle and then Newcastle, then high north to Glasgow. Barely fourteen when I arrived, Tam, my brother fifteen; working in the mills and docks, we survived and even prospered. I had a wife; Tam married and had two bairns. His wife was from here, so they came down. His sons left for the war and his wife died of consumption, so I followed him here. My wife died in Glasgow. I think.

"I've been down here nigh on a decade. I married again, a good marriage, a marriage to money. Her family made a fortune levelling the sand dunes from Kirkdale to Seaforth. Aye, there was love there as well, she wasn't the best looker but there's nothing as attractive as money when you're poor.

"Tam's lads, Bobby and Victor, came home from the war, hardened. They left again to join the Black and Tans, mercenaries in Ireland, in County Tipperary and Galway. Tam died. The wife here died, and I had some money to my name. I bought this place. The lads came home from Ireland and made this home. The lads carved out a niche for themselves by sheer hard work. Not clean work, if you ken my meaning, but money is money, clean or dirty, blood stained or no.

"I'm not the same as them. I turn my hand to making a few pound where I can but I'm not one for violence to my fellow man. This public house is useful to me and to them. More money passes through this room than ever does over the bar and it's a convenient meeting place for rogues; whether they be in the 'polis' or chased by them."

The old man sat up and taking the glass drained it.

"So, you're a learned man, Patrick. You mentioned the Irish poet, Yeats. So I guess you're a scholar. Are you as educated in mathematics as you are in your literature?"

"I'm not book learned," said Paddy, "Me mam taught me at home when I couldn't go to school. I can do me sums, adding up and the like."

"But are ye clever and quick?" Old Man Maddox said. "If I was to say I paid a guinea for each pair of ladies drawers and I'd bought a hundred of them. Now I wanted to make a bob on each pair, so I've asked you to sell them for me. One of the pairs is ripped, how much money would you be bringing back to me. And how much of that is profit?"

"I'd be selling them for a pound and two shilling. If I sold all then you'd make one hundred shillings profit. As I can't sell the one pair, the money I'd be bringing back to you would be one hundred and eight pounds and the eighteen shillings. So, you'd make a florin short of four pounds. Oh, and you can have back the pair of drawers."

"Aye, you'll do me, lad." A tired smile wandered into the old man's eyes. "I've need of someone to move some stuff on for me. Someone who is honest and straight with me. Those that aren't soon find themselves in a wee bit of badder.

"It's clean work. By that I mean, there's no skulduggery or hurting people. My aim is to cut out the manufacturer's costs if you ken what I mean. I'm always looking for one hundred per cent discount on their prices, so what we sell costs us nothing which involves a bit of thievin' nae by ourselves, ye ken. And I have a man who's a canny draughtsman, an artist if you will, and he can turn his hand to providing us with bills of sale and any licence to sell you might need. Would you fancy selling a few wee bits around the town for me?"

Paddy's hands involuntarily patted his trouser pockets. He knew it contained a fly button, string and two ha'pennies rubbed together.

"I would, Mr Maddox. What have you got to sell?"

"Have you a suitcase to carry them in?"

"I've got a cart. A hand pushed barra. Yea big." Paddy drew out the size of the cart with his hands.

"Ach wee man, I think me and you are in business." His weary smile widened. "I'll talk to my man. You be here first thing in the morning and bring your carry out, it'll be a long day."

hand in hand

In the snug, a bar area usually reserved for the wives of the drinkers who stood at the male preserve of the bar, the man with the homburg sat alone. On the table in front of him was a half pint of bitter untouched.

On entering, O'Brien saw him but went straight to the hatch and ordered a single malt. He tipped a drop of water into the glass from a jug and tasted it. He turned at the bar, passing on greetings to the couples who sat quietly on the upholstered benches around the room. They were customers at the shop, knowing all their faces but not all their names. He talked with the men of the local football teams and local politics, and to the women of the art of peeling potatoes.

The man in the homburg kept silent and tilted his head in unspoken questions towards O'Brien. O'Brien's conversations with the locals faltered and they fell back to talk quietly amongst themselves. Meet me outside in five minutes, O'Brien mouthed to the man who sat alone. The man left his drink, buttoned his coat, wished O'Brien good night and left.

O'Brien nursed his scotch and water, waiting for the tempered moment he could leave without raising undue suspicion. It didn't matter. The truth was that the customers in the bar knew him. And they knew who the man in the homburg hat was. They knew, pillar of the community that he was, that Peter O'Brien was keeping the company of a moneylender, shark, and bookmaker.

Outside, he stood in the ghost light cast by the gas lamps and waited. O'Brien left the pub and joined him in the shadows.

Peter O'Brien was one of his steady customers caught on the gambler's reel of chance. It wound out, sometimes with a winner baiting the line, but more often the hook would be wound back in empty. Each cast cost. Smaller wins and bigger losses. To the gambler, it was skill that landed the prize fish; it was bad luck when one threw the hook. O'Brien had the taste. He had hauled in big catches and had savoured the adrenalin, metallic in his mouth, racing exultant through his pulse. He relished the win. He chased the feeling. Time after time, like an addict, with each bet laid he sought the fix. He chased the dollar hoping for salvation in a win, floundering in despair at a loss. The despondency too easy to recover from, persuaded by the encouraging temptation of the 'next time'. The next time, the next time, the chorus to the song of the captivated.

"I suppose you'll be wanting money from me?" asked O'Brien, handling the roll of five pound notes in his pocket.

"I'm always happy when a man pays his debts, but I'm here really to warn you that your betting is escalating. As a friend, more than a businessman. You're a good customer of mine and that to me means you're a friend to the family. I want to ensure you're still able to have a bet, maybe a smaller amount than you're wagering at the moment, but I don't want to lose you to your debts. Do you understand me?"

O'Brien was surprised. He'd expected to be threatened, to be leant on with the persuasion of physical harm if he didn't pay off his account. "Well, that's good to hear. What's the damage at the moment?"

The bookie took a small book out of his pocket, trying to kid O'Brien that the exact figure was far away from his thoughts. It wasn't. He knew every pound, shilling, penny and farthing that was owed to him. He factored them into the odds he gave to individuals. "It's a little shy of three hundred pounds. Once it goes over that figure, I have to start charging you interest. And so the debt grows, and you may have your bets refused.

That makes it harder to pay the amount off. It's a horrible circle, descending into all sorts of chaos. The sort of pandemonium that brings problems to families."

O'Brien prickled, his jaw set firm and his back stiffened straight. "Hold on, now. One minute you're saying I'm your friend and the next you're threatening my family?"

"Mr O'Brien," said the bookie, exhaling smoke and breath upwards into the tranquillity of the streetlight, "I've issued no threats and I'm unlikely to do so to a man of your standing in the community. That sort of behaviour is reserved for the ones I have little respect for, those that wouldn't be able to service their debts; those unlike yourself who have no assets. Those assets of yours protect you, to a degree."

The smile on the man's lips read false to O'Brien. "Alright so," O'Brien conceded, he took the roll of wide white notes from his pocket and counted them out. "Here's half the money. The other half by the end of the month. Or, you never know, I'll win it back, the next time."

"The house always wins, Mr O'Brien. In time, the house always wins."

The man dropped his cigarette to the floor and casually stubbed it out with a dancer's twist of a shoe-shined foot. The lights of a car flashed its lights in response and the man tipped his hat to O'Brien and moved to the kerb. The car pulled up and, inside as the courtesy light came on, he saw in the passenger seat the face of a young boxer. His brow already marked with flat worms of scar tissue. O'Brien recognised him. He was from the Holy Cross parish and had fought three times professionally already, twice locally at the Empire and once in London. He was carrying the hopes and prayers of the people of 'Little Italy', a poor village within the city of families living around Gerrard Street, off Scotland Road, where Italian was still spoken as the first language.

So, this was the bookmaker's hard-knock. His hired hand, thought O'Brien, his Italian muscle. That's fine, I've got contacts of my own. If he or his family were to be threatened, then he would have to find men to protect them.

The car drew away. The bookmaker turned and smiled; he laid his hand on the sleeve of the boxer's jacket. "Do you like the car, Dom? You know you can use it anytime you like. Just call at my house, any time at all."

"Thank you, Mr Bernstein." The boxer, looked away, shifted his arm away from the bookmaker and changed gear. To break his embarrassment he asked, "Who was your friend?"

"Just a business associate, Dom. Someone I'll introduce you to in time. As far as I know he isn't a fan of the noble art. You'd think he would be, being Irish and everything. A nice man, a good-looking man, with a nice family. I'll introduce you to him if you'd like?"

The boxer grimaced a smile and inclined his head in agreement, but he knew this was the last time he'd share time or a car ride with the bookmaker.

As O'Brien walked home, studying each crack of the pavement in thought, the bookmaker curtained his arm around the top of the boxer's seat and turned his conversation to how the boxer kept his body so fit.

the merchant and the clerk

The cart was taken into the back entry that ran the length of the terrace. There a space allowed the boys to lay out the bed and the wheels. A spanner was required to bolt the shaft to the bed and Conroy was sent off to the local ironmongers to borrow one. They fitted the wheels and checked the spokes for rot, and dusted and cleaned the wooden planks of mildew and dirt. The name of the fruiterer who originally owned it had been scraped off by Paddy's father in faded years gone by, and the boys found paint to cover the whole finished article in blue.
"Shall we put a name on her side?" asked Conroy, "Like Conroy, Donoghue and Sweeney?"
"Not a chance," said Paddy, wiping his hands on a turps-soaked rag. "I'll be working for Old Man Maddox and you two no-marks will be working for me."
"I thought we were a workers' collective. I'll have to be speaking to my shop steward over this," said Sweeney, a smile in his voice, a furrow ploughed on his brow. Paddy ignored him.
"Let's see what work is out there first. Before we start getting ahead of ourselves. I'm to see him at nine. I'll take the cart, you two come up there with me and I'll ask if you can give me a hand."
"Right enough, Paddy, boy," Conroy agreed. They set a time to meet and Paddy reminded them to bring some scran as it would be a long day.

Paddy balanced the cart easily and, with strong arms and back, pushed the cart down to Walnut Street. With him, Conroy and Sweeney walked alongside, wanting to take turns, but the cart was Donoghue property. As they turned the corner, McClelland was shuffling away from the pub, a crimson crescent of blood across his cheek.

"You fecking divvy," he spat from between his teeth, "That tunnel in Edge Lane led nowhere. The footings of the building had walled it up and there was no entrance to the cellar. I've taken a beating for your duff information, Donoghue, and I'll be seeing you on the street. D'ya hear me, you little prick?"

Paddy nodded and wrapped his fingers around the wood and lead sap he still carried in his pocket. McClelland was the cock of the street; he was tall with a long reach and fast hands. The sort of hands that could slash a blade across your thigh or chest without you knowing, until you'd notice a scarlet bloom spreading on your trouser leg or shirt. He could throw a jab that would bloody your nose and sting your eyes before you could even imagine it. Those hands were barely controlled by a base mind that was callous to empathy and pity. A mind that could pass a kitten to a starved bulldog or stomach-kick a small child for nothing except petty devilment and, then drawing on a cigarette as the smoke filled his lungs, coolly empty his mind of any contrition or conscience.

Paddy watched him. His hand relaxed on the sap he held. He said nothing, his face blank, his thoughts loud. Aye, I'll see you no worries, not on the street though. You won't see me, but you'll get yours.

The door opened behind him and Bobby Maddox stepped out. With him were two large men. The features of their faces swollen soft by too many blows; brows criss-crossed with the tissue of hard battled scars, smooth flat smears of flesh.

"Get the feck out of here, McClelland, you scrotum. I'll be watching you." Maddox aimed a kick at him; McClelland's face turned the colour of boiled shite and he jumped to avoid the kick, leaving any small scraps of pride left in him on the pavement.

"You." He pointed at Paddy, "My uncle is waiting for you upstairs." Paddy took the stairs to the room where the old man sat in the same pose but dressed now in a heavy woollen dressing gown.

"Morning, wee man. You have your cart? Good. These papers are for you. They are proof that the goods you put on your barra are yours. The licence says the council have given you permission to site your barra at the bottom of Bold Street. You know how well-to-do it is there, so I'm expecting you to be on best behaviour. If you get pulled by the polis or the authorities, you are on your own. You won't bring any of this back to my door, d'ye ken? If you have any trouble with other street vendors, you tell them that the barra and its goods belong to Mr Robert Maddox. If they don't understand and stop you doing my business, then if you can, get their names and bring the barra back. One of my nephews will go back to your pitch with you. Do you understand what I'm asking of you?"

Paddy shifted his feet and nodded. "There is a coat over there which should fit you. It's better than the jacket you've got on. Take the cap as well. You'll look quite the part. That's the idea. Fit in, lad, be a part of the street. You'll learn quickly enough. You'll have to."

He pushed the papers over the table. The paper was of good quality and bore a number of stamps and signatures. Paddy saw his own name printed in type at the head of the license. It said he was aged seventeen. Along with the papers described by the old man was another, handwritten in neat copperplate. It gave an address in the Baltic Triangle, a side street off Jamaica Street. It listed a number of different items of children's clothing, a quantity and price shown against them. Maddox watched Paddy as his eyes ran down the paper and turned it over.

"That's what you're to sell today." Old Man Maddox's voice was flat and empty of emotion. "Where to fetch it from and what to charge. Write down what you sell and how much you charge for it. Any stock you don't sell, take it back to the same address. You bring the money to me. If you lose any of it, you'll pay for it. The shops will close at five. I expect you here with my money by seven. Do you ken?"

Paddy read the note again, he memorised the address and ripped it from the papers and crumbled it into a tight ball, leaving it on the table.

"Aye, you're a smart one, that's the truth," Maddox said, "now, off ye go and don't let me down."

The three boys pushed the cart down through the town to the area behind the Custom House. They passed the grandeur of the Seamen's Home. Grubby hands finding time to rub the gates' double-tailed bare-breasted mermaids for good luck and childish joy. They were waved on by a traffic policeman standing high in his box, with white gauntlets up to his elbows, as they pushed the cart up the busy Park Lane. They found the warehouse on Kitchen Street and knocked on the peeling paint of the door. On the dark lane, litter formed a midden from the walls to the gutter, blocking the pavement. Steam, sulphurous and stained with yellow, rose from an unknown source from within the pile.

The door opened and a woman faced them. She was fat and clean-to-the-bone ugly. Her greying hair loose and stringy, greasy as lard paper. Paddy told her Mr Maddox had sent them. She nodded and silently closed the door. The boys' faces questioned each other.

A rattle of chains and a shutter was raised in a window next to the door. She started stacking piles of clothes on the sill. Sweeney took them and put them on the barrow. Paddy found the written list and started checking them off. He told Conroy to count them as they were put on the bed of the cart. When the woman had finished she waited, still not having uttered a word. She stood in the window, filling the space with broody malevolence, while Conroy and Paddy counted, checked, and double checked the cargo. Satisfied, Paddy tipped his cap to the woman, who let the shutter down with a clattering rattle and a face as blank as a concrete beach. Sweeney pulled the tarpaulin over the goods and whistled softly. "Fecking battle axe."

The boys were in high spirits as they pushed the loaded cart through the industrial streets around Duke Street. Men stood outside the warehouses, small engineering shops and the few remaining rope making factories. Workers taking a break, smoking roll-ups and drinking from flasks of tea. The boys arrived on Bold Street and turned left, down the hill and to the space designated opposite Boots Chemist shop.

"Now what?" asked Conroy. Paddy had wedged the pieces of wood under the handles to set the barra up as a flat table. He was studying the prices on his list. His lips moved as he memorised the pennies he'd ask for the hankies, socks, shirts and collars piled on the bed of the barra.

"I've got to take the money, keep it safe, like," Paddy said, looking around, "it's well to do here so let's be polite and put our best foot forward. Two of us on the stall and the other one keep dixie. Look out for the scuffers, the police, and anyone who looks like a thief. I've got papers for the police but if we lose any of this, or the money doesn't tally at the end of day, we'll be for the high jump."

Despite Paddy's nervous trepidation the day went easily. The boys started calling out, first with nervous temerity then soon enough, shouting out the prices with charm and bravado. By late afternoon, the bare boards of the bed started showing as the sales continued. Paddy's pockets bulged with change and Conroy was sent to the bank to exchange it for a slim roll of pound notes. They called it a day at four when the pedestrian traffic thinned. Paddy sent Conroy and Sweeney to try and sell the remainder of handkerchiefs at the entrance to Central Station. He calculated the monies received, counting the coppers, tanners, shillings and florins, tallying the amount expected by Maddox. The boys returned empty handed of stock but pockets change full.

The rest of the unsold goods Paddy tallied on a piece of paper, to be returned to the fat lady in Kitchen Street. After they'd returned the remnants, Conroy and Sweeney strutted alongside as Paddy pushed the cart past the splendour of St Luke's Church and onto the steep incline of Leece Street. Paddy felt safer and more secure, protected between the cart's handles. He was carrying more money in his jacket pocket than he'd ever seen before.

"Aye, we've made a shilling or two today," Conroy said, as he bounced along the pavement. The shops and offices were closing and the few pubs and restaurants on the street were starting to fill.

When they reached the corner of Hope Street, Paddy called the boys together. They were starting to walk in meaner streets where a squabble over a sixpence could end in brutal murder. The city's main poorhouse was close by, and the homeless and sick were scattered like litter on the roads. They walked to the Walnut Hotel in a wary nervous silence.

"Sit down and tell me of your day, wee man. Nae bother, I hope?" asked Old Man Maddox.

Paddy shrugged. "None, sir. Your papers were never needed. It was a good spec. We sold nearly everything, took back the rest and I've still to add some stuff we got rid of. If you'll give me a moment, I'll hand you the full sum." He took from a pocket the notes and coppers, bits, florins and half-crowns and laid them on the table. From another pocket he extracted a piece of paper.

"Aye, right enough," Maddox said, and took up a glass to sip at his scotch. Paddy scribbled the sums on the paper. He had been scared by the Old Man's threat and had been meticulous in recording sales and money all through the day. Trust was scarce and first impressions were everything in the low life he was now involved in. He did a final reckoning and pushed the money and the note across the table.

"The final tally, lad? I'm not counting the money myself."

"What we've sold is there and the ones we've returned been taken away. Each have been tallied separate, then I summed them together to make seven pound, eighteen shilling and nine pence. I've checked it twice and it's all there."

Maddox pursed his lips and nodded in satisfaction. "That'll do me. Take a pound and eighteen shilling and the nine pence wi'ye. I can only work in round numbers. Leave me the rest and your papers. I'll have them checked in a wee while.

"But I'm right to trust you, aren't I, wee man?" A shadow slid across his face. Pale blue eyes needled into the young man's. Paddy shifted in his seat; the leather of his calliper may have chaffed his thigh raw after a day standing but this feeling of discomfort came from a primeval instinct within.

"You are, sir. I'm grateful for yer trust. I'm hoping I can do this for you again."

"Tomorrow's dry; nae stock, d'ye ken. I'm waiting for a ship to dock and then the day after she's in port, we'll be busy." The old man paused and thought on. "Aye. But come around tomorrow night, my nephews might want to use you and your cart to deliver something else. No promises but I'll speak to them. Oh, and keep your love of that Irish poet to yourself. The boys won't take kindly to hearing about him."

Paddy stood on unsteady legs and pocketed the money. He again thanked the old man, his cracked smile a thin parody of pleasure and he waved Paddy away.

Paddy limped his way down the stairs. At the door two more carts had joined Paddy's and the waiting owners nodded to him.

"How is the old bastard today?" said one.

"Mr Maddox?" said Paddy.

"Kerr-rect. There are three bastards in that place and the bastard upstairs is definitely the old one. The other two are younger, but all three are proper gobshite bastards." He spat on the ground and went through the door. Paddy shrugged his shoulders into the warmth of his coat as his fingers touched the cold reality of the coin in his pockets.

the pale unsatisfied

Paddy scowled, looking at the kitchen table with open parcels of meat and an old string bag of vegetables that lay there on the oilcloth. "Has she been here again?"

"Who is she? The cat's mother. Behave yourself. You mean Aunty Mary. She's been very kind to us all. The kids adore her and she's more than filled the void left by our mammy."

"I don't know why you still call her that. No mother does that to her children. She turned her back on us. Some Christian she is. I've seen her with her new fella and their kids, three of them now, little bastards that they are."

Shelagh cast her eyes down. She could understand the hurt her half-brother felt, but as a woman she had the grains of empathy that seeded their gender. Two years ago, her mother had been faced with a choice to make and had made it for her own reasons. Selfish in the eyes of some but, in the circumstances and from a feminine point of view, somehow understandable.

Shelagh had become an unsuspecting mother to her half-sister Bridgid, asked to fill the maternal void for her and the two other children. It was the young girl who had adapted best; Tony had grown fast and independent, by nature forgiving and understanding; Paddy brooded, unhappy with his life and those he felt had let him down.

"Fuist, hush now, Patsy, they are married now. Don't be calling her kids that word."

She knew that 'Patsy' was the name his father called him. She knew the salve the word contained. How it could be applied to calm his mood. To be used sparingly, for sure, and only at the right time to soothe troubles; applied incorrectly, too thickly or at the wrong time, it could bring about an inflamed rash of temper tantrums and sulks.

"Aye, she married in the eyes of her God, in sickness and in health, death us do part. I get all that, but before me dad was dead, and she'd already been with another man. And what did God do? Bugger all. Oh, aye, our priest tutted and muttered but she moves to a new parish and there, the priest marries them easy as anything, and then christens their bastard offspring. That's right, isn't it?"

"Not so much," she answered. "Granted, Paddy, the first was a sin but the others were when Mam was widowed and then re-married. And the new marriage was in a Protestant church."

"So, she leaves her children all born and conceived, within the eyes of your God, and just starts off fresh. And with three Hail Marys, an Our Father and a Glory Be and a hefty dropsy in the collection plate, she's back in the sight and mercy of Our Lord. Some Church, some morals, some mother."

"That's enough, so. Yer man there is not our father, he's got no need to help us out. But he does, as much as he can, so give him some tiny bit of credit, Paddy."

"He's not my man." Paddy raised his voice. "If he gives us a bean it's from Da's war pension, so don't be thinking he's some martyr to us. He's a wee evil gobshite and I'll have nothing to do with him. Nor her."

"That's your choice, but I'm asking you, Patrick, don't turn our Anthony and Bridgid against him. You may not need him, but they might do one day. So, if you can, keep that under your hot head and just let it fry your own brain and don't be giving out to the others. Are you in agreement that's the way we'll go now?"

He gave in. Paddy Donoghue's face was red with passion, his blood vessels dissipating the heat, simmering from the boil to cooling steam. He nodded and slowly unclenched his fists.

"The other thing?" he said, his voice softening, the edge frayed, "The money? I'm bringing in a few bob now, it's not solid but a good week is a good week and a bad one, not so bad. You've got your wages from the shop and we've got what the other fella gives us in dribs and drabs. So, how's the finances?"

Shelagh relaxed. Paddy's pressure cooker valve had let the simmering steam of tension escape from the room.

"We are more than managing at the minute. There's new shoes for the kids and some for school clothes and I'm putting money away. I'm not like letting on to Mam that we're sound enough; I don't want her guilt money to dry up if she thinks we're okay. So, I'll tell her a few fibs. Little white lies, you know?"

Paddy did. He'd listened to some of their conversations as he sat on the stairway when his mother visited. He didn't want to see her. He couldn't stand her, the cow; his mother, who walked away from him and her children, easy as. It was a stroll in the park for her. Aye, and to come back months after she'd left, with apologies and a sop of conscience money and presents for her abandoned children. He'd gritted his jaw and set his teeth hard between closed bitter lips and kept his counsel.

"But, Paddy, there's the other thing," Shelagh's voice trailed off leaving the question mark hanging over her brother's head.

"The money you're making off the cart," she continued, "you know it's bad money. It's money made from thievery and stealing. I'm surprised at you getting yourself involved with the Maddoxes."

"Ah, Shelagh," he whispered into his chest as his head sank, "I know, I know but I'm kidding myself that it's alright and all above board." He shook his head slowly. "How else am I to make money? Me, with a worm of a leg. Who else would give me the opportunity that Old Man Maddox has? I know it's wrong but it's all I'm ever going to do. So, I turn my own blind eye to it and tell myself there are bigger crimes done by man in the whole fecking scheme of things."

Shelagh reached across and put her arm around his muscled and sinewed wide shoulders. Memories of his mother holding him in hospital came unannounced and wet his eyes with artless tears, each a jewel of self-pity. He wiped them away with the cuff of his shirt and sat straight, Shelagh's arm falling away. "Aye, it's all I can do as a fecking useless article of a maimed man, but it'll be more than many a man will earn, and it'll keep the sharks and money lenders from the door."

"Aye, Paddy lad, true enough, and I'm sure the priest and the Almighty will understand."

"Well, they can both go and feck themselves, Shelagh. You know I've got no time for either of them. What sort of God does this and worse to little children?" He stood up and showed her, pulling at his trousered leg and leaning down on his right leg, so his torso never sat square.

Shelagh always felt the same emotion when she saw her brother's disability. In spite of his venomous rejection of the deity, she crossed herself and silently intoned the mantra, 'there for the grace of God go I'.

He adjusted the leather strap of the calliper and sat down again. In doing so, he had cold-shrugged off any sympathy he held for himself, and any that a God may feel for him and his damaged leg and spine.

"So," he said, "we're doing alright as we are." The subject had been changed and a silent vacuum fell on the room. It needed to be filled.

"So now, what was Aunty Mary doing here?" he said.

He knew Shelagh was keeping something back from him about the true affairs of the household and of her feelings about her future. He knew of her man, Jimmy. A likeable tall thin man with a penchant for Fair Isle slipovers, tweed sports coats and a hatless pate; Jimmy never let a hat, or a cap, sit atop his brilliantine-slicked hair.

And as they sat there, Paddy slipped motionless into a daydream. A smile wandered onto his lips and sat crooked stile on his mouth.

Most evenings Jimmy would spend the time with the Donoghue family listening to the wireless; helping the kids with homework and waiting patiently until they went up to bed. Then, Paddy already upstairs in his bedroom, ears all akimbo, would hear Jimmy give Shelagh a chaste goodnight kiss on the front step and an over loud 'goodnight'. The neighbours' net curtains twitched with approval and then with a slow whistling stroll down the street, Jimmy would disappear onto Prescott Street.

All quiet settled on the street.

Paddy would sometimes hear the beat bobby slow plod down the road always soft tapping the lamp post, barely a noise, to let all know the world was right. Paddy would give it a quarter of an hour or so, finish his reading and turn his light out.

He waited and listened for Jimmy's return.

There. A click. As the latch to the back gate that led from the back entry was shyly opened. Silence. Then the gasp of the back door being swung open and closed, hushed. A creak on the stair tread, a brush of material on the banister and then the slow brass click of the lock on Shelagh's door being closed. For the delight of devilment, Paddy sometimes waited for this soft tell before calling "Goodnight and God Bless, Shelagh," and laugh into his pillow when her innocent reply came back breathless and guilt ridden.

Paddy would light his lamp and read a last poem from the Yeats compendium before pulling the covers over his head to blanket out the careful sounds of cautious love making from across the landing. By the morning, Jimmy, her man was gone and Shelagh was whole, and the world turned for her with brightened chance.

Shelagh sat waiting. She watched Paddy's eyes, unsure if it was humour in those bright lights of his eyes or some remembrance of bile-laden bitterness.

"What is it?"

"Oh nothing, I was just having a thought about your Jimmy." His eyes played and jested with his sister's; his face stayed still and plain.

Shelagh folded her arms and crossed the expression on her face.

"Do you want to know why Aunty Mary was here, or don't you, you little knee scab?"

"Aye, aye," said Paddy, "that's a bit harsh. We were just talking about the savings and I just got to thinking about maybe you and your Jimmy should be thinking about getting married. Before..."

"Before what?" she said, guilt rising unseen, "Leave me and Jimmy out of this. That'll be none of your concern."

She recovered her poise. "The money. I'm putting the money that Mammy gives us away. I'm not spending it. It wouldn't do to be looking too grand on Gloucester Place, would it now? I've tallied it in a book, and you're welcome to have a look but you'll have to promise to keep it to ourselves. No one should know there's money in the house. Are you with me?"

He nodded. He agreed. Save don't spend. If you spent anything out of the ordinary, people would soon get on to it. You'd be robbed as sure as the daylight shows in the morning. Aye, in the area where they lived, they'd all look out for each other when they had all had nowt, but there was always some treacherous bastard who could smell the printed ink off a banknote. Someone who would look after himself a wee bit more than the others. Paddy knew a couple of men on the street who'd rob the soiled clothes off a dead child if given a chance.

"So, what's the grand plan? Are the savings for you and Jimmy to run away to New York?"

"Don't be half as daft as you look."

Exasperated with Paddy's feigned stupidity, she started to talk; shuffling the cards of hope and aspirations, dealing them out in a game to win Paddy round.

"New houses are being built out over by Walton Hall Park on the other side of Queens Drive. There'll be space and gardens. Close to Goodison as well. Aunty Mary was thinking we could move, be closer to the old family in Kirkdale and to her and Uncle Peter in the shop. The money we've saved would cover what we need for the move and new furniture. Maybe some over. The new house has got four bedrooms, parlour, kitchen and inside lavvy. Garden front and back."

"And your Jimmy?"

Shelagh blushed. "Well, he'd be coming with us. We're going to get married. That put us on the list, high up, and with you three kids that's why we get the bigger house. You'd have your own room. Your own key to the front door."

Shelagh thought that might be the trump card.

Paddy had to think on this. "And Aunty Mary thinks it's a good idea?"

"Yes, Paddy lad. She's the one who mentioned it. Uncle Peter is in a group, like the Young Catholic Men's League but for grown-ups. He's got a friend who can help put us on the list."

"So, Jimmy becomes our new dad?"

"No, he becomes my husband. You'll be two grown men in the same house. He's alright with that. You get on okay with him and it'll be good for you to have someone like a big brother, like."

"What about this place?"

Paddy considered the dealt cards.

He looked around the cream and dirt brown kitchen, the damp spores halfway up the wall, the coal soot on the outside of the window despite the daily washing. He thought of the old lady's bed he still slept in. How it smelt of ghosts and liniment and worse, and Anthony and Bridgid sleeping on her floor in thin mattresses and covered in their dead father's great coat.

He weighed the hand of a new life offered against the old one gone; the potential of the future against the broken vows of the past and present. The scale dropped easily on the right side of promise for his family.

"There's another thing," Shelagh said, ready to play her last card. "Uncle Peter says he has a couple of spare tickets for the first game of the season on Saturday at Goodison. He asked if you and our Tony would like to go?"

The look on Paddy's face showed her she'd won the trick.

truths that are your daily bread

When Paddy and Terry Conroy finally left the picture house, the dark of the December's night had fallen heavily on the pavements. The glister from the reflections of Christmas lights from shop windows stain-glassed the pavement in warped rainbows of colour. As the audience spilled out, coat collars were pulled tight and chins lowered into the cold. The chill of the damp made their breaths vapour above their heads and meld with the smoke of a thousand sparked cigarettes into a yellowing haze.

"Dead funny, that." Terry Conroy's face still held the smile that had been painted on while they watched the Laurel and Hardy flick at the Kensington Picturedrome. The black and white film, 'Putting the Pants on Philip', had become a favourite with the boys. This was their third visit to see the same film, twice staying put as the seats emptied to watch it again.

Hiding under the seat as the usherette's torch swept across the rows of seats between performances, then emerging when she'd moved on, with litter, dust and fag-ends decorating the knees of their trousers. Sometimes, a discarded sticky sweet would be sat on and then peeled off and saved, to be thrown into the audience when the lights went down again.

"Best bit?" asked Paddy.

"When Stan puts the coat over the puddle. The women skip over it and Ollie goes to walk on it and gets swallowed up. What's yours?"

"When Stan lifts his kilt up and the women faint."

"Deffo," he agreed, "though I'm sure those skanky yanks had

seen a fella's bits before." "Yeah, they're meant to be proper easy over there."

"Easier than Brenda?"

"Who's Brenda?" The light slowly dawned on Paddy and the blood flushed his face in a pleasure pulse of remembrance. "Oh, Dirty Undercarriage."

Terry pulled his friend towards him and rubbed his knuckles into his head. "Yes, Paddy, lad."

"Anyways," he continued, "any girl who wants to see a beast of a tally-whacker only needs to go to the bottom of Lord Street."

"Where at the bottom of Lord Street? Castle Street end? By where we put the barra sometimes?"

"You not seen it? I'll show you next time. If you stand by the First National Bank and look across at the monument, you'll see it plain as day."

Paddy, none-the-wiser, visualised the view from the pavement in front of the bank. He didn't like that quarter of town. His crippled leg, a divining rod of flesh and bone, trembled with the vibrations of underground shafts and tunnels that ran deep beneath his feet. The network of underground passageways were part of the old fortifications that had once protected the medieval city. It threw his body off kilter. It set off night time sweats and dreams he barely remembered and rarely understood. He preferred the steady ground at the top end of town where stolid sandstone formed the heavy bedrock and insulated his senses from scant memory and dream.

He shook his head. "Queen Victoria?"

"You'll see if you look, ya dope."

Laughing, the boys moved across the road, stopping to light up cigarettes, hands cupped around a shared match to save the flame, before just in time, stepping into the nearest doorway. A contour line of rain, wet-cold and hard, ran up the street to surprise scatter the cinema goers. In the porch of the shop, two girls stood looking through the window and talking quietly. Terry, peering around the girl's shoulder, recognised her face and pulled at a wet strand of hair that had curled its way out from under her beret.

"Joyce?"

The girl turned and Paddy almost swallowed his ciggie. Her face in the cold was pale translucence, framed by barely seen auburn ringlets. Her eyes ice-blue sparkled, sapphires under the lightest of red gold lashes, her mouth flushed pink in the chill of the night air.

She shook off her beauty and set her face hard, flushing the colours away with a string-pull of her upper lip. "Oh, it's you," she seethed contempt and taking her friend's elbow, sneered her way past the boys.

"See you later," shouted Terry to their turned backs as they walked into the rain. "Hope you catch your deaths," he added, low under his breath.

Paddy closed his mouth, flexing his jaw off the floor and back into its natural position.

"Who was that?" His voice danced a couple of bars above his natural tone.

"That's our Joyce." Conroy was shaking his head. "Why she's so horrible, I don't know. Just is. Me dad says she'll have to grow out of it or she'll end up on the shelf."

"Think your dad might be wrong about that, lad. Come on, let's follow them home."

Paddy shoved his hands in his new trouser pockets. It straightened his twisted gait and he almost walked tall as they made their way after the girls. The pair had splashed to a tram stop and were queuing, along with twenty-or-so stoop shouldered rain sodden people. All looked hopefully down the road hoping for the warm lights of the next tram home.

"How old is she?" asked Paddy.

Terry turned to look at his friend. The rain had sculptured his black hair to his scalp. Rain drops ran along and dripped off his nose. "Too young for you, my mate. She's only just turned fourteen. Me mam says she'll be a heartbreaker. At the minute she's a pain in the neck."

"Aye, she looks a lot older."

"Well she's not. So wind your tongue in."

Two trams were spotted as they clanked down the Kensington Road and the crowd shifted as a mass, a quick shuffled two-step of anticipation. Umbrellas were down folded and heavy drips upset on their immediate neighbours causing resentful stares and unspoken apology.

The girls got on the second tram and the boys, several passengers behind them, could only hang on the leather straps as the vehicle swayed into motion. The fug of warm breath and the damp smell of clothing filled the space. Paddy turned to face the girls. His eyes fell heavy on Joyce's face. She knew he watched her. She stared stoically ahead, the side of her mouth whispering to her friend, finding absurd flattery in the attention of the boy. On Paddy's other side, Terry Conroy's eyes drilled into Paddy's face. Finally, Paddy relented and let his eyes drop and slowly turn back to his mate.

Conroy sent rain flying from his hair as he shook his head. "For Christ's sake. She's my sister. She's just fourteen. Leave it, will yer."

Paddy did. After a few minutes, where the silence of the crowded tram was broken only by whispered conversations between friends and couples, Terry spoke again.

"How's it going with the suit fitting?"

Recently he had waited, asked to watch the barra, when Paddy had taken his money and gone into TJ Hughes department store to buy a suit. He had come out, daft face love smitten but wouldn't tell Terry what had happened.

"All good, lad. Getting a hat as well. Proper gangster hat. Fedora is what they call them."

"Aye, aye, Billy big bollocks," smiled Terry.

"Got to look the part. Next year's a big one for me. If the money keeps coming in from the Maddoxes, then I'm thinking of asking me Uncle Peter to see if he'd help me open a shop."

"A chippy? You?"

"Yes, me. Yes, a chippy. He was talking about a shop out on Muirhead Avenue. He knows they're going to be building big estates out there on the old Norris land. He's got a range to fry fish from a shop he bought from a competitor down by St Franny's and closed it down. So I'm thinking of asking him if I can put some money into it. Big opportunity for those in the know."

"Can't see you behind a counter, Paddy. Unless you were robbing the shop, that is."

Paddy's brow knitted in frustration, "That's harsh, lad. I've never done anything criminal."

"And the Maddoxes?"

"Different," Paddy snapped. But he knew inside that the work he was doing for the Scottish brothers and the old man wire-walked the thin line between criminality and legality. It was something he denied to himself but its silent admission ate away at his conscience, gnawing like a rat at a sugar loaf.

A passing stranger's foot on a grave shuddered his thoughts free of scruples. A dream formed in the brume of the heat of the tram's interior. His dream rambled blindly to the year gone; the year that was slowly coming to an end. A year when he had grown. Grown into his skin. Filling the empty spaces of his family with his own hard won responsibilities, putting coin on the table and standing tall. From a distance he heard his Da' speak two words: pride and dignity. He sweet remembered the look on his father's face as he had sat with Paddy and named the constellations. He smiled, then frowned as his thoughts soured with recall of his mother's abandonment; more bitter tasting to him after the love lavished on him in the wards of Myrtle Street Hospital. He set his jaw solid and looked up.

"There he is," said Terry, "thought you'd gone somewhere else, lad."

"For a minute I had."

"Aye, well, back to reality. It's our stop."

Terry pulled the cord to ring the bell and stop the tram. The young men stepped to the pavement and shook hands, ready to part their ways and stumble homewards. Seconds later the two girls alighted. As she passed, Joyce shy-smiled a wordless reply to Paddy's questioning stares. The smile silenced Paddy. Conroy grinned. He punched his mate on the shoulder and shouted after his sister. "Hold on, I'll walk you back."

He left Paddy standing rapt on the pavement. A grotesque in silhouette. His stance askew, his body's weight taken on his good leg; the other thin and useless; his massive shoulders hunched wet with rain and weighted heavy by endless hope.

Paddy looked from under his dripping fringe. He followed the trio that, arm in arm, ran through the wet streets. Just before they faded away into the grey damp night, she turned her head and looked to him. A spark flashed in his dark eyes and touched its bright warmth on his tinder dry heart. Paddy turned away, a grin on his lips, swinging his arms to push his lame leg homeward; his mind filled with possibilities and the wonderment of what if?

paddy donoghue's story continues in the sequel

'A Scene Upon A Painted Wall'

available on Amazon in paperback and Kindle formats.

appendix

References

The Hurricane Port: Andrew Lees

A Star Called Henry: Roddy Doyle

Reflections on Moseley and British Fascism: Various Essays

Irish, Catholic and Scouse: The History of the Liverpool-Irish, 1800-1939: John Belchem

Liverpool Sectarianism: The Rise and Demise: Keith Daniel Roberts

Police Unrest, Unionization and the 1919 Strike in Liverpool: Ron Bean

The Decasualisation of Dock Labour: Michael P. Jackson

An Eye for An Eye: Gerard Noonan The Irish Times (17th December 2017)

Tactics, Politics, and Propaganda in the Irish War of Independence, 1917-1921: Mike Rast, Georgia University

Irish narratives: Liverpool in the 1930s John Davies

https://www.hslc.org.uk/wp-content/uploads/2017/11/154-3-Davies.pdf

Northern Ireland and British Fascism in the Inter-War Years: James Loughlin (*Irish Historical Studies*) https://www.jstor.org/action/showLogin?redirectUri=/stable/30006774

http://www.nwlh.org.uk/?q=node/117

http://famouspoetsandpoems.com/poets/

william_butler_yeats/poems

A Bright Shining Star https://www.jstor.org/stable/40403602?read-now=1&seq=1

http://www.catalystmedia.org.uk/archive/issues/nerve9/bamber_mary.php

https://www.socialistparty.org.uk/articles/20962/24-06-2015/laying-the-foundation-stones-of-the-workers-movement

Printed in Great Britain
by Amazon